Live,
Laugh,
KIDNAP

Also by Gabby Noone

Layoverland

Live, Laugh, KIDNAP

GABBY NOONE

RAZORBILL

RAZORBILL

An imprint of Penguin Random House LLC, New York

First published in the United States of America by Razorbill,
an imprint of Penguin Random House LLC, 2022

Copyright © 2022 by Gabrielle Noone

Visit us online at penguinrandomhouse.com.

Library of Congress Cataloging-in-Publication Data
Names: Noone, Gabby, author.
Title: Live, laugh, kidnap / Gabby Noone.
Description: New York : Razorbill, 2022. | Audience: Ages 14 and up. |
Summary: Three teen girls get caught up in a real estate battle between
a commune and an exploitative megachurch in their small Montana town,
and they devise a plot to exact revenge and make a profit by
kidnapping the pastor's son and demanding ransom money.
Identifiers: LCCN 2021049697 | ISBN 9780593327296 (hardcover) |
ISBN 9780593327319 (trade paperback) | ISBN 9780593327302 (ebook)
Subjects: CYAC: Kidnapping—Fiction. | Communal living—Fiction. |
Big churches—Fiction. | LCGFT: Novels.
Classification: LCC PZ7.1.N64 Li 2022 | DDC [Fic]—dc23
LC record available at https://lccn.loc.gov/2021049697

Manufactured in Canada

1 3 5 7 9 10 8 6 4 2

FRI

Design by Tony Sahara
Text set in Warnock Pro

I count my blessings more than I count my money, but I need to count my money, too.

—Dolly Parton

1

GENESIS

Genesis was having an out-of-body experience.

Again.

How else could she explain why she was hovering over her own bunk bed, watching herself make out with Sage, if not through the power of astral projection? It was physically impossible for her to be up this high, floating at the top of the ceiling of the tiny A-frame cabin where she lived. Clearly, her spirit was soaring above her body to the beyond. It was as if she were a ball of light and energy floating in space.

Genesis felt a sense of complete peace wash over her, but that was quickly replaced by a sudden panic; if she was up here, then who was down there inside her actual body?

The figure in bed certainly looked like her: purple tie-dyed T-shirt and frizzy brown hair in a long French braid, freckles sprinkled across her face—but Genesis was not controlling the legs that were now intertwined with Sage's nor the fingers that were running through his glorious curls. She couldn't feel his pillowy lips brushing against her own.

"You don't know how long I've wanted this," Sage murmured,

breaking away from the kiss and staring into Genesis-But-Not-Genesis's eyes. "I'm in love with you. I love everything about you."

"But that's not me!" she yelled from the ceiling. Like a TV set to mute, though, no sound came out of her. "I'm up here! I'm up here!"

Genesis flailed her limbs, and then suddenly she was falling straight down. Just as she was about to collide with her alter ego, she woke with a start.

She rolled over on her lumpy mattress and squinted at the early morning light streaming in through the cabin's tiny windows.

"I know you're up there," Ocean said, making her own bed on the bottom bunk. "But you're gonna have to get your butt down *here* because it's our turn to milk the cows, baby!"

So Genesis hadn't been astral projecting. She hadn't even been lucid dreaming—its easier-to-do cousin in which you are able to control your actions during a dream—either.

Nope.

She'd just been having a garden-variety sexy dream.

Or, really, sexy nightmare, when she considered the likely chance that Sage was her half brother. All the kids on the ranch were raised like one big family. Genesis wished the earlier generation had really thought through this whole communal parenting concept and how awkward it would get for everyone come puberty.

She took a deep breath and pressed her head against her pillow.

"I'll be out there in a few minutes," Genesis said, reaching below the covers for her phone. "I'm just going to, um, meditate first."

"Wow, that's so . . . *dedicated* of you," Ocean said sarcastically, and went outside.

This was a running joke inside Astralia—the poorly named community Genesis called home—since nobody had actual time for spirituality anymore. They were too busy running a business. Milking the cows. Tending to the crops. Baking the bread. Not just to feed themselves but farmers market patrons across the state. It was all part of the community's image rebrand that had been going on over the last decade.

The Astralians were no longer radicals who disavowed the ways of capitalism, religion, and nuclear family in favor of communal living and a shared belief in the power of meditation and hypnosis. It had been years since the townspeople of Violet, Montana, had last cowered in fear at the sight of the members or grabbed their hunting rifles and threatened to shoot the demons they believed possessed their souls. That era ended when their founder, Jimmy Joe James—described as a "young Leonardo DiCaprio but in need of a shower" by the media, making women flock to the town in WWJJJD T-shirts—was arrested for money laundering and sentenced to thirty years in prison.

The early 2000s were an exhilarating, terrifying time, or at least that's what Genesis had heard. When all the excitement was going on, she was no bigger than an heirloom tomato inside of her mother's uterus. Sometimes Genesis was overcome with the nagging sense that she had arrived to her entire existence too late and would always feel like an outsider looking in.

This feeling intensified as she opened Instagram on her phone, her feed full of people she observed closely but had never met. As she scrolled, their posts seemed to blur together, one woman with long beachy waves clutching a latte in her hands followed by a Bible verse in a gold curly font followed by a smiling baby followed by the next woman with long beachy waves and so on. Her finger paused as the algorithm finally fed her the woman she had been looking for, the one who stood out from all the rest.

> Ree Reaps
>
> Lover of Life | Lover of Christ | Wife to @PastorJayReaps +
> Mama x5 | Bestselling Author of ACT LIKE A LADY, PRAY LIKE
> A BOSS!

Ree was the source of her spiritual awakening, something her own community didn't seem to have the energy to provide her. By the time Genesis was born, the population of the commune had dropped from over two hundred to under thirty. Those who didn't get convicted in conspiracy with Jimmy Joe James or flee after his sentencing quickly realized that keeping up acres of land required a lot more than just the ability to lead a chant or prepare a good lentil stew. Sure, they originally came here looking for the meaning of life, but at least surviving was something to do.

Genesis popped her earbuds in and pressed play on that day's devotional vlog.

"Good morning, boss babes! It's a new day. And in this moment, you get to choose how you want to show up in this beautiful world that God created," Ree said, staring in awe out of the window of her car. "Now I want to talk to y'all about something that God has put in my heart today . . . a little thing called temptation."

Genesis looked around the cabin to double-check if anyone else was present. She adjusted her pillow and sat up straight.

"So, I had just stopped by our newly opened coffee shop at Hope Harvest Market—which, if y'all haven't stopped by yet, you should! I was getting my second iced latte of the morning—'cause, you know, Mama needs her coffee—when I saw the yummiest-looking donut behind the counter. I swear to you, this donut was screaming, 'Ree. If you don't put me in your mouth right this second . . .' Look, I love to treat myself, but y'all know I am trying to be good. Temptation can lead us all day long. From that yummy-looking donut at the coffee shop all the way to that cute guy at work who is definitely not your husband."

Ree winked at the camera, and Genesis felt like it was directed at her. Cute guy who's not your husband, cute guy who might be your brother . . . those were basically the same thing, right? Genesis thought.

"Look, we're only human," Ree went on. "It's impossible to prevent ourselves from having these enticing thoughts. But, girls, we can choose how long we hold on to those thoughts. When we entertain temptation, we fantasize about ourselves eating that donut or reaching across the copy machine to kiss that guy in accounting . . . we take another step downward! One of the Devil's greatest deceptions is to tell us that just *imagining* the pleasures of our sins really isn't that bad. Satan *knows* the power of our thoughts. He *knows* those li'l fantasies can turn into full-blown obsessions! Satan ain't stupid. But you know who's smarter? Our one and only Lord Jesus Christ. When you give your temptations up to God . . . when you open yourself up to that light . . . that temptation will be gone! Poof!"

Ree flashed her manicured fingers into the air like fireworks.

"He will say to you, 'Don't do this! Come into the light, girl!' So today, I want you to go forward and give your temptations up to God! Because when you give those up to God, he will take them and replace them with nothing but blessings! Do you hear me, girls? B-L-E-S-S-I-N-G-S!"

"I give my temptations up to you, God," Genesis frantically whispered as she closed her eyes and her visions of Sage and his perfect cowboy body intertwined with hers floated up higher and higher toward the sky.

. . .

When Genesis made it to the community kitchen for breakfast, all that was left on the buffet table were the end piece of a freshly baked loaf of bread and dregs of granola.

"Early bird gets the worm," Ocean said, reaching around Genesis for her second helping of bread.

"Bet you couldn't get bread like that in the big city, huh, Ocean?" a cheerful voice said behind them. Genesis turned to find Sage in his purple apron, hoisting a plastic crate full of dirty dishes with his toned arms. She knew that here purple was every-one's color, but she felt like it really was *his color.* Something about it made his hazel eyes pop. He gave her a goofy grin, and her face flushed, then a light wave of nausea rolled through her body.

"Nine whole different grains in there," he added. "I bet Trader John can't even *name* nine grains."

"It's Trader *Joe's*, you hayseed!" Ocean exclaimed. "And they definitely sell, like, one hundred kinds of grains. Quinoa, oats, rice . . . brown rice . . . but whatever. It sucks there because you have to wait in line just get inside the store to shop for the grains, and then once you're inside, you have to wait in line around the perimeter of the store just to pay for them. God, you're right," she said, taking a bite of bread and savoring it. "I'm so glad I moved back here."

Like Genesis, Ocean had been born on the ranch, but she had left years ago to attend college in spite of protests from elder members. The Astralian youth were "unschooled" all year round, which meant their days usually consisted of six or so hours of performing a rotating schedule of chores around the ranch combined with two hours of independent reading time or, if one of the adults was feeling crafty, some kind of do-it-yourself tutorial involving yarn or beeswax. Miraculously, Ocean had gotten a scholarship to Columbia, in part because she was good at math but also because the school was seriously lacking in students from Montana and the admissions department found her origin story to be "colorful." Then last February she turned up back at the ranch in a black turtleneck, complaining about her "tech job" and how she didn't want to "deal with capitalism" ever again. She was on the verge of throwing her company-issued iPhone in the trash when Genesis asked her if she could have it instead. Somehow its data plan still functioned all these months later. Genesis didn't ask questions.

"Morning, Gen," Sage said, turning toward her. "You get something to eat?"

"No. She was too busy 'meditating' again," Ocean answered for her through a full mouth, giving her a knowing look. Genesis couldn't figure out if it was because she knew she was using the iPhone or if she'd heard her moaning about Sage in her sleep, or maybe both.

"It's fine." Genesis shrugged. "I'll just have some kombucha."

Sage gave her a doubtful look.

"C'mon," he said, nodding toward the kitchen. "I've got something for you."

Genesis swallowed hard and followed him into the massive, dilapidated kitchen, where the ranch did all of its baking for sale. Sage had recently taken over the role of head baker from one of the original Astralians who couldn't even knead dough anymore because of his rheumatoid arthritis.

He carefully dropped his plastic crate off in the dishwashing area, then led Genesis over to a metal domed cake plate on the center island.

"Just a warning, this was my first time ever making them. I want you to try one and be honest," he said, lifting the dome to reveal three glistening donuts covered in dark pink glaze.

Genesis's eye widened. Was this some kind of test from God?

"I know they look like a mess, but—"

"No. No," she said, rapidly shaking her head. "They look great. It's just . . . I'm . . . trying to . . . *be good.*"

"Seriously? Since when?"

"Since . . . now," she said unconvincingly.

"You're gonna be working out there all day, Gen. You need to eat something. And these are raspberry glazed, which practically makes them fruit, which basically makes them a vegetable."

"I don't think that's how food works, Sage."

He lifted one of the donuts and waved it under her nose. Genesis tried to imagine a Barbie-size version Ree Reaps perched on her shoulder, whispering in her ear about the power of temptation. Try as she might to avoid breathing in the sweet, yeasty smell, it only made her mouth water.

"Fine," she sighed, reaching for the donut and taking a bite.

"How is it?" Sage asked, nervously biting his lip.

"It's really good," she said at last, tears starting to pool at the corners of her eyes because she knew she had failed the test and would never receive her blessings. "Really freaking good."

"Success!" Sage exclaimed, shaking her by the shoulders and pulling her into a half hug so as to not crush the donut.

"I gotta go," she mumbled, pulling out of his grasp and heading toward the kitchen door.

"Wait, Gen, wanna come with me on the delivery route later?"

"Uh. Maybe. Thanks for breakfast," she said quickly, waving the donut behind her without looking, and bolting outside. She ran straight through the pasture, behind the barn, where only the cows could see her cry.

. . .

A dozen buckets of milk and equally as many splatters of it on her overalls later, Genesis made her way through the open door of the laundry shed, where she found her definite biological mother, Grace, and her 10 percent–likely biological father, Art, poring over a pile of purple textiles in the midst of what looked like a tense conversation.

"Okay, so what did they tell you at the clinic?" Grace asked as she folded a pillowcase.

"They said it was mal-something?"

"Malignant?" Grace froze.

"Does that mean the bad kind?" he pressed.

"Yes, Art." She nodded, her face softening.

Art placed both hands on top of his stringy man-bun in distress. He still wore it that way even though his hairline seemed to be shrinking exponentially. His face crumpled, and he began to sob. Grace threw down the pillowcase and took him in her arms.

"It's okay. It's okay," she cooed.

"This wasn't supposed to happen to me," Art blubbered. "I mean, cancer? I haven't eaten a genetically modified food in decades!"

"I know."

"Now I have to figure out a way to come up with tens of thousands of dollars to pay for them to pump me up with toxic chemicals and radiation so I can *live*? Are you kidding me?"

"We will figure something out," Grace said, rubbing his back.

The Astralians had no official leader since Jimmy Joe James, but Grace, with her diplomatic ability to defuse any community conflict with her empathetic stare and soothing voice, had become the closest thing they had to one.

"Um," Genesis said quietly, making her presence in the shed known.

Grace looked up from the hug. "Gen," she breathed. "Hi."

"I . . . just . . . I wanted to throw my overalls in with the dirty stuff . . ."

"Okay," Grace said, turning to look back at Art. "First, can you do me a small favor, Gen? Can you go check the mail while me and Art finish up in here? I don't think anyone has done that today. That would be such an important contribution, don't you agree, Art?"

Art nodded once and continued to sob, his face now nearly the same color as all the laundry. Genesis knew this was a nonsense ask for privacy; no one on the ranch regularly checked the mail. All it brought were bills and notices from the Montana Department of Public Health and Human Services. But still, she complied.

As she stumbled into the midday sun and down the hill toward the ranch's timber-and-iron gated entrance, Genesis could feel her lack of proper breakfast. When she first noticed a shiny red convertible in the distance, parked outside, she swore it must've been a low blood sugar–induced illusion.

A woman emerged from the driver's seat with wavy blonde hair and sunglasses almost as big as the handbag slung over her arm. Now Genesis *knew* she was hallucinating. She was picturing Ree Reaps again.

"Hey!" the woman called from behind the gate, waving her arm.

Genesis looked over her shoulder.

"Yeah, you!" the woman said with a smile.

Genesis began to walk the several yards toward her. As she got closer, the woman flipped her sunglasses up onto her head and squinted at Genesis. Her eyebrows and lips were painted on almost like she was a cartoon. It wasn't Ree Reaps, Genesis quickly realized; she'd watched her "Five-Minute Makeup Look for Mamas on the Go!" tutorial three times and knew she'd never be so heavy handed.

"Can I help you?" Genesis asked the woman from her side of the gate, shielding her eyes from the sun.

Just then, she noticed a big, muscular guy in a black polo shirt emerging from the passenger side of the convertible.

"Oh, Gary, stay put. It's fine. I told you it'd be *fine,*" the woman said, reaching her palm out toward him to stop. "I'm sure this nice young lady isn't dangerous," she said in a stage whisper, rolling her eyes. "Old news, Gary! Anyway, hi. Do you happen to know the owner of this property?"

"Um, well, there isn't really one owner. We all kind of own it, I guess," Genesis said, squeezing her hands inside her overall pockets.

"Hmmm," the woman pondered, pursing her lips. "Interesting."

She reached into her enormous leather handbag, which Genesis could now make out was patterned in letters of brown and gold. She didn't know what they meant, but she was sure it was something expensive.

"Ah! Here we go," the woman said, finally branding a manila folder from the bag. "Okay, so see, according to county records, this land was purchased in 1999 by a woman by the name of Grace Ogilvy."

She pointed to the name on what looked like a photocopy of an official-looking document with a red-polished fingernail.

"Do you know this Ms. Ogilvy?" she pressed.

Genesis's stomach dropped. She didn't know a Grace *Ogilvy*, but she knew a *Grace Astralian*, the only person named Grace on the ranch. She'd never known what her legal name was before she dropped it, like all devoted members did upon joining.

Genesis just shook her head. The woman stared at her critically for a moment before putting a friendly face back on.

"Huh. All right. Well, you know what, honey? Why don't I just give you my card, and you can pass it along and see if anyone else knows Ms. Ogilvy?" she asked, reaching back into her bag. "And if you find her, you tell her my client is looking to make a *veeeerrrry* generous offer for her property."

She took out a small white card from a bedazzled metal case and handed it to Genesis through the gate with a wink.

Faith Johnson

Licensed Real Estate Agent

Community Development, Hope Harvest Church

Genesis let out a small gasp. Despite living just a few miles from the church, she had never met any of its members in the flesh.

Blessings, Genesis thought as she watched the convertible speed away, leaving behind a cloud of dust. *B-L-E-S-S-I-N-G-S!*

2

HOLLY

Holly hadn't planned to lie to her friends about where she was going for the summer. Like the other lies she told them, it just kind of slipped out.

The first domino fell on the first dress-down day of Holly's first year at Hawthorne Prep. She had been struggling to make friends for weeks at her new fancy private school when Marissa Roberts complimented her shirt and asked where it was from. Holly told her she bought it at Brandy Melville, when in reality she'd thrifted it from Savers for three dollars because that was all her mom could afford. When Marissa invited her out to a fancy sushi restaurant with the rest of the group, Holly only ordered green tea, and when they asked why, she said she was vegan even though her favorite food was cheese. When they all turned sixteen and got gifted Teslas, she invented a fear of driving though she'd actually passed her license exam on the first try after practicing in her stepdad's used Kia.

After a childhood of moving around and never having a best friend aside from her own mom, Holly was now fitting in (she even got to stop lying about her secondhand clothes once the other girls decided thrifting was cool, though they certainly weren't doing it out of necessity). She planned on keeping things that way, hoping no one ever got close enough to her to find out her whole life was a construct.

The more lies she told, the worse the truth became. Now she was hiding more than the reality of her family's finances, and she didn't have a single friend she could confide in about it.

So there it was: *I'm going away this summer. To visit my dad. Um, in Iceland. I know, soooo random. Yeah. He's Icelandic. That's why my hair's so blonde. I'm half Icelandic.*

As she stared at the Bridger Range from outside Bozeman Yellowstone International Airport, she wondered if her friends would be able to tell the difference between these peaks and valleys and the Icelandic ones if she took a picture and posted it to Instagram. Maybe if she added a blueish filter? This was her stupidest lie yet. She considered not posting anything all summer, and if they asked why, she would say it was because an international phone plan was too expensive. But besides making her look cheap, wouldn't that make them question how she was still able to answer their texts?

A pickup trunk honked a few feet away from Holly, interrupting her brainstorm on how to dig herself out of this hole of her own making. She looked up and realized it was her dad waving to her through the window of a Ford F-150. He got out and walked around the front of the car.

"Hey. How was the flight?" Danny asked, giving her an awkward one-armed hug.

"Good. How was the drive?"

"Good."

He smiled at her and blinked twice, then reached for her suitcase and placed it in the back of the truck. Conversation was never his strength, but in texts and emails he'd sounded enthusiastic about her visit, even venturing to use a smile emoji once or twice. He'd told her how he'd stopped working in construction to run the town diner he'd inherited from his uncle. Holly had a hard time imagining this; one of her few vivid memories from visiting Violet was his terrible cooking.

They headed out to drive the remaining two hours north to Violet, listening to the staticky local oldies radio station.

"So, uh, do you want to talk about what happened?" Danny asked her after about forty-five minutes, staring straight ahead at the road.

"Not really, if I'm being honest," she said, giving him a tentative glance.

"Maybe some other time." His shoulders relaxed; he was relieved, as if he could cross off his one fatherly task of the year from his to-do list.

By late afternoon, they passed the NOW ENTERING VIOLET sign and turned down Main Street.

"You know, the town's changed a lot since you were a kid," Danny said, giving her a glance. "Might never compete with Los Angeles, but they sure as hell are trying."

Holly sat up in her seat, craning her head out the window and feeling like she had stumbled onto the set of a Hallmark movie.

The space where the run-down pharmacy used to be had been transformed into something proclaiming itself an "all-American gastropub." The soda fountain next door had been turned into a coffee shop with a sandwich board out front advertising matcha lattes and avocado toast. What used to be a discount appliance depot was now piled high with a display of faux-distressed signs that said words like FAMILY and FAITH. One space looked like a knockoff version of the chain of blow-dry bars where her mom, Courtney, used to work; through the windows, Holly could see a row of women having their hair stretched and curled into identical styles. The sidewalks were full of people and strollers. Most of the women wore either floral-print dresses or jumpsuits that went to their ankles.

Most baffling of all, the massive marquee above the movie theater, which frustrated Holly as a child because it was always showing movies she'd seen three years previously and never the hottest Pixar movie of the summer, was no longer advertising showtimes for films, just "Sunday Services."

"Wait, wasn't that the gum factory?" Holly asked, pointing in the distance toward a now-repurposed industrial warehouse with an enormous sign out front that read HOPE HARVEST II EST. 2017. A group of girls about her age took a selfie in front of it. Holly subconsciously slumped in her seat.

"Yep," Danny nodded. "The Reaps family bought it a few years after the accident. Turned it into some kind of church slash store slash restaurant slash who knows what . . ."

"Who are the Reaps family?" she pressed.

"You remember that church near the highway overpass?"

"Kind of." She didn't.

"Well, that's been there for years. Your grandparents used to go every Sunday. But, uh, Pastor Reaps's son took over a few years ago, and him and his wife . . . they're trying to make Violet this . . . this . . . Jesus-themed Disneyland. Basically."

Holly raised her eyebrows. "Well, at least that's good for the diner. You must get a lot more business now, right?"

Danny just frowned. As they pulled into the diner parking lot toward the end of Main Street, the answer was clear. There were only two cars, and the restaurant's vintage metal exterior was rusting—a beacon of authentic distress unlike all the reproductions being sold down the street.

"Hungry?" he asked.

"Sure," Holly said, though suddenly she had lost her appetite.

When they went inside, there were a couple of old men drinking coffee at the counter and a family sitting in the corner booth, getting yelled at by their waitress.

"Sir, I can't tell you what each of the nine grains are. We don't bake it on the premises," she said in a raspy voice. "All I know is we offer four kinds of toast: white, wheat, rye, and nine grain." The waitress paused and splayed her fingers to count the varieties. "If you're uncomfortable consuming a bread of which you do not know all the ingredients, I suggest you order one of our three other toast options to accompany your meal, which I might add, includes eggs, bacon, pancakes, coffee, and juice. Realistically, you're not even gonna get to the toast. It's too much food. People order this every day. I swear I dump their uneaten toast in the trash about seventy-five percent of the time—"

The dad raised his palms. "Hey, now what kind of hospitality is this, young lady?"

The waitress let out one humorless laugh. "You want hospitality? Go down the street and pay eighteen dollars for eggs, see if I care!"

Danny pinched the bridge of his nose and rushed over to the table.

"Zoe, let me handle this. Um, sorry about that. The grains in the bread are . . . wheat, barley, rye, quinoa, millet, oat, uh . . . shoot . . ."

The man's wife slapped her laminated menu on the table. "You know what? We *are* just going to go down the street. The only reason we came to this dump was because the wait over there was too long, but now I can see why it's worth it. Expect a *lengthy* Yelp review from us later. C'mon, kids." The family filed out of the booth and left.

"Danny, I'm sorry," Zoe said, turning toward him. "They were just totally being a pain in my you-know-what."

She was a lot younger-looking than her voice let on she and Holly had to be about the same age. Her unnaturally red hair was in a ponytail with jagged short bangs across her forehead, and eyeliner was smudged around her eyes. She wore multiple earrings up and down her ear and a pin on her apron that said JESUS DIED FOR MY SINS! WHAT AN IDIOT! I WOULD NOT DIE FOR HIM!

"That's the third time this week, Zoe," Danny whined. "And you're wearing the pin?!"

"What? It's just a joke!" Zoe exclaimed.

"You know I don't personally have a problem with it, but we've at least got to, you know, sing for our supper with this crowd, if you get what I mean."

"Oh my god!" Zoe blurted out, completely ignoring him. "Holly!"

She jumped up and swung her arms around her. Holly's shoulders stiffened, but she reciprocated.

"Uh, hey," she said.

Zoe pulled out of the hug.

"You totally don't remember me, do you?" she asked with hurt eyes. "We used to play together in my kiddie pool and braid each other's hair. All these years I've considered you my best friend, and now you're back . . ."

Holly's mouth gaped. "Well, now that you mention it, um—"

"I'm kidding! I'm totally kidding, oh my god, you looked so freaked out," Zoe said, playfully swatting her arm with her order pad. "Anyway, it's so good to have you back in town. I know Danny's been looking forward to having you here. Hasn't shut up about it for weeks!"

Danny shifted uncomfortably. "Holly, what can I get you to eat?" he asked.

"Um, I don't know. What's your specialty here?"

"Hmm. That's a good question . . ." Danny pondered for a few seconds, making it clear that this was more of an existential inquiry than Holly had intended.

"How about some pie?" Zoe interjected. "That's my favorite."

"Pie. Yes," Danny said, looking dazed and walking toward the swinging kitchen door. "You two catch up. I have to check on some things in the back. Be careful around this one, Holly," he called over his shoulder. "She's a bad influence."

Zoe stuck out her tongue, then gestured for Holly to take a seat at one of the battered red vinyl stools lining the counter and made her way around to the other side. Holly felt so instantly welcomed that it took on the reverse effect of making her uncomfortable; she wasn't used to people being so unabashedly friendly. At home she sometimes felt like she was in a contest with her friends for who could be the least earnest.

"Do you want me to be honest with you?" Zoe asked in a low voice, opening the pie case on the counter.

"Okay," Holly said skeptically.

"The pie is the only good thing we serve here. And Danny doesn't even make it. We get them from the Astralians."

"Australia?!"

"No, Astralian without the *u*. Danny's told you about them, right?"

"Wait, like that cult?"

"Yep. Jimmy Joe James was hot, but he was *so* bad at names. And following the law, I guess. Anyway, they bring us milk, eggs, and bread too. The eggs are good, but only if Danny or Arnold, the line cook, doesn't burn them. Which they both tend to do," Zoe said, scooping up a piece of apple pie with a cutter and putting it on a plate. "Whipped cream?"

"No thanks," Holly answered. "I didn't even know the Astralians still existed."

"Yeah, they're just, like, old hippie farmers now," Zoe said, sliding the pie across the counter. "Then again, I don't know. They homeschool their kids and everyone wears purple and they only move around in packs. Like, who knows what trafficking ring they could be running right under our noses?" She paused to stare out the window. "Though I'd take that over whatever the hell is happening out there. My dad freaking died in that gum factory, and now Ree Reaps is selling inspirational plaques inside of it! Totally tasteless."

"Oh. I didn't realize. I'm so sorry," Holly murmured, staring at her pie, her mouth going dry.

Zoe shrugged. "It's fine. I was little when it happened. But, hey, enough about me. What brings you here this summer of all summers?"

Holly thought about telling Zoe the truth; she seemed like the type of person who didn't judge. Or, at least, didn't judge people she liked. There was a high chance if Holly told her what she'd done, Zoe would write off Holly as a spoiled brat. Anyway, she decided opening up to Zoe would be admitting that she was her real peer, the actual type of person who could relate to her, not the girls with shiny hair back in LA.

"Change of scenery," Holly finally lied, and took a bite of pie. The crust crumbled like sawdust on her tongue. "Getting away from all the smog," she added, followed by a violent cough. "I thought it'd be good for me."

Zoe leaned on the counter and stared out the window dreamily.

"God, what I wouldn't do for some *smog*. I mean, yeah, sure, it's nice living near the mountains—the fresh air, the natural beauty, blah, blah—but it is boooring. You get to live near so much culture! So many different kinds of people! I can count on one hand the number of interesting people in this town. Two, maybe three." She looked back to Holly and cocked her head. "Four, once I've made my decision about you."

"I'm . . . interesting," Holly said unconvincingly.

"Oh, yeah?" Zoe raised her eyebrows. "What do you like to do for fun?"

Holly opened her mouth to speak but came up blank. She couldn't think of the last time she'd genuinely had fun. There were times she must have looked like she was, going to house parties, hanging out by Marissa's pool, but she was too consumed by the anxiety of saying the right things and giving off the right appearance to truly have a good time.

Before she could say anything, the bell over the diner door dinged. She turned her head to see two teenagers both wearing head-to-toe-purple outfits. They were beautiful in a unique way, like they were stopping here on their way to modeling a monochromatic runway collection for some trendy designer.

"One second," Zoe said to her, then turned her head toward the pair. "Hey, Sage!" she called loudly at the boy. "You're right on time. I just served our very last piece of apple pie. We've gotta replenish the supply!"

"Well, you know, Zoe, us Astralians are psychic. I had a vision that you would run out of pie today."

"Seriously?!"

"No. I'm just joking," he said with a laugh. The girl with him just stared at the floor, with her hands in her pockets.

"Why would you lie to me like that, Sage? I thought I could trust you," Zoe said, mock-offended. "You're one of the only men in this town I actually tolerate. If it weren't for you, I would probably starve."

"Thank you, Zoe. It is an honor to be tolerated by you."

Holly swore she saw the girl in purple roll her eyes.

"This is Holly, by the way," Zoe said. "Danny's daughter! She came all the way from the City of Angels just to eat your pie."

Holly cringed internally at this introduction. How could she always find something to be embarrassed about, even in front of absolute strangers she had no intention of ever meeting again?

"Nice to meet you," Sage said, reaching out his hand. "That's Genesis." He pointed a thumb toward the girl. She meekly waved a hand without making eye contact.

Danny burst through the kitchen doors with a dish towel slung over his shoulder. "I'll help you unload the truck. Oh, and before I forget, can you tell me all the nine grains that are in your nine-grain bread? People were asking."

"Sure. Can you walk and talk? We have to make it back to the ranch before sundown," Sage said, pushing the glass door and propping it open with a nearby doorstop. Danny pulled an order pad and pen from under the counter. "So there's wheat, barley, pumpernickel . . ."

"Pumpernickel!" Danny mumbled to himself, writing everything down frantically. Genesis followed the pair to the delivery van parked outside.

"Oh my god," Holly said to Zoe, leaning over the counter. "They're, like, really beautiful."

"I know," Zoe agreed. "It has to be the result of inbreeding or something."

"Do you think so?"

"I mean, I don't think they take new members anymore. They all have to be cousins to keep repopulating, right? He's brought that girl Genesis with him ever since he took over for this old weirdo who used to do the deliveries, and I can never tell what their deal is," Zoe said, turning her back to pour two cups of coffee from the pot behind the counter. "Like, I think she's his sister? But, like . . . is she his wife? One of his *many* wives? His daughter?! Okay, maybe not daughter, but he hasn't explicitly said otherwise. And she never speaks. Obviously, I think Sage is great, but I don't actually *know* him. Part of me is like, blink twice if you need rescuing, girl."

Zoe turned with mugs in hand and jumped an inch, her eyes going wide for a second.

"You can just set those on the counter," she said, recomposing her face with a small smile. Holly turned to see Genesis standing still behind them with a stack of three boxed pies in her hands, staring straight at Zoe and scowling.

"And don't forget about the amaranth, Danny. That's the least of the nine grains, but it still plays a very important role," Sage said, following Danny through the door, both of them carrying flats of eggs.

"Got it," Danny said, taking a deep breath and setting the eggs down. "I'll settle up with you in a second."

Danny went behind the counter to the register, then came back around with a small bunch of bills and gave them to Sage with a handshake.

"See you all next week," Sage said. "Nice to meet you, Holly." He looked at her and waved. Genesis pushed herself out the door without acknowledging any of them.

As the Astralians' delivery van pulled out of the parking lot, Zoe put her head in her hands. "She heard me talking crap, didn't she?"

"No, no, definitely not!" Holly reassured her.

Zoe looked up and searched her face. "You don't have to sugar-coat it."

Holly felt exposed. Was she always this unconvincing, or was everyone in her life just not really paying attention? "Okay, she definitely did."

"Ugh. I want today to be over," Zoe groaned. She rubbed her eyes, further smudging the eyeliner around them. "Hey, do you have any plans tonight?"

Holly pretended to rack her brain, knowing full well her only plan was to crawl into bed and ideally stay there for the next three months. "I have a FaceTime date with some friends later," she lied. "Can't miss it."

"Well, if you get done early, you should come hang out with me and my friend Delia. Her parents aren't home tonight, and she has a firepit. We're gonna make s'mores!"

"Oh." Holly was taken aback. She wasn't sure exactly what she expected Zoe to do with her free time. Probably something closer to ax-throwing than s'mores-making.

"We never make new friends," Zoe went on. "So many people have been moving here lately, but they're all clones of each other. Your arrival is thrilling."

"Well, I should also unpack all my stuff tonight. After the Face-Time, so—"

"How much do you have to unpack, anyway?" She sipped her coffee and eyed Holly critically. "Let me guess: half a dozen crop tops, some scrunchies. Maybe a pair of Crocs? I heard they're cool now, but I'm refusing to believe it."

"No!" Holly blurted. "Well, actually, yeah. Minus the Crocs. They were cool, but then they became so cool that it made them uncool again. Is that what you think people from LA wear?"

Zoe shrugged. "It's just what I've inferred."

"From what?"

"The internet. We do have that here in Montana."

Holly stared at Zoe's purple-painted fingernails bitten down to the quick gripping the sides of her coffee mug. Under normal circumstances, they wouldn't be friends, but it was clear Violet was an alternate universe.

"All right, then," Holly relented. "I guess that means you can text me your friend's address."

3

ZOE

Zoe Peters parked her bike against the chain-link fence surrounding the tiny plot of land her family called home. She wiped the sweat on her forehead with the back of her hand and got a whiff of her armpits combined with her overall aroma of bacon grease and coffee grinds. What she wanted more than anything in the world was a shower. But first she had to navigate the tower of packages blocking her front door.

They all had the same return address:

Hope Harvest, LLC

1600 Faith Way

Violet, MT 59789-3001

She reached over the packages to unlock the door, then kicked them into the entryway with zero concern for their contents.

"Hey, Mama," Zoe called into the little blue house, a blast of cool air hitting her face. "You got some more stuff in the mail."

"Just leave 'em there," Marla called back from the living room.

Zoe stacked the boxes with the approximately two dozen others that sat unopened, completely eclipsing the space that was once their dining room. She walked into the living room, where her mother was creating her own personal hole in the earth's ozone layer by blasting the window AC unit, watching a home renovation show on the TV, scrolling Instagram on her iPad that was plugged into its charger, and sticking her feet into an electric foot massager all at once.

"How much more junk are you gonna order from those people?" Zoe said, flopping down on the couch next to her.

"It is not junk, Zoe," Marla protested, shifting her eyes from the iPad to the unveiling of a new sparkling kitchen on the TV. "It is a business opportunity!"

"Yeah, that's what you said about the makeup. Then the diet shakes. Then the essential oils . . ."

"Those were different. That was just pushing products. With the Reapses, it's like . . . I've been going to church with these people all my life. I trust them! And we both believe in the same thing: to reach and influence the world by building—"

"The greatest Christ-centered, Bible-based organization in the world, by encouraging people to lead, changing their mindsets to grow, and empowering their hearts, stomachs, and wallets with the best country-inspired meal kits on the planet," Zoe finished her sentence robotically. "Yeah. I know."

She stood up, walked over to the packages, and started ripping the tape off one of them.

"Zoe!" Marla exclaimed, finally peeling her eyes away from her devices. "Don't mess with my inventory!"

Zoe ignored her mother and pulled a smaller box out of some

packing peanuts. The front was printed with a photo of Ree Reaps clutching a steaming casserole dish of mac and cheese with two gingham pot holders.

"Ree's Super-Creamy Country Mac and Cheese?" Zoe said, reading the box. "Do you really believe that's what's inside here? That this is anything special?"

"Of course!"

"Hold on. Let me prove it to you." Zoe stormed into the kitchen and rifled through the cupboard until she found what she was looking for.

"Ah! See," she said, a box of Kraft Macaroni & Cheese in one hand, Ree's in the other. "Look at the ingredients list. They're both made of enriched macaroni product, riboflavin, whey, milkfat, milk protein concentrate, salt, sodium tripoly-something—all the same. Except then the Hope Harvest one randomly has even more preservatives I can't pronounce. One we can just buy at Walmart for a dollar and change, the other you get charged hundreds of dollars a month for."

Marla sighed and pushed her pink plastic glasses up her nose. "You're not accounting for that this mac and cheese doesn't expire until 2035. And it's organic. It's a miracle."

"There is no way any of that can be true. Who is actually going to buy this stuff from you? If everyone else in town is trying to sell it, who is your customer?"

"Well, your aunt Sharon said she might be interested. And six people tuned into my last Facebook live. But that's only the beginning."

"I'm just saying, you have to be careful with your money. Daddy's workers' comp payout is only going to last so long."

Zoe's father had been the factory floor manager at the Violet Gum & Mints plant and one of the casualties from the explosion. Because he knew of his wife's impulsive buying habits, he had gotten his will in order years before. It stated that Zoe and her older brother, Tom, would split half of his remaining assets when they each turned eighteen and that Marla would receive the other half, their house, and any workers' compensation resulting from his death. The "remaining assets" amounted to about twenty thousand dollars split between the siblings.

"You don't have to worry about my money, Zoe. God is always going to provide," Marla said, turning her head back to the TV. "Oh, would you look at that!"

Zoe glanced at the screen to see a walk-in closet the size of their living and dining rooms combined, filled with shelves of shoes and handbags arranged in rainbow order.

"The things I would do for a house like that . . ." Marla sighed. "I bet that's what Ree Reaps's closet looks like."

"Mama, you know what the tenth commandment says: thou shalt not covet."

"Oh, really?" Marla asked, raising her eyebrows. "Surprised you still remember the Ten Commandments given that you haven't come to church with me in a while."

"Just because I don't go doesn't mean I don't think about them," Zoe mumbled under her breath, walking back into the kitchen and putting the box of normal mac and cheese back in its place.

She opened the cupboard where the drinking glasses and mugs lived, pausing to consider how everything in their kitchen, possibly their entire house, that could have an inspirational phrase on it did. Pot holders that said HOPE, magnets that said PRAY, wineglasses that said DANCE LIKE NO ONE'S WATCHING. Since Zoe's dad died, it was like Marla needed constant instruction from the objects around her on how to be a person. It certainly didn't help that the sermons she listened to every week contained just about as much depth as her soap dish that simply said FAITH.

Zoe smiled to herself as she imagined swapping out the stone engraved with the Ten Commandments in front of Hope Harvest's original location with another that said *1. Thou shalt live. 2. Thou shalt laugh. 3. Thou shalt love.* She doubted anyone would even notice.

From the cupboard, she settled on a blissfully simple mason jar and held it under the faucet, but when she turned the knob, no water came out.

"Hey, Mama!" she hollered.

"Yeah?" Marla answered.

"The water's not working. Are they doing some construction outside again or something?"

There was silence.

"Mama?"

"I don't know, honey."

Zoe walked back into the living room, the empty glass in her hand.

"Did you pay the water bill last month, Mama?"

Marla just stared intently toward the TV screen. She was good at bending the truth, at distorting the circumstances of her own reality, but because of her Christian convictions, she would never, ever straight-up lie.

"No," she said at last.

"Why not?"

"I maxed out my credit cards for the month. It was between the water and the electricity bill, and, well, I couldn't go without . . ." Marla gestured to all of her devices.

"Were you not going to tell me?" Zoe raised her voice. "Just hope I didn't notice? We're just supposed to live without water?"

"We just have to make it till next month, Zoe."

"It's the fourteenth. That's over two weeks away."

"I've got bottled water in the fridge," Marla said, pointing to her own Dasani on the coffee table. "And we've still got those jugs in the basement from when I tried being a Wellspring salesperson. And I figure, you're at work all day. You can get water there."

"How are we supposed to wash our hands? How are we supposed to shower?" Zoe asked, thinking of the outer layer of grease that had formed on her body after a day at the diner.

"You can stay over at Delia's, right?"

"I can't *live* at Delia's for the next three weeks," Zoe cried. "Did you not realize that this is, like, inhumane?" Zoe stared up at the ceiling and sighed. "How much is the water bill, Mama? I don't want to make a habit of this, but I can lend you my paycheck until the next workers' comp check comes in."

"No, no. I don't want to make you do that."

"Just tell me how much."

"Don't worry about it, Zoe."

Just then, she heard her brother's bedroom door open down the hall.

"Tom, did you know about this?" Zoe cried, following him into the kitchen. He was wearing his signature noise-canceling headphones, so he couldn't hear her.

"Tom!" she yelled, pulling them off his ears.

"Owww," he whined. "What?"

"Did you know we don't have any running water?"

"Oh," he said, squinting. "I hadn't noticed." He reached into the fridge and pulled out a Glacier Freeze–flavored Gatorade, his preferred beverage.

"What have you even been doing all day?" Zoe asked, cringing as she watched him slurp down the antifreeze-looking liquid.

"I was just, like, online and stuff." He shrugged, then wiped his mouth with the back of his hand like he was recovering from running a marathon instead of browsing Reddit.

"*Online and stuff?*" Zoe groaned. "Are you ever going to get a job?"

"Jobs are just . . . humiliating, Zoe." Tom leaned against the fridge and sighed. "I have no aspirations in life because I have no material needs, okay? I'm not like you, obsessed with the idea of moving from your so-called nowhere town to some elite coastal city that's going to get sucked up by the rising tides in a few decades anyway. Besides, you forget jobs aren't the only way to make money."

"Oh, is that so?"

"Yeah. There's investments. Like, I've got a case of pre-ban Four Loko sitting in the basement that I bought all the way back in middle school from the guy down at the gas station when it got recalled. Full ABV. Full caffeine. It's been aging like a fine wine since 2010. When the moment's right, I'm going to sell it on eBay for thousands. Possibly tens of thousands."

"Wow. Silly of me to forget!" Zoe mocked. "So in the meantime . . . Gatorade and headphones just grow on trees?"

"Of course not," he said incredulously. "That's why I order the few things I do need on Amazon, then claim they never arrived and receive a refund."

Zoe closed her eyes and stuck her fingers through her bangs. "I never thought I'd say this, but everyone in this house desperately needs Jesus."

. . .

There was one reason and one reason only that Zoe was grateful to Hope Harvest Church: it was why Delia Johnson's family had moved to town.

Delia's parents both worked for the Reaps family empire and brought in hefty salaries. So in an indirect way, the money Hope Harvest squeezed out of Zoe's mom was at least used to pay for the pizza rolls Zoe was eating in Delia's canopy bed.

"If getting scammed were a talent, I swear my mom would win awards. Pageants, even," Zoe said, wiping tomato sauce from her hand onto the plush bathrobe she'd borrowed from Delia. "A big old sash across her chest that says, 'Miss Easy Money.'"

"It's not her fault," Delia said, pulling a comb through Zoe's wet hair. "These schemes are designed to prey on people like her: no education, no job prospects, no ho—"

"Hope?" Zoe finished Delia's sentence, turning around to glare at her. "Ironic, isn't it?"

"I'm sorry, Zo. I wish I could do something to help."

"This isn't your fault," Zoe said, her eyes softening. "You're doing enough by letting me shower here."

"You know you're welcome to shower here anytime."

"I know."

"Literally anytime. Even if you're not dirty. Maybe you're just in the neighborhood and wanting to shower recreationally? No problem. We could even shower . . . recreationally . . . together . . ."

"Oh yeah?" Zoe asked, smirking at her. "That sounds kind of gross. Like showering in gym class."

Delia put the comb down. "I assure you this would be like showering after an extremely fun, hot, sexy gym class."

"Ewww," Zoe snickered, then leaned in to kiss her.

Suddenly there was a heavy knock at the door. "Delia?"

Delia swore under her breath and jumped off the bed. "Yeah, Mom?" she called. Zoe shifted into her best attempt at "acting natural."

The door opened, and Faith Johnson poked her head in. "Hey, sweet—oh, hi, Zoe. You look comfy."

Zoe looked down, realizing she was lying across the bed, reclining Venus-style, though holding a pizza roll rather than a bundle of roses.

"How've you been? Haven't seen you at church in a couple of weeks," Faith added.

Try months, Zoe thought. "Yeah, I know. They've got me working weekends down at the diner. I'm trying to save up for college. But, you know, praise the Lord I can still fit in youth group on Saturday nights." She raised her hand toward the ceiling. "Delia was generous enough to do my hair for the occasion."

Anytime Delia was hanging out with Zoe, she lied and told her parents she was at youth group. Zoe wasn't terribly convincing, but it didn't matter; Faith Johnson's eyes were zeroing in on a pizza-sauce stain on Zoe's robe, probably already calculating how much OxiClean it would take to get it out.

"So what's up, Mom?" Delia asked. "I thought you and Dad were going out for dinner tonight."

"Well, we were, but then Mrs. Clark called and let me know she's sick and can't host Girls Ministry anymore. She asked me if we could swap weeks, so we're having it *here* tonight."

Zoe's stomach sank. Girls Ministry was an offshoot of the main Hope Harvest youth group in which just the girls ages fourteen to eighteen went to someone's house for a bonding activity and an intimate discussion about a topic that was apparently unfit for boys' ears.

"Oh. Nice," Delia said coolly, hiding what Zoe recognized as disappointment. "What's tonight's topic?"

"It's, um, let me check my email again." Faith pulled out her phone from the pocket of her jumpsuit. "'How to Keep Up with the Trends while Staying Modest.' Oh, perfect! You know, D, maybe this will be inspiring for you. That little jump start you need to start dressing with pizzazz!"

Zoe could scream. Did Mrs. Johnson not realize that her daughter exclusively wore baggy flannel shirts and Vans? That "pizzazz" for her meant cuffing the one pair of Levi's she wore every single day? Did she ever pause to consider that the reason young Delia watched her DVD of *Freaky Friday* so much that it broke wasn't just because she loved the movie's excellent soundtrack but because the part where Jamie Lee Curtis goes through a makeover montage was the source of her sexual awakening?

Even worse, Zoe thought, Mrs. Johnson probably *did* realize. She just chose to blatantly ignore it.

"I'm comfortable in this, Mom," Delia answered patiently.

"Oh, but how will you ever get Dustin Reaps's attention in that?" Faith pouted. "She hates when I say it, but, Zoe, don't you just think Delia and Dustin would make the cutest couple?"

"Definitely!" Zoe answered through an enormous fake smile. "Their ship name could be Double D!"

"Ha!" Faith exclaimed. "Double D. That's cute."

Delia's face contorted like she was half stifling a laugh, half trying not to vomit at the thought of herself with Dustin Reaps, their pastor's oldest son, who looked like he could be the third-most attractive member in any given boy band. "You both seem to be conveniently forgetting that he has a girlfriend!"

"Yeah, precisely. A *girlfriend*. Not a wife." Zoe wiggled her eyebrows. "You've got a solid couple of years until they get married to slide into that relationship."

Faith frowned at Zoe and cleared her throat; the girl had taken the joke a bit too far. "Why don't you two come help me set up some chairs outside when you get a second?"

Once the door had closed again, Zoe flipped over and dug her face into a pillow. "Uuugh! I know I say this, like, every day, but is she completely oblivious?"

Delia sat back on the bed. "She sees what she wants."

When Zoe first realized she definitely liked girls, she turned to Pastor Marcus, Hope Harvest's youth pastor—who inexplicably always wore a wicker fedora and would end his prayers with "talk to you later, big guy" instead of "amen"—and asked for guidance. He looked at her with panicked eyes, like she was suddenly made of radioactive material, told her not to panic, and that they could pray about it together. This was really the final straw in a series of unsatisfying nonanswers to Zoe's other concerns like "If it's God's will for his people to prosper, then why do one percent of Americans hold ninety-nine percent of the nation's wealth?" and "Literally why does anyone need to own an assault rifle other than murder?"

Zoe often got in trouble for her running commentary, or just running her mouth, as some people at church saw it. But when Delia moved to town, it was like she finally had a deserving audience, someone she could make knowing eye contact with during the cringeworthy parts of sermons and who actually laughed at her jokes. During a youth camping retreat, while Pastor Marcus was yammering on about the dangers of using Snapchat for lustful purposes, Zoe and Delia snuck off to the woods and made out after many Sundays of pent-up tension and eye contact that became not just knowing, but meaningful. Two years later, their relationship was still going strong *and* undetected.

Delia was scared to tell her parents that she wasn't interested in the pastor's son, nor anyone's son for that matter, because she knew it would shatter their world. But Zoe was always waiting with a boulder in her hands, prepared to shatter it the moment she had Delia's permission. Keeping their relationship a secret was an everyday battle between Zoe's brain and her mouth.

More and more, she stopped going to youth group and started taking on Sunday morning shifts at the diner. Some days Zoe still believed in God, others not so much, but she was certain that Hope Harvest's lighthearted approach to such heavy questions about human existence wasn't for her.

Without mentioning Delia, Zoe came out to her mom, whose stance on being gay was about the same as Hope Harvest's official written stance toward LGBTQ people: "While we believe marriage can only exist between a man and a woman, we welcome all people, regardless of their beliefs, values, or personal identity, into our doors." (They never really elaborated on what would happen once you were actually inside the doors.)

"I know your mom doesn't like me," Zoe said. "Not that I care what she thinks of me or anything, but this whole *I'm your bad-influence friend who you're quietly guiding back to the light of Jesus Christ* routine is getting exhausting."

"Well, at least she thinks you're funny, like with the Double D joke—which, excuse me, what was that?!"

"I was trolling her!" Zoe exclaimed. "It's how I stop myself from saying other things like, 'Mrs. Johnson, if you would pause for a second to use more than a single brain cell, you would clearly see that it's actually me and Delia who make the cutest couple!' It's how I cope when everything sucks."

"Everything does not suck."

"My mom has been brainwashed into selling fake artisanal Hamburger Helper to support a pyramid scheme, and now my family's broke. Your mom will not stop until she's forced you into a marriage to Dustin Reaps and you've given birth to some ugly blond toddler named, like, Deklynn. Everything *does* suck!"

"First of all, Zo, if I married the pastor's kid, you know I'd also be forced to name our demon spawn James Dustin Reaps III—or Dustiny, if it was a girl. Second of all, that is not going to happen." She reached out and grabbed Zoe's hands. "Because I love you."

"Yeah, I love you too," Zoe sighed. "But sadly our love can't pay the bills."

Delia just sat quietly; she didn't know what to say to that. Zoe loved that, unlike everyone else in town, Delia wasn't obsessed with material things, but she never once had to worry about money or consider how much it cost to keep the water running in her own family's house.

She chewed on a pizza roll, contemplating. "It's crazy to think that Dustin Reaps could probably pay my family's water bill by selling just *one* pair of his designer sneakers."

"Zoe . . ." Delia rolled her eyes.

"I know. My mind."

"We're done talking about this."

"What?" Zoe said, glancing at the heavy wooden bedroom door. "They can't hear us!"

"Just . . . enough with the Reaps talk! You know I agree with everything you say about them. So let's just savor these few moments we have together until our night is totally ruined." She wrapped her arm around Zoe.

"Fine." Zoe started to nuzzle into Delia, then paused. "But can I get one more thing off my chest and then I'll stop talking about them forever?"

"*One* more thing . . ." Delia sighed.

"It's just the Reapses' money doesn't even belong to them anyway! They are not as 'hashtag blessed!' as they claim! They're emotional manipulators. I bet you Ree hasn't worked an honest day in her life. I wouldn't be surprised if she's not human but an experiment born in the same lab where Starbucks concocted the pumpkin spice latte."

"Listen, Zo, I know it's easy to get hung up on these people, and you're not wrong for it, but soon they won't be your problem. Your mom is an adult. She's made her choices, and soon you'll be an adult too. When you turn eighteen, you'll get that money your dad put aside for you. We'll get out of this town. We just have to be patient. Really, there's nothing to worry about."

In her head, Zoe had designated the ten grand from her dad as her Get Out of Violet fund. On days when her tips from the diner were meager, when she had to listen to men loudly spout right-wing talking points over their eggs, when another one of her mother's frivolous purchases showed up on their doorstep, the thought of her inheritance sitting safely in the bank was like a fluffy, immaculate hotel bed for her tired soul.

Of course Zoe wasn't naive. She knew that a couple thousand dollars didn't get you as far in the world as you would expect; she was prepared to apply for financial aid and an ungodly amount of student loans to pay for college. Still, combined with the little money she was able to save working at the diner, it was enough to pay the toll over the imaginary bridge that would get her and Delia out of Violet. She often daydreamed about them zooming out of town in a convertible, a sign on the back of the car reading SEE YOU NEVER!!!

"My birthday's still nine months away," Zoe whined. "That might as well be forever."

"Patience is a virtue," Delia said ironically, but also, Zoe could tell, a little bit seriously.

"No one actually gets anything in this world by being virtuous," Zoe answered, reaching for two more pizza rolls with one hand.

4
GENESIS

In the passenger seat of the delivery van, Genesis pressed her forehead to the window and watched the distant mountain range pass her by.

Blink twice if you need rescuing, girl.

The words from the waitress at the diner bounced around in her head like a rubber ball. Against her better judgment, she joined Sage on his delivery route out of her fangirlish hopes that she would get a glimpse of her hero, Ree Reaps, mingling with the locals on Main Street. Now she was regretting it.

How dare Zoe assume Genesis was just some helpless sister-wife! She was a real person with real thoughts and real hopes and real dreams! Not that she could ever share them with anybody.

Yet even though Genesis felt misunderstood, a small part of her felt *seen*. Zoe's comments meant she'd been watching her. She'd thought about her. Genesis never considered that someone out there in the world was thinking about her.

"Everything all right, Gen?" Sage asked, glancing at her from the driver's seat.

"Mm-hmm," she answered.

"You're quiet today."

"I'm always quiet."

"Not with me. What's on your mind, Beginning?"

Genesis sat up and half smiled. "Beginning" had been Sage's nickname for her ever since they were little kids and he'd asked her what her name meant. She pretended to hate it but secretly loved that he had a nickname for her that he only used when they were alone.

"Oh, I'm just imagining what life would be like if the ranch ceased to exist," she said, trying to make her tone sarcastic but failing.

Sage raised an eyebrow. "That's pretty intense."

"It's just, this is the only life we've ever known. What if something were to happen and we were all forced to just become a part of the real world? Would we be able to handle it?"

"Ah, the elusive real world . . ." Sage mused.

"Seriously. And what if that could actually be a good thing? What if the ranch is past its expiration date?"

The Astralians still met for daily yoga and meditation, but gone were the daylong meditation marathons and wild visions. They still wore purple, like Jimmy Joe James dictated them to after he had a particularly memorable hallucination in which he envisioned everyone he knew growing on a vine like grapes, but now they rarely made their own clothes or sourced their own dyes from berries; instead they would just order sweatshirts in bulk from Amazon. The most communal thing about them was probably that they all shared a single Prime account.

"Where is this all coming from?" Sage asked, taking his eyes off the road to look at her.

"I don't know," she lied. "Just like, once upon a time, some guy decided we're going to live like this? And now we're just going along with it?"

"Are you thinking about leaving?"

"No!" she blurted. "I'm just—look, you asked me to tell you what was on my mind, and I did."

Sage winced and turn his head back toward the road.

"I wouldn't judge you if you wanted to," he said after a moment, "but you saw what happened with Ocean. And Wolf. And Cosmo. They all came back. Nothing out there can compare to the life we have here. Sure, ole triple-J had his flaws, but maybe it's not about him. Maybe it's about the community we've all built together."

"What if that's just what we've been taught to think? What if we just don't know any better? I mean, doesn't anything bother you about the ranch?"

Sage thought it over and shrugged one shoulder. "I'll admit it would be nice if we could wear other colors besides purple sometimes, but on the other hand, a uniform keeps things easy. I can't complain."

"Do you ever think about what you want to be when you grow up?"

"What do you mean 'when you grow up'? I *am* grown up. This is it."

Genesis considered her own life on the ranch. She didn't love cooking and baking like Sage. No matter how hard she tried, she couldn't forge an emotional connection with the cows, chickens, and goats she tended to every day. She was too shy to ever lead a group yoga or meditation class. She didn't know what she was good at, and she couldn't seem to find it here. Every day she felt the ranch gates closing in on her, the whole place feeling smaller and smaller even though it remained the same fifty acres it always was.

There was a passage in Ree Reaps's e-book, *Act Like a Lady, Pray Like a Boss!*, that Genesis turned to so many times, she'd nearly memorized it:

> *For far too long, us gals have been told to hide our ambition. That our only place in this world is the kitchen, but I'm here to tell you: it's not. God created you to have dreams. He created you to do the things you don't think you're qualified to do. He made you to be a leader in your community, your home, and the world. One dream of mine was to create a meal-kit company that would help reduce the amount of time women spend in the kitchen so you can go out there and live your dreams. So ask yourself: What are my dreams? Dreams + prayer + hard work = SUCCESS.*

Genesis asked herself over and over again, "What are my dreams?" but she couldn't come up with any, only curiosities. What would it be like to go to an actual school? Or have parents who doted on her? Or not keep her faith a secret? Or have a crush on someone who she was definitely not related to?

She sat up in her seat. "Do you think this is the life your parents dreamed you would have?"

"My parents? Well, I consider all of the elders my parents," Sage answered. "So yeah."

"But . . . your biological parents . . ."

"Ralph is a father to me because he taught me how to make bread. I consider Art my father because he taught me how to do Savasana. Arnie showed me how to herd cattle . . ."

Genesis pressed her head back to the window, nearly banging it in frustration. "I mean, aren't you curious about where they came from? Who they were out in the world before all of this?"

"Gen," Sage said, a slight condescending laugh in his voice. "What does it matter? All that matters is who we are right now, in this very moment."

She put her hand in her pocket and touched the business card inside, remembering the person she did want to be, the place she wanted to go.

"You're right," she said, looking away as they finally pulled up to the ranch gate. "It doesn't matter."

. . .

Every evening before dinner, the Astralians met for community announcements and guided meditation, in that order. That way if any of the updates sparked debate, they would all be forced to calm down and breathe deeply. Though there hadn't been a real disagreement in a long time; mostly the announcements just consisted of housekeeping updates and reminders to pay attention to the chore charts and limit electricity use.

Genesis and Sage quietly shuffled into the back of the meeting room when they arrived a few minutes late, and sat on the floor with their legs crossed.

"Everyone, please be aware there have been some grizzly bear sightings by community members. Nothing to freak out about, but just, you know, use the buddy system. Also, the kitchen crew heard your feedback about serving too much squash at dinner," Art said to the crowd. "Their response is they cannot help it that this summer's harvest has been so prosperous, but they have heard you and will preserve some of it for the winter. Any questions?"

No one in the small sea of purple raised their hand.

"Great. So, before we move on, we have one more special announcement. Grace?"

Genesis's mother jumped up from the pine floor and walked to the front of the room. "Namaste, my family," she said, tucking the streak of white that ran through her long dark hair behind her ear. "As many of you know, we've kept a quiet presence in the world since our Ultimate Learning Experience in 2003." Grace paused solemnly, and other members briefly bowed their heads. "Since then, we have healed. We have rebuilt trust. We have thrived."

Next to Genesis, Sage nodded along in agreement. Had they really thrived? To her, it felt like they barely survived. With Hope Harvest's takeover of the town, the Astralians increasingly ran out of places to sell their goods. They had started driving hours away to sell at weekend farmers markets, and even there, people were hesitant to buy because their reputation preceded them.

"Lately, I've been reflecting a lot on the progress and the peace we've formed since then," Grace continued. "You see, it's come to my attention that there is a popular podcast detailing and deconstructing the events that took place here so many moons ago. This initially gave me pause, as I believe we, here within these gates, are the real bearers of truth. I was worried. However, I have been surprisingly overcome by an outpouring of correspondence from listeners of this podcast reaching out to us, feeling seen in our mission of communal living and higher purpose, asking if we accept visitors . . ."

Genesis sat up straight. In all her life, the only visitors she'd seen permitted inside the gates were the USDA inspectors and the Montana Department of Public Health and Human Services, who each came around once a year to ensure the welfare of the animals and children, respectively.

"So I spoke with my fellow elders, though you all know I'm hesitant to call us 'elders' because, for one thing, we're not very old." She paused to smile. "And another, as evidenced by all the brilliant youth here, I think wisdom can exist at any age. But yes, us elders discussed the matter and decided . . . we are going to open up the ranch." Around the room, members glanced at one another fearfully. "I know. We have kept this is a closed, safe space for decades now. And we don't want to let in anyone new who would disrupt the peaceful space we have worked so tirelessly to maintain. That is why we are planning on opening the ranch to *paid visitors* for *limited stays* only. The Astralian Ranch will be expanding to become a meditation retreat center!"

Genesis and Sage glanced at each other with narrowed eyes.

"You have got to be kidding me!" Ocean exclaimed in front of them. All around, members grumbled among themselves. Grace raised her palms to signal for everyone to settle down.

"We encourage everyone to take the next twenty-four hours to gather their thoughts and feelings on the matter, then at tomorrow's evening meeting, we will open up the forum for discussion. This opportunity will provide the community with a new revenue stream beyond our usual food production, which will allow for things like a new tractor, refurbished kitchen appliances, and to support the healthcare costs of our members who, yes, are not very old but *are* incurring new healthcare costs as they age. And, most importantly, this will be an opportunity for us to expand our horizons, something we haven't done in a long, long time."

"Well, it looks like the real world is coming to us," Sage whispered in Genesis's ear.

. . .

"This is utter nonsense," Ocean mumbled through a mouthful of squash. "The ranch is going to become swamped with idiots in expensive leggings and Patagonia jackets looking for a weekend of spirituality. And you know who's going to have to clean up after them? Us!"

"I don't know exactly what that all means," Sage said, passing the basket of bread down the table, "but I know it's not good."

"It could be kind of cool," Cosmo admitted. "We could meet people from all over the world without having to leave home."

Last year, on his eighteenth birthday, Cosmo left the ranch for three months and returned with a dolphin tattoo with the name

"Sheena" written above it and zero explanation of where he'd gone or what he'd done. He hadn't been outside the gates since.

"We're going to be like zoo animals to these people," Ocean continued. "And we'll have to wait on them hand and foot, probably. This place won't be a commune anymore."

"Technically, we haven't been a real commune since they started selling food to the public for money," Genesis said. She pushed the lentils around her plate one by one, imagining that each one represented a lost soul flocking to the ranch looking for a fake spiritual awakening. "Or maybe it was when there was a majority vote that we needed a TV."

Ocean dropped her fork on her plate with a clang. "Face it, people. We're waitstaff now. But the worst part? Out there is not so much better. The only way to survive is to be a total cog to the man. We're screwed either way, on the ranch or outside of it."

She pushed her chair back and stood. "Ready to go watch *The Bachelor* in the main house? We need to take advantage of these privileges now. When those guests show up, we're going have to pretend we're totally off the grid for the sake of appearances, I'm telling you."

"Sure," Cosmo said. "You know I have to see who makes it to the Fantasy Suite."

"No thanks," Genesis said, feeling like her mind was full of enough garbage for one day.

Sage shook his head. "I need to be up early in the kitchen."

Ocean and Cosmo took off, leaving the two of them behind.

Genesis picked up her plate and walked over to the compost bin to dump her half-eaten meal.

"Gen," Sage said from behind her, placing his hand on her shoulder. Even the smallest touch from him ignited her skin. "Do you want me to walk you back to your cabin?"

"Why would you want to do that?" she asked, furrowing her brows.

"The grizzly bear sightings. Buddy system. Also, I thought we could talk. Alone," he said, lowering his voice. "To be honest, Ocean was really hogging the conversation, and I was curious what you think of this whole visitor thing."

"I think it's bad. Really bad. In fact, um, I am going to go talk to my mom, I mean, Grace, about it right now. So you can go ahead without me."

. . .

The door to Grace's office was open, but Genesis still knocked.

"Come in," Grace said without looking up from her clunky desktop computer. To call it an office was generous; really, it was a glorified closet where Grace did the ranch's bookkeeping. Behind her was a framed copy of the local newspaper with the front-page headline *Om on the Range,* published months before Jimmy Joe James was arrested.

"Hi, Grace," Genesis said.

"Namaste, Genesis." Grace turned and smiled. "To what do I owe the pleasure?"

"I just wanted to talk to you about tonight's meeting," Genesis said, sitting down on a tufted cushion on the floor.

"Look, Gen, I can't grant you special privileges. You're going to have to wait for tomorrow's open forum. I'm sorry."

"I understand. I was just thinking about what you said. The costs of running this place and taking care of everyone and everything. I know this will sound crazy . . ." She paused and took a breath. "But what if we sold the ranch? That is . . . if someone here owns it. I never thought about if we paid rent to someone or something like that," Genesis lied.

"We all own this land, Gen," Grace said with an amused look, getting up from her chair and sitting down next to her on another cushion. "So, to entertain your idea for a moment, we would all have to agree to sell it. Every member. And that would be, well, a complete . . . dissolving . . . of the community!"

"But how do we all own it?" Genesis pressed. "I wasn't around to, you know, help buy it. Neither were a lot of us younger members. How does that give us equal say?"

"Well, sure, you know, if you believe in big banks and land deeds and all that, then yeah, you don't own this land, Gen. But you know we don't believe in any of that. Those are all structures created by a profit-driven society to make us feel worthless. You own a part of this land because you give this land what it needs with your own hands. And that's real power."

"But someone had to buy the land in the first place, right?" Genesis persisted.

"Sure"—Grace waved her hand—"if you want to get into the boring details. You know, I've always appreciated your sense of curiosity, Gen." She smiled, then flattened her mouth into a hard line.

Genesis reached into her pocket and took out the business card.

"This morning, when I went to get the mail, a woman drove up to the gate and approached me," she said, sliding the card across the floor. "She told me someone named Grace Ogilvy was the owner of this ranch and asked if I could pass along her info because she had a client who wanted to make what she called a, um, 'very generous offer' for the land."

Grace narrowed her eyes and reached for the card.

"Was that your last name before you moved here? Ogil—"

"Who I was in the past is not who I am today." Grace paused and inspected the card. "That information is neither here nor there. Genesis, you listen to me. If this woman approaches you ever again, you tell me immediately. We want nothing to do with those people. The only way we would ever sell this land to Hope Harvest Community Church is not only over my dead body but over the entire death of the celestial bodies in the universe. Do I make myself clear?"

Genesis gulped, then nodded.

"Grace!" Opal, an elder member, poked her head in the door. "The show's starting!"

"I'll be right there," Grace said with a sigh, looking up at her, then turning her eyes back to Genesis. "Let this be a learning experience." She tore Faith Johnson's card into two, scattered the pieces on the floor, then followed Opal down the hallway.

Genesis waited until she heard the host's voice saying, "Last week on *The Bachelor* . . ." echo from the gathering room, then quickly grabbed the remains of the business card and put them back in her overalls. She pulled out her iPhone from the chest pocket where she hid it, turned it on, opened the internet browser, googled "Grace Ogilvy," and clicked the first link, which was, to her shock, a Wikipedia page.

> **Grace Ogilvy** (born February 20, 1978) [1] is the grand-daughter of American candymaker, businessman, and philanthropist Martin Ogilvy. She became nationally known for her involvement in the Astralian community, specifically using her vast inheritance to purchase the cult's ranch. In 2003, she was arrested and charged with conspiracy to commit money laundering but found not guilty. It is speculated that she was pregnant at the time with Astralian leader Jimmy Joe James's child.

5

HOLLY

"When my uncle died, in addition to the diner, I got his old car." Danny pulled the garage open to reveal a burgundy Buick Roadmaster, one of those sedans where the hood and trunk of the car were as long as the middle. Without opening its doors, Holly could already tell it reeked of cigarette smoke. "I didn't tell you about this sooner because I didn't want to get your hopes up, you know, in case you don't like it. If you want to use it while you're here, you're more than welcome."

She felt some tears poke at the corners of her eyes. Maybe she was just tired from traveling, but Holly was oddly moved by her dad's offer. Yes, the car was a hideous gas guzzler, but it meant freedom. The weight of What the heck am I going to do all day? was slightly lifted off her shoulders. At least now she could make solo treks to Walmart or Goodwill and drive around, just staring at empty fields, listening to music. Alone. The tears intensified as she remembered her friends back home, jumping into one another's infinity pools and having the time of their lives. Sure, maybe she didn't have the most authentic relationship with them, but being alone among other people was better than being alone with herself.

"I'd love to use it," she said, her voice squeaky. "Thanks, Danny."

"No problem." He smiled without making eye contact.

Holly unpacked her things in her new but technically old bedroom, then collapsed onto her twin-size bed. It was covered in a sun-faded Disney-princess-themed bed in a bag that Danny had purchased when she'd visited as a toddler. On the walls were glow-in-the-dark plastic stars that Courtney had applied when she was first pregnant. Lying there, Holly felt a creeping sensation like she was staying in the room of a baby who had never been born, not a room that was designated for her, the actual baby all grown up. She'd considered bailing on Zoe, but now she felt an overwhelming need to get out of the musty bedroom and go somewhere, anywhere. Besides, she'd be running into Zoe a lot at the diner this summer, so it'd be better to just get this one awkward hangout over with. At least she could tell her mom she'd tried making friends in Violet.

She grabbed her phone from the edge of the bed to check the time. It was 7:10 p.m. Zoe told her to come by at seven thirty. Holly changed out of the leggings she'd worn on the plane into a pair of denim cutoffs and a striped baby tee, then threw her hair into a ponytail with a scrunchie.

Inside the Buick, which indeed smelled of cigarette smoke plus the unexpected addition of whiskey, Holly typed in Delia's address on her phone. She followed the directions and ended up in a cul-de-sac that looked nothing like Danny's street, where the houses were all squat one-stories with metal siding and detached garages. These ones were brand new but trying to look old, like farmhouses but with big shiny windows and intricate light fixtures. Behind them, Holly could see the wood skeletons of more of the same kinds of houses in progress.

She parked the car on the street and texted Zoe.

Here!

After ten minutes, Holly received no response, which was unnerving, given Zoe had been so insistent on them hanging out. She got out of the car, walked up to the front door of the house, sniffed herself only to confirm she reeked of old man with multiple substance addictions, and rang the bell.

A woman with immaculate blonde highlights peeked through the glass window of the door. She furrowed her perfectly symmetrical eyebrows and gave Holly a judgmental once-over from head to toe.

"Hi there!" the woman said, opening the door and plastering a smile on her face. "Can I help you, sweetie?"

"I'm looking for Zoe and . . . Delia?"

"Oh! You must be here for Girls Ministry! I've never seen you around before."

Holly frowned. If making s'mores was miles away from what she predicted Zoe would do with her evenings, going to Bible study was light-years.

"I—I just moved here. Well, back here. For the summer. I'm Holly," she said, awkwardly waving her hand. "My dad is Danny Hart. He owns the diner."

The woman briefly narrowed her eyes, then nodded in recognition. "Oh. That place is so . . . rustic!" She shook her shoulders with fake enthusiasm. "I'm Faith, Delia's mom. The girls are all out back. C'mon."

Faith led Holly through an open-concept kitchen and living room that was all distressed wood and high ceilings and canvases with Bible verses painted in gold calligraphy hanging on the walls.

They went through a pair of sparkling sliding glass doors onto a patio where about eight girls were sitting around a firepit in Adirondack chairs. Holly's stomach clenched; Zoe hadn't said anything about a party.

"Delia!" Faith called. "Your new friend Holly's here!"

All of the girls turned their heads and stared, most of them giving Holly the same once-over that Faith had given her.

"Who?!" Delia asked at the same time Holly said, "No, no, I don't know—"

"Holly!" exclaimed Zoe's raspy voice. She jumped out of her chair and pulled Holly in for a hug.

At first, Holly thought it was just the dimmed light from the setting sun that made her unrecognizable, but then she realized Zoe wasn't wearing any makeup and her ratty hair was clean and brushed straight. Her jagged bangs had been pulled back into a waterfall-style braid across her hairline, and she wore an embroidered peasant blouse.

"I'm so, so sorry," Zoe whispered urgently into Holly's ear. "Some stuff happened with my mom, and then Delia had to host youth group at the last minute, and I totally forgot to text you.

Please do not judge me for what you will witness here tonight."

Zoe pulled away. "Everyone, this is Holly," she called out loudly before Holly could say a word back to her. "She's staying in town for the summer. Let's all give her a warm welcome."

The girls let out a chorus of hiiii's. Like Zoe at the moment, they all looked alarmingly wholesome, like they drank a glass of milk with every meal.

Zoe took a blanket from the back of her chair and laid it out on the ground next to her, motioning for Holly to take a seat.

"We just finished the icebreaker, but that's okay, you can still do it!" a girl in white shortalls said. "We shared our seven-word biographies. So, you sum up your life in seven words. So, like, I'm Heather. My biography is: Born. Accepted Jesus. Learned to ride bike." She splayed her fingers out to count. "What's yours?"

"Oh. All right." Holly raised her eyebrows and nodded slowly. "Um. Let's see. Born . . . moved. Moved again. Moved . . . again. Here. I think that's seven."

The girls chuckled politely. Holly glanced at Zoe, who gave her a small mea culpa smile.

"That's great! Well, let's get into it. Let me pull up tonight's discussion points, written for us by the queen herself, Ree Reaps," Heather said in a singsong voice, pulling her phone out of her pocket.

"Okay, so tonight is all about untold truths about dressing modestly. Summer is here, and the days are longer and clothes are getting . . . you guessed it, smaller."

Some of the girls chuckled. Holly glanced down at her cutoffs and crop top, then at everyone else's outfits. She'd never considered her clothes to be remotely provocative, but looking around, she realized just enough of a difference; the shirt and shorts were each about five inches shorter than everyone else's.

"If there is one word that's been totally lost in our society today, it's modesty," Heather continued. "What do you girls think when you think of modesty? Personally, I used to think it was this old-fashioned thing. Like, ew, I don't want to dress like my grandma."

"Same!" said another girl, who was wearing a T-shirt that said SISTERHOOD in repeating blocky pink letters. "One time I even cried about it, but then I realized just because I'm covered up doesn't mean I have to be unfashionable."

"Exactly!" Heather exclaimed, then looked back down at her phone to continue.

"Sorry, Heather," Zoe said. "Could you explain what modesty is for some of our newcomers here tonight, in case they're not familiar?"

"Sure!" Heather's eyes lit up. "Basically, modesty means honoring God by not wearing revealing clothes and treating your body as a temple. That's what's at the heart of it, but it also helps to stop guys from being struck by temptation when they see you, and it honors your future husband."

"Aka Dustin!" one of the other girls snickered.

Heather blushed and looked down at her phone. "Anyway—"

"When do you think he's going to give you a promise ring?" another girl pressed.

"C'mon, girls, we're getting sidetracked."

"Who's Dustin?" Holly piped up, desperately wanting to keep the conversation off topic so she wouldn't have to endure a lecture about the sins of wearing spaghetti straps.

"My boyfriend," Heather said politely.

"She's being modest—no pun intended," the girl in the SISTER-HOOD T-shirt cut in. "Dustin is the Reapses' son. He's just the greatest guy. You can tell he's going to be the most amazing pastor and father one day. Sometimes I can't believe he's only our age. He carries himself with such maturity and faith. It's honestly inspiring. You're so blessed, Heather!"

Holly had never heard gossip about a boy as underwhelming as this. She looked over at Zoe, who was barely concealing the cringe on her face.

"I *am* blessed, Kaitlyn," Heather said with a smug smile. "But we're getting distracted! Let's get back to the origins of modesty. See, practicing modesty shouldn't be a chore. When you understand why we wear clothes in the first place, it becomes so easy. We have to go all the way back to the book of Genesis, in the garden, where the first clothes ever came from . . ."

Holly had never been to church in her life, at least that she could remember. Sunday mornings with Courtney had always meant watching Bravo reruns, eating Pillsbury canned cinnamon rolls, and painting their nails. As Heather went on and on, Holly's cheeks turned hot with shame, followed by anger. She shouldn't even be here, not just around this firepit, but in this town, this entire state. The reality of her whole day fell on her: she'd taken a plane just to end up here, worrying about the length of her jorts in front of a bunch of people she didn't know or even care to know. It was all so unfair.

"Just remember: God is the author and designer of all things beautiful," Heather continued. "We cannot use our beauty in a way that selfishly draws people to us. True beauty is found in a girl that loves Jesus. Wear fashionable clothing but know to avoid sexual styles. Wear makeup but don't go overboard. Chase the glory of God, not likes and faves online." She took a thoughtful pause and smiled serenely. "So what do you think? Have any of you guys struggled with modesty?"

"I know that when I'm looking on social media, it can be hard," a younger girl spoke up. "Like, seeing pictures of beautiful influencers, I'll think, 'Ugh, I wish I could look like that.'"

The group nodded in agreement.

"But this is all really encouraging to hear," the younger girl added. "It's important to remember, I don't wear clothes or makeup for attention. I wear them to honor God's glory."

Holly glanced at Zoe. She looked like she was going to burst a blood vessel. Delia quickly patted her arm, then lifted it away.

"Sometimes shopping can be hard, though," an older girl in glasses admitted. "Clothes these days aren't really designed with modesty in mind. And the ones that are, aren't exactly cute. But I've found that layers are a girl's best friend. If I find a dress with straps that are too skinny, I can always wear a shirt underneath!"

"That's such a good tip, Mary," Heather said with a smile.

Zoe took a deep breath. "I just wonder why . . ." she started.

Several of the girls made eye contact with one another, as if to telepathically communicate, *Here we go again.* Heather frowned.

"Why is it that all of this work to dress modestly is put on us? Why can't you just wear what you want and call it a day? It's not like this for guys. No one says they're being sexual when they're swimming without a shirt. You mentioned earlier, Heather, that one of the reasons you're supposed to dress modestly is to help guys avoid temptation, but doesn't that sound like a personal problem for them, not you?" The words started to spill out of Zoe. "You can be completely covered up and having tons of sex, and you can wear a bikini and be a virgin. Whatever combination, it's your choice. Have you considered that they're just clothes? And it's how we treat people that determines whether or not we're 'glorifying God'? Maybe it's not actually God who's judging our outfits, it's just each other."

Zoe's eyes darted around the firepit, searching for anyone else to agree with her. "I mean, if you want to dress modestly, that's totally cool. I just think it should be a personal choice, not a command, you know? There's so many things to worry about in life, should your exposed belly button really be one of them?" They all stared at the ground or the sky, as if she didn't exist.

"So as usual you're all just going to ignore me until I shut up, is that the plan?" Zoe snapped. "No one wants to even *engage* in some discourse tonight?"

"Zo, c'mon," Delia muttered.

"I'm just wondering why we're letting ourselves get so preoccupied by this stuff when we could be funneling our energy elsewhere."

"It's because we are *children of God,* Zoe!" Heather exclaimed, gripping the arms of her chair.

"Oh, really? Is that why you're dressed like an actual child? Nice *shortalls,* Heather. Did you do the fingertip test before you left the house in those? God forbid a *man* see your *kneecaps*!" Zoe gripped her chest in mock horror.

Heather winced. "This is why I pray for you, Zoe."

Zoe looked to Delia with pleading eyes, but Delia just stared away and stayed silent. Zoe stood up from her chair and pushed it back, then stormed off to the side of the house.

A heavy silence fell on the group. The sun had fully set, and the fire had burned down to embers. Goose bumps erupted on Holly's skin. She wondered why Zoe had dressed up to look like these girls in the first place if she disagreed with them so much. She could clearly hold her own in an argument, so why was she suddenly so upset now? Nothing was making sense.

Heather cleared her throat. "So. Who's up for s'mores?"

"I think I better go," Holly said, lifting herself from the stone patio. "It was nice meeting you all?" She said it more like it was a question.

Holly raced across the backyard and around to the street. Zoe was halfway down the block on a bike, aggressively pedaling.

"Hey!" Holly called out, jogging after her. "Are you okay?"

Zoe stared back and slowed down. A disappointed look briefly washed over her face, but then she half smiled.

"Yeah. I'm fine." Though her eyes were wet. "Sorry again about the mix-up and that you had to see me like . . ." She gestured vaguely at herself.

"Do you want to talk about . . . whatever that was?" Holly asked.

"Honestly, right now I just need to bike this out." Zoe swatted her face as a tear finally fell down her cheek, then she pedaled away before Holly could say another word.

*   *   *

It was Saturday night, and Holly had a car but no friends and nowhere to be. She got back inside the Buick and hand-rolled down all the windows, hoping that would do something about the smell.

For the first time since she'd left California, there was a text from her friends back home.

> Hey bb just so u know we started another group chat so we're not like blowing up your phone and messing w ur data while ur in Iceland while we discuss boring local stuff lol. Hope ur having an amazing time!!! Send pics <3

Holly sighed and rested her head on the steering wheel.

Still not ready to return to Danny's sad little house, she googled the nearest discount store so she could pick up the shampoo she'd forgotten to pack and maybe one of those little Febreeze air fresheners you could stick on your dashboard. There was a twenty-four-hour Walmart twenty-five miles away.

As Holly drove to the outskirts of Violet, the reception on her phone turned spotty, and the map stopped loading. She kept going, thinking she'd come across the exit onto the highway eventually but instead ended up on a long, unlit dirt road. She slowed down, trying to identify anything but fields, until she came across a battered, carved wooden sign next to a locked entry gate.

ASTRALIA

EST. 2001

"BE BEYOND THE BODY"

A chill ran down her spine. In the distance, she could see a few lights on in a big dilapidated-looking house. Though Zoe had told her the Astralians were probably harmless, Holly still felt like this was the start of a bad horror movie.

She drove into the space in front of the locked gate to turn the Buick around. As she was about to make a full one-eighty, something made an impact with the back. She poked her head out of the open window to assess the potential damage. The extra-long tail of the car had hit the thick wooden gate.

"You didn't break anything," a bored, low voice said from somewhere.

Holly whipped her head toward the voice and jumped, her foot slipping off the brake, and jolted forward into the road, then she slammed on the brake again.

"Sorry. I didn't mean to scare you," the voice said.

She looked around until she spotted its source through her open passenger window: a tall figure wearing all black was languidly leaning against the outside of the fence, smoking a cigarette.

"Are you lost?" he asked, bending his head down to make eye contact.

"No," she blurted out too quickly, turning her eyes away and shaking her head. She cursed the ancient car for not having automatic windows.

"It's okay. I'm not a serial killer. I promise." He stuck his hands up to prove he had no weapon. Tentatively, Holly looked back at him. He was young and had a chiseled jaw and floppy blond hair like he was a series regular on a CW show; not what she expected at all.

Her cheeks flushed. "That's exactly what a serial killer would say."

He gave her a crooked smile. "Do you need directions?"

"Yeah," she admitted with a sigh. "My phone's being weird." Then she internally reprimanded herself for letting this strange boy know that her phone was compromised. It was like she was starring in a public service announcement video about how to not get murdered.

"Where are you headed?"

"I was just trying to get onto the highway to go to Walmart." She immediately cursed herself for not lying and saying something more safe, like her dad was expecting her to be home any minute.

The boy exhaled a cloud of smoke. "If you give me a ride, I'll guide you to the exit you need to take."

"Uhhh." She hesitated and glanced at the lock on the passenger door. "I don't know. Can you just tell me how to get there?"

He laughed once and ran a hand through his hair. "Sorry. Yeah, I'm putting myself in your shoes and this is definitely creepy. So, turn around and take a right, then another right at the next stop sign and then a left at the next intersection, keep going for like ten minutes, and then you should see some signs leading you to I-90. Got that?"

She nodded, though she was too busy staring at his perfect face to actually retain any of the instructions.

"Good luck." He waved his hand and started to walk away.

"Wait!" Holly blurted out. The boy froze and turned.

Some kind of gut instinct came over her. Not the safe kind of gut instinct that tells you to not talk to strangers and lock your doors. The kind of gut instinct that says somehow you have encountered the hottest boy you've ever seen in your life on a dirt road you weren't supposed to turn on and maybe you should invite this stranger into your car because it's the exact opposite of what those girls back at youth group would do and it's Saturday night and you're seventeen years old and screw your parents who think you need to be shipped away for your bad behavior like it's the 1800s or something . . . this is the kind of thrilling adventure you *deserve.*

She leaned over and unlocked the passenger door.

"Get in."

The boy took one last puff of his cigarette and stomped it out on the ground.

"Jeez, your car reeks of cigarettes," he mumbled, sliding into the front seat. "You know, smoking is really bad for you."

Holly smiled. It was the first time she'd genuinely smiled since she'd landed in Montana. Or maybe the first time she'd genuinely smiled in months.

"I'm not responsible for the smell. My lungs are perfect," she explained, surprising herself with how natural the sass flowed out of her. "It's my dead uncle's car."

"I'm sorry for your loss." The boy assessed the dusty dashboard and nodded toward the road. "So like I said, you're going to want to turn around, then make a right."

Holly lifted her foot off the brake and turned. "What are you doing out here?"

He shrugged. "Went for a walk."

"Seems like an awfully weird place to go for a walk."

"Seems like an awfully weird place to accidentally drive by."

"Touché."

"You know what that is?" He nodded in the direction of the ranch.

"I've heard about it, but I'd never seen it in person until now."

His eyes traveled up and down her face. "You're not from around here, are you?"

"Technically I am," Holly said. He raised an eyebrow. "I was born here, but I moved away as a baby. Now I'm just visiting for the summer," she elaborated.

"Wow, what a vacation. *Take a thrilling getaway to Violet,*

Montana," the boy said in a voice like a radio announcer. *"A premier community that hearkens to a simpler time for our nation's Christian families."*

Holly cringed. The boy stiffened and straightened in his seat. "No offense if you're a Christian."

"I'm not." Holly shrugged dismissively. "I'm not anything."

"Huh. So just visiting . . ." he pondered. "Who do you know in Violet?"

"My dad."

"Do you visit him often?"

"Not really. It's been a while. We're not exactly close."

"So is he dying or something?"

She grimaced. "What? No! He's alive and well. Why would you ask me that?"

"I'm just trying to wrap my head around why someone who's not religious or close with anyone who lives here would willingly subject themselves to this place."

Holly considered giving him the same excuse she'd given Zoe: fresh air, a change of scenery, blah, blah, blah. Then she realized what a rare situation she was in; alone with a complete stranger who didn't know her name or have any expectations of her. Like to a priest during confession, she felt like she could say anything to him.

"I was banished by my mom and stepdad," she said flatly, staring straight ahead at the road.

"Banished?" he echoed.

"For about the last six months, I was stealing cash from my mom's purse to buy Adderall from this senior at my school. My mom didn't notice for a long time because she's pretty disorganized. The kid selling it got caught, and he ratted me out to the principal and the school searched my backpack and found the pills that weren't prescribed to me; I don't have ADHD. Then I got put on academic probation and lost my scholarship, which is just so *ironic* because the only reason I was buying the Adderall in the first place is because I was drowning in work and keeping up appearances and needed perfect grades to *keep* my scholarship."

The boy was silent.

Holly glanced at him, her cheeks going red. "I know. It's really bad."

"It's not that bad," he said finally.

"What?!"

"Well, did anyone press charges against you?"

"No . . ."

"Then you're fine."

"But I lost my scholarship! I still haven't told any of my friends that I'm not coming back to school! They know about the pills, but they told me to just shrug it off. Which is easy for them to say—they're not on a scholarship, they get in trouble and their parents can just write a check for a new tennis court. Happens all the time. No way can my mom do that. Especially now that I've been *robbing her*. I am a complete and utter disappointment!" She gripped the steering wheel like she was trying to rip it out of the dashboard.

The boy raised a finger and smiled. "Counterpoint: you're not in juvie. Kids get sent there all the time for buying and selling.

Trust me, it could be so much worse for you right now."

Holly could practically feel red flags flashing before her eyes. "What do you know about juvie?"

The boy shrugged noncommittally and smirked out the window. "So what was it like?" he asked, looking back at her with a serious glint of curiosity in his eyes that let her know he wasn't just making small talk. "I mean, when your parents found out you had completely disappointed them?"

Holly was a little thrown off by his interest. "Uh, well, my mom was just really sad and quiet about the whole thing. My stepdad wouldn't even hear me out about *why* I was buying the pills. I know if it was still just my mom, she would, but sometimes I think she's kind of insecure about having had me at a pretty young age, so she defers to him out of some fear she didn't discipline me enough and fed me too many sugary cereals. But I turned out pretty well adjusted long before Rick came along, you know? I mean, I could argue that it was his whole disciplinary attitude that made me think if my grades dropped, my life would be over and actually *drove me* to buy the Adderall, but . . ."

He shook his head. "It's messed up that they just sent you away. This was clearly a cry for help, and they ignored you."

"Right?! Thank you!" Even if it was simple, the boy put into words exactly what she was feeling. She wanted to burst into tears from actually being understood. "My mom and stepdad are pregnant with their first kid together and, you know, it's high risk because she's older now. He said it'd be a good idea for me to 'get some fresh air and stop stressing her out.' So that's why

I'm supposedly here, but I can't shake this feeling that Rick is annoyed by my existence. Like he was waiting for an excuse to get rid of me. A seventeen-year-old stepdaughter is an imbalance throwing off his dreams of a perfectly symmetrical life with his dependable job as an accountant with a nice beige house and a pretty wife and a golden retriever and a baby with a big round head and . . ."

The boy chuckled. Holly took her eyes off the road and glanced at him. "Sorry," she said. "Now I'm just rambling."

"No, no, don't apologize. This is the most fascinating conversation I've had in months."

She truly could not tell if he was being sarcastic or not; he was completely messing with her sense of judgment.

"So what's your deal?" she asked him.

"Me? Well, I was just going for a nighttime stroll, and then I let myself get picked up on the side of the road by a common thief. First she took money from her mother's purse, then an entire Buick from God knows where." He flashed her another crooked smile. *"Dead uncle's car my ass."*

"I swear on my dead uncle's grave that this is his car!"

"Really?" the boy asked, then reached down to open the glove compartment. "Then what was his name?"

"George," Holly blurted out, though she had no idea. She had never met the guy.

The boy pulled out a wrinkled piece of paper and squinted at it. "Says here this car is registered to someone named Gerald Hart."

"George was his nickname," she added.

"You're a terrible liar."

"If only I was. Then I would've never gotten myself into this mess."

He shook his head, then suddenly peered at the road. "Make another right up here, and that'll take you to the highway ramp. You can just let me out at the corner."

Something in Holly's chest deflated. She was disappointed that the highway had materialized so soon.

She stopped the Buick at the corner and looked around. There were no houses, nowhere this boy could possibly be going, just a gas station in the distance.

"Well, thanks for the ride . . ." the boy started.

"Holly." There went her anonymity, but suddenly she didn't care.

He reached out his hand. His fingers were long and bony. "Orlando."

Without thinking, Holly made a face.

"What?" he pressed.

"Nothing. I've just never met anyone named Orlando."

He grinned and looked away like he thought of something only he knew was funny. "Yeah, well, what can I say? We exist. Orlando, Florida, and Orlando Bloom hog the spotlight, but there are lots of us."

Holly grabbed his hand, and they shook.

His touch was surprisingly cold, but then he said something that made heat shoot up her arm like a tree stump invaded by fire ants.

"I hope you get lost around here again soon, Holly."

6

ZOE

The last place Zoe wanted to be on a Sunday morning was in a sanctuary full of families dancing while a DJ hyped them up to an EDM remix of "Our God Is an Awesome God."

Yet there she was.

Praise and worship was Zoe's least favorite part of every church service precisely because it was the part that used to be her absolute favorite. When she was a kid it felt completely natural for her to raise her hands up in the air, close her eyes, and feel the presence of God as she sang along to the contemporary Christian ballads she'd memorized all the words to. She looked forward to that time all week long, where she could release whatever fears and anxieties were swirling around in her head and give them up to Jesus. But eventually everything started to sour for her when she began questioning why the church was so obsessed with raising money not to help others but to build and build and build; or why her father had died so tragically if God really had a plan for everyone; or why, if being attracted to other girls hurt no one and brought her joy, did Pastor Marcus insist on telling her it was wrong?

Praise and worship became excruciating to Zoe, like having to participate in the karaoke birthday party for a person she barely knew.

So there was no worse punishment she could have received for getting home past one a.m. the night before than being forced to attend the nine a.m. service with her mother.

Zoe had tried to explain to Marla that she didn't mean to be out so late; before she knew it, she had stress-biked miles away from home and gotten a flat tire, so she had to haul herself back by foot in the dark. Marla didn't question what would compel Zoe to do something like that, she just recognized it was a clear sign that maybe her daughter needed the Lord, now more than ever.

Zoe hadn't heard from Delia since the night before. She looked toward the front of the "sanctuary"—i.e., the old movie theater that the Reapses had refurbished—to see if Delia was there sitting with her family, but she couldn't make out much with the flashing light display coordinated to the DJ's music in her eyes. The only people she recognized through the spectacle were Heather and freaking Dustin Reaps standing together in the front row. She figured their courtship must have been getting pretty serious if they were at the sitting-together-at-church phase, something she and Delia could never dream of doing.

She hadn't remembered the service being *this* showy. Zoe could remember a time when Hope Harvest was a run-of-the-mill Charismatic Christian church with only about a hundred members who just sang along to CDs played over a speaker. Then when Pastor Reaps Sr.'s son Jay went away to a Christian college in Texas, he met Ree, the daughter of a famous televangelist who presided over a stadium-size congregation. They married and returned to Violet because they believed it was God's purpose for them to revitalize the town in his vision. Zoe had a hard time believing that vision somehow included a smoke machine.

After a few more praise songs, the DJ slowed down and was replaced by a band with acoustic guitars for the worship portion. Then they shifted to an instrumental as Pastor Marcus came out with a microphone to share prayer requests.

"It's incredible to see all of you here today! Let's give it up for the Praisemakers!" The congregation erupted in roaring applause. "Now, so many of you have written in this week asking God for healing, with help with job applications; someone here even asked God for the grace to finish doing their laundry. That might've been me." He mock-tugged at his collar. "Hashtag bachelor problems!"

Everyone around Zoe chuckled, and she rolled her eyes. This was a classic church dynamic: no matter who was speaking, the person tasked with prayer requests took the time to display some light stand-up comedy. Pastor Marcus's jokes were the worst offenders.

"Just to put some faith in your spirit this morning," Pastor Marcus continued, "I'm looking over here, and we have Cindy Phillips with us today."

A spotlight shined on one of the singers behind him.

"As some of you know, Cindy has been battling cancer for

several months now, but today she is back up here with us. Through the power of prayer and God's healing, she has entered remission!"

Everyone, even Zoe, clapped. Though she couldn't help but think of the GoFundMe page for Cindy that Marla had shared on her Facebook. Being sick made Cindy lose her job, so she lost her insurance and went into tens of thousands of dollars in medical debt. Zoe wondered why Hope Harvest didn't just offer to foot the bill in addition to the prayers, but she knew the answer.

"It's just so cool to see you up here again, Cindy," Pastor Marcus said, putting an arm around her. "Just so, so cool."

He let go of Cindy, and the spotlight returned to him as he walked to the center of the stage. "We believe in a God who can take the worst situations and turn them around for good. With faith this morning, stretch out your hands and let's believe together, right now." He closed his eyes, and the congregation followed suit as he led them in prayer.

"Amen! Talk to you later, boss." He raised his eyes to the ceiling and stared solemnly for a moment. "A big warm welcome to Hope Harvest if you are new or visiting or maybe you're just kind of hanging out. Let's continue in our giving right now with the wonderful Ree Reaps."

Marla clapped and hollered next to Zoe. Ree walked onto the stage, and even Zoe had to admit that she looked incredible. She wore a flowy tangerine jumpsuit with bell sleeves and peep-toe booties. Her hair was pulled back into a low ponytail, showing off a pair of gold hoop earrings.

"Thank you, Marcus," she said, grabbing the mic. "Well, good morning, y'all! It's an honor to share a few verses this morning as we share our giving, but first, I am so thrilled to reveal that the Hope Harvest giving app is *finally* live!"

On the screen behind her, a video appeared with an image of the church's logo on an iPhone. The sight of it made Zoe's stomach turn. She knew people throughout history gave 10 percent of their income to their church; it wasn't some predatory new idea, but on top of all the other ways Hope Harvest brought in money, seeing it streamlined like this just felt so cold and calculating.

"You just have to download the app, select your tithe amount, and enter your billing info. You even have the option to choose the recurring giving option, so you don't have to bother fussing with it every week! No matter how you give, whether through our app, website, or in person with an envelope, it doesn't matter. What matters is what's in your heart."

Ree paused and lifted her Bible. "2 Corinthians 9:6 through 7 says, 'Whoever sows sparingly will also reap sparingly, and whoever sows bountifully will also reap bountifully.' So today, I encourage you to be a cheerful giver! Amen?"

The congregation shouted "Amen!" back to her, and she grinned like it was the most delightful sound to her ears. Ree exited the stage as the band began playing some background music and the congregation whipped out their phones.

As Marla reached into her purse, Zoe grabbed her arm. "Did you forget we currently don't have running water?" she hissed between her teeth.

Marla froze like a child with their hand caught in the cookie jar. She sighed and slumped back into her seat. Zoe crossed her arms and glowered at all the happy congregants giving each other hugs and confirming brunch plans for after the service.

The thing Zoe wished she could tell her mother was that she didn't enjoy being the bad guy. She didn't get a thrill out of hating church, like everyone might assume. In fact, she *missed* when this all felt so true; she wished that she could just go about her life, praying and handing over her dollars without thinking, hoping that wherever it went it was doing good. She didn't know the right words to explain to her mother, without sounding like a total jerk, that having a conscience was exhausting. But then maybe that confirmed her worst fear of all: that all these people were right, and she *was* a total jerk.

.   .   .

When Zoe got to the diner Monday morning, the place was empty except for an elderly man eating eggs at the counter and Holly sitting alone in a corner booth, drinking coffee and reading.

"Hey," Zoe said, sliding in across from her. She nodded to the book in Holly's hands, *Independent People* by Halldór Laxness. The cover was an abstract oil painting of sheep on a hillside. "Is that any good?"

Holly looked up. "Uhhh, apparently it's the most popular Icelandic novel of all time," she said. "It's basically about a guy who buys a farm and goes off the grid."

"Huh."

"I'm trying to learn about Icelandic culture," Holly elaborated.

"Why?" Zoe pressed.

"Um. For school. I'm doing a summer project on Iceland."

"Cool," Zoe nodded. They sat in awkward silence for a moment. "Look, I'm sorry about Saturday night. I really didn't mean to bait and switch you into coming to youth group. I owe you an explanation."

She told Holly about her mom, about the water shutoff, about the meeting place for Girls Ministry switching to Delia's house at the last minute. "I was so livid, Holly, I totally forgot we made plans."

Holly stared out the window thoughtfully. "I'm still confused. Why did you stay at Delia's house for youth group? It kind of felt like you were only there to pick an argument. Don't get me wrong, I totally agree with everything you said that night, but that's exactly why I would never knowingly go to one of those meetings."

"I stayed because Delia's my best friend," Zoe answered matter-of-factly.

"Well, some friend she is," Holly said, looking back to Zoe and shaking her head. "She didn't even stand up for you. I just met you, and I'm the one who ran after you to make sure you were okay."

"She's an *amazing* friend!" Zoe snapped, pounding her palm on the table so it shook Holly's mug of coffee. "You don't even know her."

Holly shrank into her seat. "You're right. I don't know her at all," she said quietly. "Sorry."

Zoe looked around the diner. The old man at the counter was still the only one there. She leaned across the table toward Holly.

"Delia isn't my best friend," she whispered. "Well, I mean, she is. She's my best friend in the entire world. But she's also my . . . we're . . ."

Holly raised her eyebrows with understanding. "Oooh."

"I'm assuming because your dad is pretty chill that that's not weird or anything to you, but if—"

"Of course it's not!" Holly said, eyes wide. "Why would that be weird?"

Something in Zoe's chest loosened that she didn't realize had been tight.

"It's still weird to people at Hope Harvest, though they've figured out much more polite ways to say so. Not like you know anyone here, but please don't say anything. She's rightfully scared of what her parents will say or do. So when we're in front of other people, I just have to pretend we're friends and leave it at that. Even if she agrees with me in private when I speak up about stuff, she's so reserved in public. Keeping up the whole charade is *exhausting*."

Holly nodded emphatically. "I know exactly what you mean."

"Do you?" Zoe asked, eyes narrowing.

"I—I just mean, I can imagine. Lying to people about who you are all the time. That must really take a toll. Especially when it's something you shouldn't even have to lie about in the first place."

"Yeah, well, the good thing is this is the last summer we're going to have to spend like this. Once we're both eighteen, we are getting out of here." Zoe exhaled deeply, like she was detoxing the whole town from her body. "Anyway, how was the rest of your weekend? I hope I didn't completely ruin it."

"It was . . ." Holly paused and chewed on her lip. "It was weirdly good."

Zoe blinked twice. "How so?"

Holly blushed and started to giggle. "I picked up some guy on the side of the road."

"Oh?"

"And he was, like, surprisingly hot? He was smoking. I mean, like, literally smoking a cigarette, but I guess figuratively too. Ew. Ugh. Honestly, I've never actually seen someone our age smoke. I've only seen them vape, which always looks stupid. He looked *so* cool doing it, Zoe. Like James Dean or something." Holly covered her eyes with her hands. "Does that make me sound like an idiot?"

"Well, do you want me to be honest or—"

"Nothing happened between us or anything! He just gave me directions for a few minutes and then I dropped him off near the gas station."

"How romantic!"

"No, well, it kind of was? I know it sounds underwhelming, but it was nice."

"Did you get his number?"

"No," Holly said ruefully. "It all happened so fast. I think he's from around here, though. He knew enough about the back roads to give me directions."

"A hot guy who smokes cigarettes . . . from Violet." Zoe pursed her lips and twiddled her fingers. "I'm getting nothing. Though I generally think most men look like feet, so I may not be the best judge. Did you catch his name?"

"Oh. That was the thing," Holly said, leaning in conspiratorially. "His name is *Orlando*."

Zoe burst out laughing, her spittle flying into Holly's face. "No! *What?* No one named Orlando lives in Violet. *I* would know."

Holly took this in and sat back in the booth, deflated. Zoe sat up and gave her a sympathetic look. "It sounds like you just encountered a very attractive drifter."

"Probably for the best," Holly admitted, taking a sip of her coffee and looking wistfully out the window.

In that moment, Zoe felt relieved that God created her exactly as she was.

7

GENESIS

Genesis sat in child's pose on the floor, blocking out the sounds of the class leader and praying to God in her head. This was the closest thing she had to actually going to church.

For most of her life, Genesis had treated yoga the same way lots of regular American children regarded gym class: as a useless chore. She had thought it was just some exercise regimen that Jimmy Joe James had invented himself, unique to the ranch. It wasn't until she got her iPhone that she learned it originated with Hindus in ancient India and eventually got co-opted by JJJ and rich white people, the kind who would probably pay to visit the ranch when it eventually turned into a for-profit retreat center like Ocean predicted. It was just one of the many revelations she'd had by typing a few things into her phone, though not as earth-shattering as the newest revelation that, according to various news sources, Jimmy Joe James was her biological father.

Recently, though, she'd started to look forward to yoga every day. Or maybe it wasn't the yoga; it was just that she really liked to pray. Sometimes she felt like she liked it so much, she was convinced she had to be doing it all wrong; it was too easy. At the ranch, whenever she spoke up, her voice wasn't heard. Everyone was discouraged from rocking the boat, and everything stayed the same. Yet when she prayed, she could say whatever was on her mind and ask for what she needed without feeling judged.

Dear God, she thought. *Thank you for this world you've created. Thank you for the sun in the sky and the oats I ate for breakfast. Thank you for my health. I have so much to be grateful for, but Lord, I've got to be honest with you, I'm really struggling right now. I ask that you show me the way to the light. I just found out my father might be a man who's spending time in prison for doing some really awful things. I worry that means I'm awful too. I am still having unclean feelings toward Sage, who doesn't share my beliefs, and he might actually be my half brother. Every day I keep a secret from everyone, and it's that I have a phone that I use to learn about the outside. I feel like I'm hiding something, but if I'm hiding my relationship with you, God, is that so bad? Is my life here really as horrible as I think it is? If people from the outside want to get in, then what am I complaining about? I ask for your help to guide me through this situation, to show me a life beyond these gates, if that is your will for me. Lord, I am terrified to leave, but I believe through you all things are possible. Amen.*

Genesis opened her eyes, and when she looked around, she realized most of the class was huddled around the big window in the meeting room, staring out into the front of the ranch.

"What's going on?" she asked, collecting herself from the floor.

"Grace is fighting with some lady," Cosmo said without peeling his eyes away from the window.

Genesis craned her neck so she could see through the cluster of purple-wearing bodies. Instantly, she recognized Faith Johnson's convertible at the edge of the long driveway. She was standing on one side of the fence, while Grace stood on the other with her right hand on her hip and her left angrily pointing a finger.

"Oh no, no, no," Genesis said to herself. She ran out the side door of the house and crouched behind the old Subaru station wagon in the driveway so she could listen to the argument between the two women.

"And if you ever come here again," Grace's voice echoed in the distance. "Or try to talk to any of our children, there will be consequences."

"Is that a threat?" Faith asked, lowering her sunglasses to make direct eye contact with Grace. "You know, the county sheriff is a member of our congregation."

Grace stood up a little taller. "There is absolutely no need to get the police involved. This is private property—it is not for sale—and *you* are the one trespassing."

"I don't think you understand, Ms. *Ogilvy,* we are making you and your . . . family—or groupies or whatever they are—*a once-in-a-lifetime offer.*"

"I don't think *you* understand that we don't give a flying *fuck* about your offer. No!" Grace screamed.

Faith leaned back, scandalized by Grace's language. "You are going to regret this," she said slowly. "This was the easy way out, but now you leave us no choice but to make it hard. God's will shall be done, and he will not let you idol worshippers get in the way. And neither will I."

8

HOLLY

"Should I be offering you more, um, what's the word?" Danny asked, shaking salt on his fries. "Activities?"

Holly shook her head, assessing the cold yet burnt grilled cheese in a Styrofoam container on the TV tray before her. "Oh. No, no, I'm fine."

"Well, what have you been getting up to during the day? I worry about leaving you all alone."

Holly's first week in Violet had been about as uneventful as she expected it would be. She got into a routine of eating breakfast at the diner, going home and reading or watching Netflix, then quickly regressing into scrolling on her phone to see what her friends back home were up to. She didn't allow herself to watch their Instagram stories as soon as they posted them and instead forced herself to wait eight hours to account for the Iceland time difference, in case they were keeping track. Though a small part of her knew they weren't.

When she wasn't monitoring her friends' iced coffee runs and outfit selfies, she was googling "Orlando Violet Montana" and hoping that maybe the fiftieth try would magically yield results that could lead her to the strange, beautiful boy she picked up on the side of the road.

"I've been looking into local hiking trails," she said to her father.

This wasn't a total lie. Caught in daydreams of an alternate reality where she and Orlando had the kind of summer that teen movies were made of (going to drive-in movies, making out underneath the stars, licking cotton candy from each other's lips at the top of a Ferris wheel at the county fair, watching the sun set from the top of a mountain), Holly had also searched for "most romantic hiking spots Montana."

Each time someone entered the diner while she ate breakfast, Holly looked up, hoping it was Orlando, but it never was. Twice now, she'd made up the excuse around bedtime that she needed to run to Walmart for something urgent only to drive around for an hour, looking for him with no success. Danny's clueless bachelor lifestyle worked in her favor—she genuinely did need to buy things she had assumed he would have in the house when she packed for the move, like clothes hangers and hand soap.

"Besides," she added. "I'm not a little kid anymore. You don't need to worry about entertaining me, Danny."

He stared ahead at the show they agreed upon, but neither was particularly excited to watch. "You know, you can call me Dad, if you want."

Holly's mom, Courtney, had left Montana with her as an infant to pursue her dream of becoming a movie star, which turned into her reality of being hairdresser on the set of reality shows sometimes but mostly at Supercuts. Danny sent Holly birthday and Christmas gifts, but he was never exactly a hands-on parent. To start calling him Dad now would feel like putting on a pair of shoes that she had outgrown years ago.

"That's, um, really nice, but seriously, don't worry about this summer," Holly said. "I'm fine. I know you're just doing Mom a favor. Don't let me interrupt your routine. Consider me a room-mate."

Danny frowned just the tiniest amount. "Sure."

"You're giving me a place to stay with internet access and a car and unlimited pie," she added. "What more could a girl want?"

Danny smiled to himself as he lifted his burger to his mouth. Holly's words seemed to genuinely touch him, though there were plenty of things Holly wanted besides Wi-Fi and stale lemon me-ringue. She wanted to be comfortable in her own skin. She wanted her parents to pay closer attention to her so that they would know something was wrong without her having to spell it out dramati-cally. She also wanted a certain hot mysterious stranger to jump her bones, but this was not something you revealed to your father, let alone your father you barely knew.

Later that night, she FaceTimed Courtney. "I think I've reached the phase of pregnancy where I have to buy those stupid jeans with a thick elastic waistband," her mother said upon answering. "I don't even remember what I *wore* when I had you. 2003? Did I just keep buying velour track pants in ever-increasing sizes as the months passed?"

Holly felt an ache of homesickness in her chest, not for LA, but for her mother's presence. She missed her warm hugs and her smell—a combination of her musky vanilla perfume and hair burnt on a flat iron. Her taste in décor that Holly used to cringe at when compared to the luxurious houses of her friends—matted faux-fur pillows and coffee mugs that said things like SHE BELIEVED SHE COULD, SO SHE DID—now felt so thoughtful and warm compared to the coldness of Danny's house and the religious undertones of Violet at large.

"Anyway, how are you?" Courtney asked. Holly knew if she revealed how she truly felt, her mother would break down and cry. The better strategy was to just pretend that the visit was not so bad and keep their conversation shallow.

"I'm actually great, Mom," Holly lied. "I'm making friends with this girl who works at the diner. Danny got me a car. If I'm not careful, I might end up spending the rest of my life here."

"Don't you even think about it!"

They made plans to watch some new mindless reality show in which couples met through the interface of a VR game together. It was twelve episodes long, with one coming out every week. Holly could finally feel a light at the end of the tunnel. She just had to get through the show, and the summer would be over.

Even so, she tossed and turned all night because she still couldn't stop thinking about how Orlando was out there somewhere. She replayed their brief interaction in her head so many times that she was certain she'd overinflated it. If she ran into him again, she'd probably realize he was really a fifty-year-old man with horns and that she should get her eyes checked. Or Zoe had definitely been right and she had just picked up a hitchhiker;

nothing more, nothing less. Still, the Buick sitting in the driveway called out to her like a zit she knew she shouldn't pick at but desperately wanted to. She told herself she'd just go for one more late-night ride to completely get it out of her system and then she'd never think about him again.

Holly crawled out of bed, took off her pajama pants, and changed into her cutoffs. Then she put on her nicest bra underneath her oversize sweatshirt, feeling like a clown. Then swiped on some lip gloss, feeling like an even bigger clown. She told herself that if she got caught sneaking out, she'd just tell Danny she got her period in the middle of the night and had to run to Walmart for tampons. For this, she felt like the biggest clown of all.

She crept out of her room with her sneakers in hand. The gap underneath Danny's bedroom door was dark. She tiptoed down the hall, grabbed her keys from the kitchen counter, and slipped out the back door as quietly as she could. Inside the Buick, her heart raced like she'd just pulled off a heist.

She drove the car into town and down Main Street, past the movie theater turned church and all the boutiques. It was completely dead; even the flashing lights on the Hope Harvest marquee had been shut off. When she got to the gas station near the highway, the absurdity of what she was doing hit her: this wasn't cute or exciting—she was being a *stalker*. She pulled into the gas station parking lot to turn around.

The lights of the twenty-four-hour mini-mart glowed, neon signs hawking beer and cigarettes. It was probably the only remaining business in Violet that was as unsightly as her dad's diner.

It crossed Holly's mind that she should probably go in and buy some tampons for her alibi, just in case she got caught sneaking back home. Plus, it would make so much more sense that she would come here in an emergency than the Walmart miles and miles away.

She parked the car and went inside. A balding guy with a soul patch working behind the counter winked at her. The stark fluorescent lighting made Holly feel exposed, like she'd just been forced awake from a nap even though she hadn't yet gotten a wink of sleep. She crossed her arms and hunched over, avoiding eye contact with the man. The tampons were locked behind the counter, stuck between the condoms and cigarettes, and there was only one variety, some off-brand with cardboard applicators. What was she thinking, that she could just waltz in by herself and find a box of Tampax Pearl in this kingdom of beef jerky and Mountain Dew?

Holly turned down one of the three aisles, determined to buy something, anything, to add some legitimacy to her trip out. If Danny asked, she would just tell him she had an undeniable craving for Cheetos and that Courtney let her go to the grocery store in the middle of the night all the time. She angrily snatched a bag as if the cheetah mascot on the package were responsible for this entirely fabricated and pointless scenario she had put herself in.

"Nice choice," a voice said behind her. Holly froze in place. At first she thought the bald clerk had followed her down the aisle, but this voice was familiar.

She stared at the floor, taking in a pair of white Converse so dusty they'd turned brown. Her eyes wandered up a pair of worn-in jeans and a faded black T-shirt, all the way up to a devastatingly handsome face.

She swallowed once. "Orlando."

He smiled at her crookedly. "I was wondering when I'd run into you again." He gestured for her to hand him the bag of Cheetos, and she did, speechless.

Orlando walked to the front of the store with the Cheetos and a bottle of Coke in hand. The clerk nodded at him like they knew each other and rang up the items.

"And a pack of Marlboros," Orlando said nonchalantly. Holly noticed him slide the guy an additional twenty-dollar bill.

Orlando stuffed the cigarettes in his back pocket and grabbed the snacks. He looked at Holly and nodded toward the entrance. Her feet were still glued to the floor in front of the chip display. She poked her palm with her car keys to ensure sure she wasn't dreaming, then followed him outside the mini-mart.

"Thanks," she said. "You didn't have to do that."

"No problem." He shrugged and handed her the bag. Orlando twisted the top off his soda and took a sip. He looked like he'd been generated in a lab by the Coca-Coca Company to star in an ad consisting of this very moment.

They stood on the pavement in silence as a surprisingly cold blast of wind blew in their faces. Holly pulled her sweatshirt sleeves down to her fingers. "Do you want to go for a drive?" she asked.

He took another sip and swallowed. "Where?"

"I don't know. I'm still pretty new around here. Maybe you can give me a tour?" she asked, peering up at him.

He laughed once. "It'll be hard to see much of anything in the dark."

Holly's face fell. Once again, she worried she had totally misread the situation. "Yeah. You're right, um—"

"Let's do it," he said. "Lucky for you, my favorite spot in town looks best at night."

They got inside the Buick, and Holly put her keys in the ignition.

"Which way should I go?" she asked, trying to keep her hands from shaking.

"Drive in the direction of the mountains," Orlando said. "May I?" He pointed to the car's antique stereo system, and Holly nodded her permission. Orlando adjusted the radio dial until he hit an oldies station playing Fleetwood Mac.

"So why do I only see you out at night?" Holly asked, turning back onto Main Street.

A smile danced on Orlando's lips. "I could ask you the same thing."

"Okay, so we're both vampires," she said dryly. "Great. Glad we could get that out of the way."

"I have trouble sleeping," he admitted.

"So you went out to buy nicotine and caffeine. Is that some kind of homeopathic remedy for insomnia?" she asked, eyeing the Coke in the cupholder.

"Nobody's perfect, Holly." Her name rolling off his tongue made her feel like she was going to pass out.

They hit the only traffic light in town. Even though no one else was around, Holly still obeyed the law and stopped. "How old are you, Orlando?"

"Seventeen. You?"

"Same."

Orlando breathed a loud sigh of relief.

"What?" Holly pressed.

"I'm just relieved we're the same age. You wouldn't believe how many scrapes with older women I've accidentally gotten into."

Holly's eyes went wide. "Seriously?!"

"No," he admitted after a few seconds, shaking with laughter. "I wish you could see your face."

Holly shook her head and took her foot off the brake.

"Forgive me if you told me before," Orlando said, relaxing into his seat, "but where do you live when you're not being banished to Violet for the summer?"

"Los Angeles," she said.

"*Los Angeles*," he repeated. "I can see that."

"How so?"

"I don't know. You just seem like a California girl."

"I can't tell if that's supposed to be a compliment or an insult."

"It's a compliment," he said.

"Thanks," she said quietly. Holly kept looking toward the empty road, but she could feel his eyes grazing her body. She turned to meet them, and surprisingly he looked down at the floor like he was embarrassed.

Orlando cleared his throat. "Are you planning a trip to Iceland?"

Holly froze. "Excuse me?"

He gestured to a pile of books on the passenger-seat floor. The novel Holly had been reading at the diner sat alongside a *Rick Steves Iceland 2014* guide that she'd stumbled across at Savers before she left for Montana.

"Oh." She sighed. "No. I'm just . . . researching."

"For what?"

Holly contemplated repeating the summer project excuse she'd given Zoe, but she had told him the truth before. Why start lying now?

"I told my friends I was going to Iceland for the summer instead of telling them I was coming here," she admitted. "I thought I should read up on the culture in case they asked me questions, but the thing is, since I've gotten here, they've barely even contacted me. So the books are pointless, honestly."

"Why couldn't you just tell them you where you were going?" Orlando pulled his brows together.

Holly chewed on her lip, deliberating her answer. "I didn't want to have to explain Violet to them."

"But you would read entire books about Iceland so you'd be ready to explain that to them?"

"I was worried they'd make assumptions about me. Like that my family is basically white trash."

Orlando winced.

"Not that I think they are or that that's an okay thing to say. And, you know, clearly this is becoming a pretty fancy place to live and all," Holly said quickly. "It's just . . . that's how they would see me regardless. It's why I never told them about my scholarship."

"Then it sounds like they're not your real friends."

"Well, no!" Holly protested, her voice getting high. "They're actually super nice."

"Super nice," Orlando echoed, reaching into his back pocket, "but you just can't tell them a basic fact about yourself or else they'll completely change their opinion of you because they're classist jerks."

It stung deep, but Holly knew he was right.

"Maybe I'm just a country bumpkin," he went on, "but I thought the cool thing was for rich kids to pretend to be poor these days, right? So they don't get eaten when the revolution comes or whatever."

Holly half smiled. "Yeah, but they don't have to pretend when they're only in the presence of other rich kids. Or least they think they are."

He held up the pack of Marlboros. "Do you mind if I? And would you like one?"

Holly shook her head. "No and no."

Orlando rolled down the window, then lit a cigarette. "What made *Iceland* seem like a better place to tell them you were going than Violet, anyway?"

"I don't know." Holly sighed again. "It just came out of nowhere. I guess I figured if I told them I was going somewhere *they'd* go on summer vacation, they would start grilling me, and it'd be clear I was a big fraud. Iceland felt so random that it seemed believable, you know?"

"Yeah. I could see that." That look, like he was thinking of some inside joke, came across his face again.

"I even told them my hair is this blonde because I'm half Icelandic, but the thing is, my mom bleaches it over our kitchen sink! Like, what is my problem?!" She shook her head incredulously at herself. "Maybe it's not their fault for not being my real friends. Maybe it's *mine*. Who would want to actually be friends with me, a person who's just desperately pretending to be someone they're not?"

"I would."

Holly's heart skipped a beat, but she tried not to give anything away and rolled her eyes. "You're just saying that to be nice."

"No. I'm really not. This is the thing—sure, you were pretending to be someone you're not—but everyone's doing that all the damn time. Unlike most people, you"—he pointed at her with the cigarette in his hands—"are waking up to it. You can see through all the bullshit. Better you deal with it now, when you've got your whole life ahead of you, rather than wake up an old lady and realize your entire life has been a lie. I've been in your shoes; believe me: what you're going through—it feels like you're having a crisis right now—but it feels amazing when you come out on the other side. When you stop living for other people's expectations and just start living for yourself, that's when your life really begins."

"You make it sound so easy."

"It *is* easy, Holly! You just have to think, 'What would I be doing right now if I wasn't trying to please everyone else?' And then you do it. So . . ." He looked at her expectantly.

"You mean like right now, what would I be doing?"

"Exactly."

"Well, I wouldn't be in Violet, for one thing—"

"This isn't a hypothetical question. I'm not asking what you would do if you could change the past. I mean this very second."

"I—I don't know. It's like I've just been going along with what I think everyone else wants me to be for so long that I've completely lost touch with who I actually am and what I want. Maybe the damage is permanent. I'm never going to recover like you have. I'm just going to be this boring, floating blob with no identity of her own forever."

Orlando dragged on his cigarette and rolled his eyes. "That's a load of crap."

"What do you mean?"

"You have an *extremely* unique personality. Boring people don't just pick up strangers and share their deepest secrets with them. I think you're just trying to avoid the question."

Holly pursed her lips for a long moment. "Right now, if I were doing what I wanted, I would drive this car straight out of here."

"Where? Back home?"

"No. Home doesn't really feel like home right now. I'd go somewhere new. Maybe I would keep driving west, through that skinny part of Idaho, all the way through Washington, until I reached the coast."

He raised an eyebrow. "Then what?"

"I guess I would go to the beach. I'd figure out the rest after taking a really long nap on the sand. Recover from all the driving."

"Could I join you?"

"Sure, but you can't chain-smoke the whole way there."

"All right." He sighed, then reached over and stubbed out his cigarette in a tiny square on the Buick's center console, brushing her arm. Even through her sweatshirt, Orlando's brief touch made a wave of warmth roll up Holly's arm.

They had driven all the way through town and were approaching the mountains. Up ahead, an SUV turned onto the street. Holly squinted at its bright headlights, and Orlando shrank down into his seat.

"Holly, I'm sorry to do this," he said in a low voice, "but can you drop me off at that next corner up ahead?"

"What?" Holly panicked.

Orlando glanced at the clock on the dashboard. It was a quarter until three. "I completely lost track of time."

"Do you want me to drop you off at your house?"

He shook his head. "No, no, don't worry about it."

She pulled over and idled the car. Orlando opened the door and jumped out, then turned around and peered back inside.

"Will you accept a rain check?" he asked. "I still want to show you my favorite spot."

Holly gulped back her worry. "I'll think about it," she said, though she knew she would 100 percent be there.

"Well, if you decide the answer's yes, meet me at the gas station tomorrow night around twelve. I hate to be such an early bird, but you know I just *can't* be late to church on Sunday morning."

With that, he winked at her and disappeared into the night.

9

ZOE

On Saturdays, Zoe worked at the diner from seven a.m. to three p.m. She set her phone alarm in five-minute increments from six a.m. onward even though she almost always ended up scrambling out of bed at quarter till. The first warning blared, and she rolled over to shut off her phone, a flurry of notifications filling the screen.

— Low Battery —

— 10% of battery remaining —

Delia: Hey.

I miss you Zo.

Can we talk?

Delia
— Missed Call (2) —

Holly: SJFJGJFHGBJ RAN INTO ORLANDO AGAIN

He bought me a bag of Cheetos . . . should I consider that a date?

Ok I just realized I didn't even get his number smh

Zoe rubbed her eyes. It was too early for her brain to truly process any of the texts. She needed at least another half hour of sleep. But first, she had to deal with the low-battery warning. She swore she'd plugged in her charger before going to sleep, as she did every night. Zoe leaned over the side of her bed to push the plug into the outlet behind her nightstand, but it was already snuggly pressed in place. So then she tried pulling the USB connector in and out, but still the phone wouldn't charge. She sat up and turned on her bedside lamp (also plugged into the outlet), but no light came. Great, she figured, the outlet was busted.

Zoe picked up her phone and charger, got out of bed, and stumbled into the kitchen. She plugged the charger into the outlet next to the microwave, yet still that little green icon didn't appear. Her battery had dropped down to 7 percent. It was then that she realized the display clock on the microwave was totally black. She walked over to the light switch, flicked it on, and watched the bulbs in the ceiling fan do absolutely nothing.

"Mama," she called, nearly tripping over the pile of packages as she walked through the dark dining room into the living room.

Marla was passed out on the couch, clutching her iPad to her chest. Zoe shook her gently by the shoulder. "Mama," she whispered.

"Mmm, what is it, honey?" Marla murmured, her eyes closed.

"The power's out," Zoe said.

"Oh. Must've been a storm or something."

Zoe crossed the room and peered through the front window. The sun had just started to rise, but all the streetlights were still on. Across the way, she could see her neighbors drinking coffee and watching the morning news in their living room.

"Doesn't look like it," Zoe said. "When you were drying your hair last night, maybe you blew a fuse or something?"

Marla sat up straight and touched her hair, as if it would provide an answer itself. "Maybe," she said quietly.

"I'll go check the circuit breaker."

Zoe opened the door to the basement and grabbed the flashlight her father had thoughtfully hung on the back of it when he was still alive. She crept down the rickety wooden stairs and was faced with the graveyard of her mother's failed attempts at being her own boss: boxes upon boxes of essential oils, makeup, weight-loss powders, spandex leggings, and more leftovers from schemes that had lured Marla in with promises of financial independence only to put her deeper into debt.

After wading through it all, Zoe made it to the circuit breaker. She opened it up and shined the flashlight directly on it, but none of the switches were in an off position, meaning nothing had been disrupted.

"Well, everything looks normal down here," she said, climbing back up the stairs. "I don't understand."

"I do," Marla said. Now she was fully awake and sitting up straight, with her eyes solemnly staring down at her folded hands.

Zoe's empty stomach started to churn. She knew something was deeply wrong. "What happened?" she asked breathlessly.

"There was a . . . miscalculation," Marla said.

"With what?" Zoe pressed, though she already knew.

"The electric bill." Marla rifled through a stack of catalogs and open envelopes on the coffee table, pulled out a piece of paper, and handed it to Zoe.

"Two thousand and forty-seven dollars?" Zoe screamed.

"I haven't paid in ten months," Marla admitted sheepishly. "They're always saying 'Your final warning this, your final warning that,' but they've never *actually* shut the electricity off."

"What about 'God is going to provide'? Huh? Because this looks a lot like God not providing."

"It's okay, Zoe. That new shipment I got last week, I'm going to multiply my investment with it. We will be fine."

"We will *not be fine*! You haven't multiplied any investments ever. You're insane, Mama. This is the literal definition of insanity. Doing the same thing over and over, expecting different results."

"Zoe, that is no way to talk to your mother."

Zoe took a deep breath and sat on the recliner opposite the couch. She closed her eyes for several moments, trying to think of a course of action.

"I'm sorry," she said at last, opening her eyes. "I know it's still a couple months until I turn eighteen, but what if we dip into my inheritance from Daddy? The ten thousand. I pay off the bills. You promise me to cancel your Hope Harvest subscription and not buy any nonessentials for a few months while you pay me back."

Marla curled up into a ball on the couch and mumbled something into a throw pillow.

"What's that, Mama?"

She mumbled again. Zoe got up and pulled the throw pillow out of her mother's arms.

"I said I already spent it," Marla cried, tears beginning to pour of her eyes. "I'm so sorry, Zoe. I figured that by the time your birthday came around, I would have multiplied your money tenfold. I was planning on giving you a little something more."

Zoe just stood there, motionless, her face frozen.

Her Get Out of Violet fund.

Her fluffy bed to land on when things got out of hand.

Her future with Delia.

Gone.

. . .

Delia was sitting on the steps in front of the diner when Zoe pulled up on her bike a few minutes after seven. At the sight of her, Zoe felt an ache in her throat.

"Hey," Delia said, standing up.

"Hi," Zoe croaked, locking her bike to the step railing.

"I didn't mean to sneak up on you like this. It's just . . . we've never gone this long without talking to each other. And you didn't respond to my texts last night, so I felt like I should come here and do this face-to-face."

Zoe took her bike helmet off and shook out her hair. "Do what?"

Delia peered around the parking lot; it was empty. She grabbed Zoe's hands and held them in hers.

"I'm sorry that I didn't take your side at youth group. I'm sorry that I just let you be humiliated. I'm sorry that I never stick up for you. I act like a coward because I'm scared of how people would react if they knew the truth. And that's not fair to you. I shouldn't be scared of them. The only thing I should really be scared of is *losing you*."

Tears formed in the corners of Zoe's eyes. "You didn't do anything wrong. Sometimes I forget that it's just better for the both of us in the long run if I keep a low profile. I shouldn't go around making a big scene when we're so close to—" Her voice hitched, knowing that without the money, what she was saying was no longer true. "So close to being free."

"I love you so much," Delia said, pulling her in for a hug. "I can't wait until we leave this place forever," she said into Zoe's hair, "so we can live together in a cute little house with zero inspirational décor and an old dog, where we never have to hide again."

A stream of tears poured down Zoe's face. "Me neither."

10

GENESIS

In theory, harvesting produce was Genesis's favorite job on the ranch. Seeing fully formed vegetables come out of the dirt felt biblical to her, as if each leaf of kale was a miracle in itself. The vegetable garden felt like undeniable proof that God existed, that it was a direct descendant of the gardens described in the book of Genesis itself, even if it lived in the midst of such a twisted place.

In practice, Genesis hated harvesting produce after about forty-five minutes. Standing hunched over the crops in the midday sun with nothing but a layer of Art's questionable homemade sunscreen to protect her skin from the rays was excruciating. Genesis had never been inside a supermarket, but she knew that's where regular people got their produce. She wondered if they ever stopped to think about the sweat and tears that went into a bunch of spinach.

She sat down on an overturned bucket, then reached for her metal water canteen and took a drink.

"Hey, Ocean?" she said, wiping her mouth with the back of her hand.

"Yeah?"

"Was it weird the first time you went to a grocery store?"

"Ha!" Ocean barked from the plot of Swiss chard she was steadily picking away at. "What do you mean?"

"Like all the foods you could ever want are just sitting out for you to grab? And they're all clean and ready to eat? It must have been exciting."

"Honestly? It was super weird. Everything looks fake. The apples are too shiny. They have these automatic sprinklers above the lettuce that just spurt out water for no reason. The meat is all wrapped in plastic. I thought I was gonna barf the first time I saw it. Then when I got to the checkout, I realized I'd accidentally put hundreds of dollars' worth of food in my cart. I had to put most of it back. Humiliating. Granted, I later learned Whole Foods is, like, the most expensive of the stores, but I'd never paid for food in my life, you know? How would I have known?"

Genesis nodded thoughtfully. Each time she asked Ocean about an element of the outside world, it was like opening a nesting doll filled with hundreds more. "When you left the ranch, how did you even have money to pay for anything?"

Ocean paused and placed a handful of leaves in the barrel. "It was so brutal, dude. Sometimes I don't even know how I pulled it off. None of the elders were supportive of my decision. They said I was handing over my brain to an 'elitist ivory tower,' which, spoiler alert, they ended up being totally right. My scholarship covered tuition and room and board, but let's just say I was no stranger to selling my undergarments on the dark web."

Genesis cringed. "What's the dark web?"

"Oh, muffin," Ocean cooed. "How I wish I was still as innocent as you." She got up and wiped her hands on her lilac pants. "Be right back. I need to pee."

Genesis took another sip of water and peered around the vegetable garden. It was deserted, so she snuck her phone out of her pocket and pulled up Ree Reaps's Instagram profile to see what she was doing.

Minutes before, Ree had posted a photo to her feed of all of her kids jumping into an enormous in-ground pool together. Genesis knew all their names and ages: Chloe, three; Eden, seven; Gabriella, ten; Ella, thirteen; and Dustin, seventeen. She imagined jumping in with them and how refreshing the cool water would feel on her hot skin.

First pool day of the season! the caption read. So blessed to call this weird and wonderful crew my kiddos! #Gratitude

Genesis kept scrolling even though she'd already seen the other posts and had practically memorized their captions.

A selfie of Ree in her tangerine jumpsuit, laughing at her reflection in the mirror:

Proverbs 31:25. Strength and dignity are her clothing, and she laughs at the time to come. #SundayFinest

A carefully arranged spread of food on a kitchen island next to a vase of fresh flowers:

For what it's worth . . . I LOVE to cook, but oh my WORD, sometimes I just get tired of making dinner. Thank the Lord for these country-inspired meal kits. Just add hot water, toss a salad on the side, and dinner is DONE and

> my kiddos' bellies are HAPPY. @HopeHarvestKitchen
> #SuperCreamyMacAndCheese

Ree and Jay Reaps drinking coffee out of matching mugs that said HUBBY and WIFEY:

> "Don't talk to me before I've had my coffee" is the motto in our house, right after "Praise God." So blessed to wake up every day and drink coffee with this guy (even if his bedhead can get a little out of hand 😊). New his and hers mugs now available in the merch shop @HopeHarvestMarket.

What Genesis admired most about Ree was how full her life seemed: She took great care of her kids. She wore incredible outfits. She ran her own business. She was in happy, fulfilling relationships with both her husband and God. It seemed like wherever she went, sunshine followed. Genesis couldn't decide if she wished Ree were her mother or if she wished she *were* Ree. Maybe it was a combination of both.

She scrolled back up to the photo of the kids by the pool and zoomed in on Dustin, the child closest to her in age. Genesis believed that God had a reason for her circumstances, but for just a moment she let jealousy wash over her. How was it that Dustin Reaps was born into a loving, supportive, *perfect* family while she was thrown into this ragtag band who seemed to forget about her half the time?

"Gen?" a voice called. She jumped, and her phone slipped out of her fingers, bouncing off her knee and onto the dirt. Genesis reached to grab it, but her hand was met by another.

"What's this?" Grace asked, staring at the phone. Genesis had fallen so far down the rabbit hole of Instagram fantasyland that she hadn't noticed Grace enter the garden.

"It's . . . um . . . I—"

"Where did you get it?" Grace asked, picking up the phone.

Genesis didn't want to rat Ocean out. All things considered, she was a good roommate, and it was kind of her to give Genesis the phone in the first place. Genesis knew lying went against the Bible, but because her phone was her gateway to the Bible, she figured maybe it'd be okay to lie just this once.

"I found it." She shrugged after a moment of silence.

"You *found* this?" Grace repeated like she were talking to a small child. "Where?"

Genesis just gestured vaguely.

"You know, Gen, I hate having to remind you one of our core principles is disavowing the use of unnecessary technology that tampers with our individual enlightenment. And I'd say this certainly counts."

Something snapped inside Genesis. The phone was her escape, the thing that led her to God, the only thing that made her feel anything vaguely resembling enlightenment.

"So is the television set that you all watch trashy reality shows on necessary technology?" Genesis asked, standing up from her bucket seat. "Huh?"

Grace held up her palm and closed her eyes. "Gen, let's not get combative here."

"I'm serious. It seems like there's a real picking and choosing of what rules we follow. It's almost like there's no core philosophy to anything we believe in and it was all just made up by some guy picking rules as he saw fit. We're called *the Astralians,* but when's the last time any of us astral projected? If any of us have ever even done it at all?!"

"Gen, we are a community. We decide as *a community* how to live. If that is how you feel, I welcome you to share it with the *rest* of the community during our next open forum."

"I know that you're the owner of the ranch," Gen blurted out. "I know that your real last name is Ogilvy. I know your parents are very rich. Is that why you don't want me to use technology? Because then I'll find out more of the truth?"

Grace took a deep breath. "The past is in the past, Genesis."

"If that's true, then maybe you wouldn't mind telling me who my real father is. Because if that's in the past, I guess it doesn't matter really, does it?" Genesis asked.

Grace winced. "That's enough. I know you're feeling angry and confused because you have been caught breaching our trust. I think you should take the rest of the day to go back to your bunk and process those feelings by doing some breath work. Meanwhile, I am going to take this," she said, holding up the phone. "And I am going to destroy it. And after you've calmed down, you will be on dish duty for the foreseeable future. Is that clear?"

"Oh, so now you decide to be a parent?"

"Genesis, believe me, I know growing up comes with so many questions. When you are ready to have a calm discussion about these topics, I will be available. I hope one day you'll learn to appreciate the incredible path that the universe has chosen for you." With that, Grace turned and left.

The reality of life with no phone sank in for Genesis. She had no access to her Bible PDF. She couldn't watch Ree's vlogs or the Hope Harvest sermons. When she had a question about life on the outside, she would only have Ocean's jaded answers.

Her chest started to pound, and she began to hyperventilate, curling up into a ball on the dirt beneath the kale plants.

Genesis knew she couldn't continue to live like this; it was time for her to forge her own path.

11

HOLLY

"Make a right up here," Orlando said to Holly, pointing toward a dark road. "We're almost there."

Her time was now divided into hours she spent waiting to meet up with Orlando and hours spent with him. All day long she'd turned their last two conversations over and over in her head, realizing that she had revealed her most private thoughts to Orlando, yet she still knew so little about him. Tonight she was determined to change that.

"Okay, right up ahead, you're just gonna pull over on the left side."

Holly did as he said, then put the car in park.

"Now if you look over there, you will see a complete portrait of Violet, Montana."

He had taken them to a lookout point from which they could see the whole town glowing under the moonlight: the church marquee, her dad's diner, even Astralia on the edge of town.

"Whoa," Holly whispered.

"I like how small it looks from up here. Like it could fit inside a snow globe," Orlando said quietly. "It reminds me how big the universe is. How nothing that happens here really matters at all."

Holly leaned forward onto the steering wheel, resting her chin at the top to better stare out the front window. "I think I see it as the opposite," she said. "It's kind of terrifying to think how somewhere so small can have such a big impact. Like a pin in a grenade. I mean, all it took was for that cult leader guy to go nuts and the whole country's eyes were on Violet. And now all these people are moving here just because of one single church. It might not be so small for long."

Orlando was quiet in his seat, frozen. "Wow," he said finally.

"Not that your interpretation is any less true," she said quickly. "Maybe I'm just a pessimist and you're an optimist."

"No, I'm definitely a pessimist." He chuckled. "You know, I've read some stuff by Jimmy Joe James. Someone uploaded a bunch of his pamphlets online. A lot of it *is* nuts, but some of his ideas hold up. You know, we should sneak onto the ranch one of these nights and explore. I've always wanted to do that, but I've been too much of a chicken."

Holly tilted her head and stared at Orlando. The moonlight cast a perfect shadow on his jaw.

"What are you thinking?" he asked quietly.

"I'm thinking maybe you actually are a serial killer," she said. "And I've just driven myself to the site of my own murder."

Orlando smiled wickedly.

"Seriously, you are kind of a mystery to me. I told you my life story, but I don't have the faintest clue about you."

Orlando's face became serious. It felt like the air had suddenly been sucked out of the car with a vacuum. "What do you want to know?"

"Whatever you want to tell me. You've been a good listener for me. I want to do the same for you."

"It's just hard to talk about myself."

Holly gave him an encouraging glance. His eyes softened, and he stared down at the town.

"Both my parents passed away when I was a kid," Orlando said. "In the gum factory explosion. Now it's just me and my grandma."

Holly thought of Zoe and her dad, then felt like a brat for resenting all three of her very-much-alive parental figures. "You too? God. I'm sorry, Orlando."

"So I wasn't being totally honest with you last night: I'm not just living life for myself. That's not really possible when I have to be there to make sure Gammy takes her meds and has something to eat and doesn't confuse Windex with mouthwash." He smiled sadly, then crunched up his nose like he was trying to hold back tears. "This place is full of too many bad memories, but I have to stick around. We only have each other."

Beneath the cloud of smoke covering Orlando, there was just a boy who had lived through tragedy and cared about his grandma. Holly felt like her heart was going to burst.

Instinctively, she reached across the center console and took Orlando's hand. "I'm here, if you want me to be."

Orlando stared down at their intertwined fingers for an excruciatingly long minute.

Then he pulled Holly into his arms and kissed her.

. . .

"A T-shirt under spaghetti straps? How *modest!*" Zoe exclaimed as Holly walked up to her in the lobby of Hope Harvest.

Holly cringed and tugged at the bottom of her leopard-print sundress. "I look okay, right? This is the only nice thing I packed."

"Oh, yeah. You look great. And you're using all those helpful tips you learned at youth group." Zoe turned and scanned the crowd of people congregating outside the sanctuary doors. "Let me wrangle my mom and we'll go inside. Thank you so, so much for coming today. I owe you one."

"Don't worry about it. This will be an . . . interesting cultural experience," Holly said, looking around warily at all the manicured families.

Attending a church service had not been on Holly's summer bucket list by any means. By now, she knew to actively avoid Main Street for most of Sunday, when it became flooded with socializing churchgoers. But then Zoe had asked her for a favor: apparently her mom was hemorrhaging money to the church, and Zoe needed someone to effectively help babysit her mom, a second set of eyes to watch her every move to ensure she wasn't giving a dime more. Holly thought her idea sounded a bit ridiculous, but she couldn't ignore the desperation in Zoe's eyes. Plus, Zoe told her about the DJ and the light show, and Holly thought the whole thing sounded so ridiculous that she had to see it for herself, just this once.

She'd been a lot more easygoing since her late-night meetups with Orlando began. He didn't have his own phone, but Orlando was reliable; they met up in the gas station parking lot every night and drove around together. Danny hadn't caught Holly sneaking out; he was too busy keeping the diner from burning down to notice that she'd been sleeping in until two in the afternoon.

For once, everything felt right; she was seventeen and falling in love. She barely thought about what her friends were up to back in LA. The world seemed a little lighter.

Holly followed Zoe and Marla into the sanctuary. It was already packed with hundreds of people, so they took seats closer to the back, much to her relief. The lights went low, and the DJ began. Then the band followed suit and played the slower worship songs. Holly swayed along to the music, having a semi-fun time. Yes, she'd much rather be singing along at a Harry Styles concert, but this really wasn't as bad as she'd imagined church would be. Granted, she had no idea if most churches were like *this*.

Pastor Marcus came out to say his corny jokes and read prayer requests. It took a second for Holly to realize what was happening when everyone around her bowed their heads and closed their eyes. Then Ree Reaps took to the stage to collect tithes and offerings.

All of Holly's concerns about her outfit being too loud were quelled when she saw what Ree was wearing: a pink floral pantsuit with a belt that she immediately recognized as Gucci.

"Good morning, everybody! It is so good to be here today," Ree said, walking to the center of the stage. "I want to tell y'all a little story this morning. So yesterday, I was talking to my oldest, Dustin, about the verse I was preparing to share this morning. And that verse is Matthew 17:20, which I'm sure many of you have heard before: 'If you have faith like a grain of mustard seed, you can say to this mountain, "Move from here to there," and it will move. Nothing will be impossible for you.' Meaning, your faith is so powerful that like a little tiny mustard seed, it can grow and grow until it changes the world." She moved her manicured hands out wide to mimic the shape of a globe. "And y'all know what Dustin said to me? He said, 'Oh, Mama, nobody plants mustard seeds anymore.'"

The congregation laughed. Zoe looked at Holly and rolled her eyes.

"But then he said something really powerful, y'all," Ree continued. "He said, 'I think faith is a lot like a pin in a grenade. It might look small, but it sure has a big impact.'"

Holly's spine went rigid.

"Well, I was just touched by that. I'm so proud of Dustin and this next generation. You know what a grenade causes? A mighty big fire. And this next generation of believers, they are on fire for Jesus! Dustin, why don't you come on up here? Oh, he's shaking his head no. Y'all know sometimes he's a little shy. Let's give him some applause of encouragement. C'mon! Heather, help me drag that boy up here, won't you?"

The congregation clapped uproariously. From the side of the stage, the girl who had led Girls Ministry emerged holding hands with a tall, handsome boy wearing a button-down shirt and expensive-looking sneakers.

A tall, handsome boy who up until that moment Holly had only known as Orlando.

12

ZOE

Dustin Reaps embodied everything Zoe thought was wrong with the world: he was a corny straight white guy whose entire life had been handed to him on a silver platter. She'd resented him since they were little kids: men laughed when he didn't say anything particularly funny; old ladies pinched his cheeks like he was a cherub who'd just fallen from heaven; most of the girls at youth group harbored lifelong crushes on him, and, honestly, so did their moms.

As Dustin appeared onstage, Zoe looked to Holly and discreetly made a gagging motion. She thought Holly was going along with her joke and fake-barfing at the sight of him too, but then she realized that Holly genuinely looked like she was going to be sick: her mouth curled up in disgust, and her entire face went pale.

"What's wrong?" Zoe whispered. Holly stood up from her seat and squeezed her way out of the row without even muttering an "excuse me."

It was terrible timing. Zoe had brought Holly here specifically to help her keep an eye on her mom, and she bailed just as it came time for the tithes and offerings collection. But her conscience tugged at her; she knew she should go check on Holly and see if she was okay.

Zoe reached, grabbed Marla's purse, and got out of her seat. "Hey!" Marla snapped. A few heads turned their way.

"Do you want me to make a scene, Mama?" Zoe whispered through her teeth. Marla clenched her jaw and turned her attention back to Ree and Dustin, the image of a perfect mother-child relationship.

Zoe burst through the exit into the church lobby; it was empty except for two ushers slash security guards. "Did either of you just see a girl run out of the sanctuary?" she asked one. He pointed in the direction of the women's restroom.

"Holly?" she called as she pushed through the door.

"Mm-hmm?" Holly's voice responded from a stall at the end of the row.

Zoe started to walk over to her but paused when she noticed a different, familiar-looking girl splashing her face with water at one of the sinks.

"Hey," Zoe said, pushing her eyebrows together. "I know you, right?"

The girl froze as they made eye contact in the mirror. Zoe tried to place her—frizzy brown hair in a braid crawling down her back, thick eyebrows, and wide brown eyes like she was a runway model. Suddenly, it clicked.

"You're Sage's . . . friend. Genesis, right? Sorry, I guess I didn't recognize you because you're not wearing purple." Zoe eyed her outfit: a big floral sack that looked three sizes too big for her. "Wait, do you go to church here?"

Genesis opened her mouth to speak, then closed it again. She shook her head and stalked out of the bathroom.

"Nice to see you too," Zoe mumbled, making her way to Holly. She tapped at the stall door. "Holly, are you okay?"

From behind the door, she could hear her taking a jagged breath. "I know. It can be really overwhelming in there. Do you need anything?" Zoe asked.

The door lock clicked open and Holly poked her head out. Her face was drenched with tears.

"That's him," she said, sniffling.

Zoe bent down to meet her face at toilet level. "Who's *him*?"

"That boy on the stage," Holly said, her voice cracking. "That's Orlando."

"*Dustin?!*" Zoe exclaimed.

"Yeah. I mean, if *that* is even his real name," Holly said hysterically.

"Are you sure?" Zoe asked, putting her fingers to her temples. She mentally compared the all-black-wearing, cigarette-smoking James Dean look-alike Holly had described with clean-cut Dustin. It just didn't compute.

"Unless this Dustin person has an identical twin, I'm positive," Holly said, blotting her face with toilet paper. "Of course his name isn't *Orlando*! Zoe, I literally want to die. I want to melt into a puddle and be flushed down this toilet. This is so embarrassing. Who does this happen to? I got catfished, but in real life! What is even the word for that?"

"Dustin comes from a long line of scammers," Zoe explained.

"These people are skilled in the art of the con. You did nothing wrong."

"God, I'm such an idiot. He has a girlfriend! He's rich! He even has *parents*! He told me they died in the gum factory explosion!"

"No!" Zoe said, grabbing her by the shoulders. "You are not an idiot—Wait, what was that last thing you said?"

"He said he was an orphan. That his parents died in the accident, just like your dad. Oh, I'm going to be sick . . ." Holly slipped out of Zoe's arms and lurched for the toilet.

Rage bubbled up through Zoe's veins. Lying to Holly about his identity was bad enough, but pretending to experience the same tragedy that Zoe did just to elicit sympathy was straight-up diabolical. Dustin had everything he could possibly need and more. A girlfriend who openly adored him. Endless money, part of which he had taken from her family. Now he was trying to steal Zoe's grief, too. In that moment, Dustin escalated from just an annoying acquaintance to her mortal enemy.

"What should I do now?" Holly asked, wiping her mouth with the back of her hand and staring up at Zoe like a helpless puppy.

"Now? You're gonna clean yourself up. You're gonna walk over to the diner and drink a glass of ginger ale. I'll meet you there when the service is over."

"Okay. Yeah. I can do that. That sounds good."

"And then . . . we are going to figure out a plan to ruin that boy's life."

13

GENESIS

Genesis slipped back through the sanctuary doors and to her seat. She reminded herself that she hadn't dug through the main house attic until she found a box of clothes from before the Astralians all started wearing purple, snuck out at the crack of dawn, and walked the three miles to Hope Harvest in her torn-up Birkenstocks just to chicken out and turn around. She'd never expected to run into that girl Zoe and her vulgar mouth at a place as sacred as Hope Harvest, but the sight of her was a reminder to Genesis that she wouldn't be that meek, silent cult girl Zoe thought she was; today, she was going to be brave.

She'd streamed dozens of church services on her iPhone and knew some of the praise and worship music by heart, yet the service in person wasn't at all what she'd expected. The lights and the volume and the size of the crowd overwhelmed Genesis; she'd never been in a room with so many people in her life. While she thought it would be uplifting, somehow it felt wrong to experience the thing she'd had such a personal connection with alone in her bed in this room full of complete strangers. Not to mention, she suddenly felt drab and dirty and very aware of the fact that she wore homemade, aluminum-free deodorant.

By now, Ree and her son were gone from the stage. Her husband, Pastor Jay, was speaking behind a plexiglass podium. He was wearing an outfit that made no functional sense to Genesis: his muscular arms were bursting out of a too-tight suit vest over a T-shirt with jeans and a belt that matched his wife's, with a pair of cowboy boots that had sneakerlike soles. Genesis would listen to his sermons when she'd stream the Sunday service, but she didn't go out of her way to seek out Pastor Reaps's content the rest of the week.

"As many of you know, we have been working hard to spread the love of God even farther than we have ever before," he said, hands gripping the podium. "Well, last year, God blessed me with a vision that I want to share with you all today. In this vision, I saw people from all over the world traveling here, to little old Violet, Montana, to partake in a beautiful gathering never before seen in our lifetimes. I saw people dancing, singing, and rejoicing with one another, but not just in the way we dance, sing, and rejoice here every week. No, no." He paused, making meaningful eye contact with the crowd. "This was something different. Something special. Now, my kids will make fun of me, but in my head, I gave this gathering the working title of 'Christian Coachella.'"

Chuckles flowed throughout the congregation. Genesis had no idea what was so funny.

"You see, I believe the next step in God's vision for Hope Harvest is a kind of resort, kind of summer camp, and something never done before. While the rest of the country, even the world, is descending into chaos, we have created this haven here in Violet, Montana. So then God told me what we need: we need a ranch."

Pastor Jay nodded to someone in the distance, then on the screen behind him appeared a satellite map of Violet.

"If only, Lord, there were a ranch. Sitting right here on the edge of our town."

Whoever was operating the screen zoomed in on the map. It took Genesis a second to realize: they were zooming in on *her* ranch.

"God has rehabilitated the town of Violet to be a shining beacon of his grace, but there remains a remnant of its dark past. The demonic influence of the Astralian *cult* still lingers." He slammed his palm down on the podium for emphasis. "It's not as loud as it once was, but it is there."

Genesis's stomach dropped. She looked around self-consciously, as if people knew who she was and where she came from.

"Members of this cult still live there today. Across the county, they sell fruits and vegetables to support themselves, much like Satan tempting Eve with an apple. Even some local businesses, though none of *ours*, sell the bread baked by the very hands of these idol worshippers. These Astralians are breaking bread among us, but this is not the bread of life. No." He paused solemnly. "It's the bread of death."

No, no, no, you've got it all wrong, Genesis thought. She wished she could speak up and tell him there was really no need to be so dramatic. Maybe the Astralians were demonic once, but they were tired now. There was no force to be reckoned with.

"But you all know, like Jesus, we believe in hating the sin and loving the sinner. Myself and Ree, we went to these Astralians. We invited them into our home. We started a conversation. We asked them if they would like to open up their hearts to Jesus Christ. We thought maybe God would want us to build something in his vision together. But they refused. Instead, they said many, many unkind words to us that I shall not repeat here."

Genesis's whole face flashed red. The pastor was lying; he had never come to the ranch. If they had come, Genesis would've poured her heart out to them. She would have jumped at the chance to eat dinner at their house. It would've been the best day of her life.

But all they did was send their real estate agent.

"A kind of resort, kind of summer camp" sounded an awful lot like the Astralians' grand plan to open a meditation retreat. *Is this all religion is?* Genesis wondered. *Just an excuse to get people to open up their wallets?* She felt so close to God when she prayed in her humble cabin, and it didn't cost her anything. Maybe the only difference between the pastor in front of her and Jimmy Joe James rotting in jail for money laundering was that the former had a good accountant.

"So after many talks with God, and with Ree, I have decided to launch something we have never done before. We will be launching One Hundred Days of Prayer for the Hope Harvest Ranch. Starting this week, we are asking groups of you to flood the gates of that ranch with prayer for one hundred days or until it is handed over to us by God. Whichever comes first."

The screen behind him shifted to an animated graphic that slowly echoed the phrase *100 Days of Prayer*. Pastor Reaps clapped, and the congregation followed uproariously.

On the side of the stage, a figure appeared and ran to the podium. It was the redheaded waitress from the diner. She lurched for Pastor Reaps's microphone.

"Hi," she said as a wave of feedback clanged in everyone's ears. "I just want to ask, how do you plan to pay for any of this? Will it involve more scamming? More lying? For instance, will it involve—" Two large men in black suits pulled her back by the waist, cutting her off and dragging her down the side of the stage. The congregation clapped for them like they'd just scored a touchdown.

"And we will be praying for that young lady as well, it seems," Pastor Reaps joked.

Genesis didn't know what exactly she'd just witnessed, but she felt in her heart that God wouldn't like any of it. She got up from her seat and left the sanctuary for the second, and last, time.

· · ·

Outside the church, Genesis put her hands over her eyes and stared into the late-morning sun. She was thirsty and hungry and not looking forward to the walk back to the ranch, not to mention the rest of her entire life. She couldn't go back to the way things were, especially without her phone, but she couldn't picture a way forward either. Hope Harvest had always been the escape hatch in her head, the place she'd go when she'd finally worked up the confidence, but now it felt like an escape hatch that just led her down an endless rolling hill.

She asked God for a sign, any sign, to lead her where she was supposed to go.

And then that darn waitress came bursting out of the front doors of the church.

"Okay, okay!" Zoe said, tugging her arms from the usher's grasp. "I got it. I'm leaving." The doors slammed behind her. She took a breath, straightened her shirt, and looked around. "Hey!" she called, noticing Genesis standing out front.

Any other *sign*, Genesis pleaded silently to God.

"Did you know about this BS? Them trying to take over the ranch?" she said, pointing a thumb at the church. "Is that why you're here?"

Genesis reluctantly shook her head. "No."

"Oh," Zoe said. "Then what *are* you doing here? And how did you even get here? Is Sage here?" She craned her neck to look around.

"No. I came here *alone*," Genesis said, staring at her feet. "I don't think you'd really understand."

Zoe raised her eyebrows. "Try me."

14

ZOE

Holly and Zoe sat next to each other on one side of the vinyl booth, staring at Genesis on the other side rapidly sucking down the final inch of a chocolate milkshake with a straw, like she was some sort of alien creature they'd just rescued from another planet.

Zoe peeled her eyes away to glance at her phone.

Delia: WHAT WAS THAT?

Zoe: I thought you said you weren't scared of what people think anymore!

Delia: I'm not . . . but that doesn't mean we still shouldn't keep a "low profile" in the meantime.
i.e. not physically attacking Pastor Reaps?!

She had yet to tell Delia about the money situation, which would at least offer some kind of explanation as to why she'd acted out, but she didn't want to tell her until she was absolutely positive there wasn't some way she could recoup it.

Genesis let out a large belch. Zoe looked up and flipped her phone facedown on the booth. "Sorry," Genesis said, placing her hand over her mouth.

"Don't apologize." Zoe eyed Genesis's skinny wrists and her floral dress that seemed to swallow her whole body, then leaned in across the table. "Are they feeding you over there?" she whispered.

"Oh, yeah," Genesis said, reaching for her second glass of ice water. "It's just generally macrobiotic. We sell most of the good stuff. And we never have ice cream."

"Huh." Zoe nodded. "Well, now that we've sufficiently raised your blood sugar, do you think you're ready to tell us why you were at church?"

"I just always wanted to go." She shrugged.

"But *why*?" Zoe asked. Her usual judgment had dropped from her voice. She was genuinely curious, like this was truly a puzzle that made no sense.

"Well . . ." Genesis stared down at the table and fidgeted with a paper straw wrapper. "Over the last year, I've accepted Jesus Christ into my heart and become a born-again Christian."

"No shit!" Zoe exclaimed. "Sorry. Excuse my language. I meant: *no way*. How? Don't you guys believe in having like a hundred gods and ten wives?"

"No," Genesis said. "The Astralians don't believe in *any* god, or marriage."

"Then how did you . . ."

"I did my research and decided I wanted to believe in something else."

"Wait," Zoe said, raising her hand. "How did you research?"

"On my iPhone."

"You guys have iPhones?!"

Zoe considered the elusive corners of TikTok where she'd come across short videos of Amish teens or men in prison filming themselves doing trendy dances. She'd always wondered how they'd managed to get their hands on such technology without getting in trouble.

"No." Genesis shook her head. "Just me. Or I did. Until Gr— My, um, mother took it and destroyed it last week."

"Destroyed?!" Holly repeated, as if taking a hammer to an iPhone was a form of manslaughter.

"That's why I decided to finally go to the service today. Without my phone, I can't access the Bible. I can't stream Hope Harvest services. I can't look at Ree Reaps's daily Instagram devotionals. Though after today, I'm not sure I'd even want to. They *lied*. They never came to visit the ranch. They never invited us over. Believe me: I would've gone."

"I know this must be hard," Zoe said. "But they're no better than Jimmy Joe James. In fact, they're running a multilevel marketing scheme. Which is worse, in my opinion." She explained to Genesis the way her mother had been manipulated into giving away all her money and how Dustin had faked his identity to Holly.

"I think Orlan—*Dustin* knew exactly what he was doing," Holly said. "The first time we met, it was when I got lost and ended up driving past Astralia. He was hanging out outside the gate, smoking a cigarette. It was like he *wanted* someone to notice him." She clenched her jaw and stabbed the ice at the bottom of her cup of ginger ale with a straw. "The other night he told me he had always wanted to sneak onto the ranch and see what it's like. That just feels sick. He made fun of his parents' church all the time. What does he really believe? Does he just get some sick thrill out of doing bad-boy cosplay and taking advantage of random girls?"

Genesis leaned on the table like she couldn't sit up and take in all this news at once. "Maybe this is just a big misunderstanding," she said, pressing her hands to her temples. "I'm sure they didn't intend to stop your mother from being able to pay her bills. If they knew, they'd probably feel terrible. For all I know, maybe the Reapses *did* come to the ranch and try to talk to us, and I just missed it. As for Dustin, I don't know . . . maybe if we just tried calmly sitting down and talking to them all, we could get an explanation."

"Genesis," Zoe said, staring into her eyes. "When you've ever asked an adult in your life for a reasonable explanation to an irrational problem, did they give you one?"

Genesis stared back at Zoe for a moment. Her eyes turned wet, and she slumped back into the booth. "No," she admitted quietly.

Holly took a swig of ginger ale. "I wish the Reapses could just write us all a check for emotional damages and call it a day."

Zoe froze, then slowly pivoted her head. "Holly. You're a genius."

Holly narrowed her eyes. "I was joking."

"Blackmail," Zoe whispered through her teeth. "Dustin has no idea that you know who he is. The congregation's too big and the lights were shining in his face. There's no way he saw you. Maybe you can take advantage of that. Hang out with him again. Get him all vulnerable. Record him talking about how much he hates the church or whatever try-hard stuff he does to look un-Dustin-like. Then we'll threaten to share it with the world unless he pays us off."

"This is escalating very quickly," Holly said slowly, leaning back from Zoe. "If we were to do this—theoretically, of course—how would I inconspicuously get clear footage of him? We only meet up in the middle of the night in my dark car. I would have to turn the flash on. Then he'd know something was up."

"You just have to take him somewhere well lit," Zoe said.

Holly shook her head. "Clearly, he doesn't like going to places that are. He can't get recognized."

"What about the mini-mart?" Zoe went on. "You ran into him there, right? Record him buying cigarettes!"

"Is that actually explosive blackmail material? I'd have to, like, zoom in on the box of Marlboros for it to be truly damning. I have really shaky hands. I don't know, Zoe."

"Okay, *okay.*" Zoe sighed, rubbing her eyes. "We need to think harder. There has to be somewhere this could work."

"Maybe you *could* take him somewhere dark," Genesis piped up, "but where you could use the excuse of your flash being a flashlight. Somewhere he told you he wants to go. Somewhere like . . . the ranch."

15

HOLLY

Holly drove to the gas station as if she were under the influence, nearly swerving into Hope Harvest Market on her way, envisioning a tragic crash in which she died surrounded by a sea of handcrafted ceramic crosses and potted succulents. When they last parted ways, Orlando aka Dustin and Holly agreed to meet up again on Monday at midnight. She'd left feeling as if there were electricity running through her veins, unsure that she'd ever be able to fall asleep again. Now she felt the same way but for entirely opposite reasons.

She pulled in behind the gas station, where the dumpster sat. Dustin was standing with one foot against the wall, smoking as usual. He nodded at her and took one last puff, then threw the cigarette on the ground and put it out with his toes. Even knowing the truth, she still found him overwhelmingly attractive, but now it was a rotten kind of attractive, like a loaf of bread that looks perfect on the outside but is actually teeming with spores of mold between the slices.

Holly took a deep breath, then leaned over to unlock the passenger door.

"Hey," Dustin said, sliding in and closing the door shut behind him. He leaned in to kiss her jaw.

Holly stiffened and steered her head away from him. "H-heyyy!" she said in an unusually high voice.

"Everything all right?" Dustin asked her.

"Yep," she said, smiling with too many teeth showing. "Great."

He glanced sideways at her. "All right. So where are we headed tonight, Holly?"

She swallowed hard. "I actually have a surprise for you."

He raised an eyebrow. "Oh?"

"Mm-hmm." She shifted the car back into drive and pulled out of the parking lot.

"Can I have a hint?"

She shook her head.

"Not even a little one?" he pressed.

Holly looked both ways to turn onto the road. At this point, she just wanted to see how far Dustin was willing to take his act. "Okay, I'll give you a hint on one condition. You have to tell me what you want to be when you grow up."

Dustin laughed once. "What?"

"I just want to know. I like getting to know you; is that so bad?"

He raked a hand through his hair, and it tumbled back down his forehead in a messy wave. "Uh, to be honest, I have no clue. I want to do something that helps people, not harms them, you know? But so many jobs are just useless or just, like, actively bad, you know? I firmly believe it's impossible to be rich in this country without exploiting others."

Holly snorted through her nose. She couldn't help it. He was just so full of it.

"What?" Dustin pressed.

"Nothing. It's just . . . that's such an . . . *Orlando* answer."

He smiled, clearly pleased that his whole act was working on her. "So now do I get my hint about where we're going?"

"Well, you don't need one now," she said, turning down the road that led to the ranch entrance. "Because we're here."

Dustin's smile fell an infinitesimal amount. Holly kept driving past the entrance and down the road. She pulled over next to a patch of trees and parked the Buick, as if she weren't internally freaking out about what she was about to do.

"You told me you always wanted to sneak into the ranch. Let's just say I got us an in."

"What do you mean an 'in'?" He looked around as if he were waiting for someone to pop out of the trees.

"You'll see." Holly poked at his shoulder. She was less nervous now; he was a liar, but she had the upper hand. "What? Are you scared?"

He just gave her a smoldering look and got out of the car. Holly internally recited the directions Genesis had given her—the reverse of the ones Genesis herself used to sneak out of the ranch—then got out and took Dustin by the hand.

She turned on the flashlight on her phone and led them through the trees and up what appeared to be a mountable hill but was actually a steep climb. Holly's breath went short, and she paused, gripping her kneecaps.

"You all right?" Dustin asked.

Holly nodded. "How come you're the one who smokes like a chimney and I'm the one who's out of breath?"

"I suppose some of us are just blessed with strong lungs."

Holly resisted the urge to roll her eyes into the back of her head. Dustin reached out his hand and helped pull her up.

They made it to the top of the hill, where a chain-link fence with a rusty NO TRESPASSING sign separated them from about a dozen tiny simple wooden A-frame cabins lining the other half of the hillside. Genesis had explained that they had gone unused since the days when the Astralians' membership numbers had been in the hundreds. They were out of view of the main house or the larger cabins the remaining members still inhabited, meaning Holly and Dustin could sneak in undetected.

Some of the windows had been punched in, a few had been tagged with graffiti, and the ground was covered in weeds. The sight of it took Holly's breath away, gone as it already was; maybe she had just gotten used to the squeaky-clean feel of Main Street Violet over the last few weeks, but this place felt downright haunted. She walked along the bottom edge of the fence, her hand shaking as she held her phone out until it illuminated a human-size hole. Then she knelt down and crawled through, motioning for Dustin to follow.

"This is *sick*," he whispered, emerging on the other side.

"Let's go inside one," Holly said, though she dreaded they'd open a cabin door to find a dead animal—or worse.

"Which one?"

"Your choice."

He took her hand again and led them to the least dilapidated-looking of the cabins, in the middle of the hill. They stood on the small porch in front, and Dustin reached for the doorknob. It twisted but wouldn't turn. Dustin tried again, casually trying to break the lock with his elbow.

Holly nervously glanced over her shoulder. Genesis had promised she would keep a lookout, but without a phone, Holly had no way of confirming she really was. They'd agreed on a time at the diner, and she put her faith in Genesis following through.

"Let's try another one," Holly suggested.

They moved next door to a cabin with a broken window and partially collapsed stairs. The knob turned seamlessly.

Holly flashed her phone inside before they entered: a wooden double bed frame sat in the corner with a water-stained mattress on top. Some weeds had managed to grow a foot high between the floorboards.

It was showtime. Holly wore a denim jacket with a front pocket. She discreetly started recording and stuck her phone inside, pretending the flash was just the flashlight. They walked through the cabin entryway, and Dustin perched himself on the edge of the bed.

"This is wild," he said, staring up at the ceiling. Holly leaned against the wall opposite the bed with her arms crossed at what she hoped was an angle that could capture his face.

"Can you imagine living here?" she asked.

"Oh yeah. Totally off the grid. That's the life." He leaned back with his head resting in his hands like he was relaxing at a poolside resort and not on a mattress that was probably housing multiple kinds of termites.

"Even in the winter?"

"Sure."

"How would you stay warm?"

"I don't know. Light a campfire. Maybe I'd do that survivalist thing where you sleep naked with another person to absorb each other's body heat." He gave her a mischievous grin.

Holly reminded herself that she was there to get footage of him smoking, maybe saying a few dirty words, and that would be it. She leaned against the wall, trying to keep as much distance from him as she could in the small cabin. "Speaking of fire, um, can I have a cigarette?"

Dustin sat up on his elbows and squinted at her. "I thought you didn't smoke."

"Yeah, well, you just make it look *so cool*. I'm inspired to try."

"No." He snorted.

Holly squared her shoulders. "Why not?"

"You're serious?"

She nodded. Dustin reached for his back pocket and paused. "I don't want to be the reason you develop a lifelong habit."

"Believe me: you won't."

He took a cigarette out of the box and motioned for Holly to join him. She peeled herself off the wall and sat down next to him on the mattress, her heart speeding up. Dustin handed her the cigarette, and she put it between her lips. Then he pulled a lighter from his pocket and flicked it with his thumb. As he leaned toward her, carefully cupping the small flame that illuminated his face, he didn't feel to her like Dustin, the spoiled-rotten brat she knew he was. For a second, he was once again Orlando, the boy who seemed to only exist in her own head.

He paused and flinched away from the light coming out of her phone.

"I don't think we need that anymore."

Holly looked down at the phone camera poking out of her pocket. The profound ridiculousness of the plan overwhelmed her. What was she thinking, trying to commit blackmail? She didn't want revenge; she just wanted to pretend she had never been humiliated.

So she shut the flash off, pulled the unlit cigarette out of her mouth, and leaned into Dustin. It would be her last hurrah. She would believe for one last time that Dustin was Orlando, then she'd never pick him up at the gas station again, pretend he was just a glitch in the simulation, and try to forget this summer ever happened.

"Hi." He smiled, then dragged his mouth across her jaw, then to her lips.

She kissed him back urgently, heat racing through her body. She reached for a handful of his T-shirt, feeling the warmth of his skin through the threadbare material. One of his hands cupped the back of her head, and he kissed her harder. She wrapped her legs around his waist, and he let out a low groan.

But then the face of Heather, Dustin's girlfriend, sitting at home in a pair of modest pajamas patiently waiting for her promise ring, filled Holly's head. She suddenly pushed Dustin away from her and jumped up off the bed, slamming her feet to the floor.

"We can't do this! I know who you—"

The whole cabin started to rattle, like the beginnings of an earthquake, and a beam fell loose from the ceiling. Holly ducked and covered her head with her hands.

"Agh!" Dustin yelled, his voice muffled by the terrible sounds of a crushing collapse followed by something snapping in half.

Without looking, Holly reasoned it could've been wood, bones, or both. She prayed to the God she didn't believe in that it was only wood.

16

GENESIS

Genesis raced from her perch behind a tree at the bottom of the hill. She was worried something had gone wrong when she saw the glow from inside the cabin go out, then her fears were confirmed when she heard something that sounded like a pile of logs falling on one another. She rushed to the cabin doorway, then peered through the window: Holly was pulling Dustin Reaps's unconscious body out from under a collapsed ceiling beam.

"Oh no," Genesis gasped.

Holly looked up and noticed Genesis, her eyes going wild. "I don't know what happened," she sputtered. "I jumped up and then the ceiling fell."

Genesis knelt down to inspect Dustin. A purple bruise was beginning to form on his forehead, with a drop streaming down from a gash in the middle. She placed two fingers below his jaw. "He has a pulse." She put her ear to his mouth. "And he's breathing."

Holly heaved a sigh of relief.

"But I have no idea if all his bones are intact," Genesis added. "This was a lapse in my judgment. These cabins should be condemned. I should have never let you come up here."

"What should we do? Call 9-1-1?!"

"I don't know," Genesis admitted. "My heart says yes, but my head says if they come to the ranch and find Dustin Reaps knocked unconscious, not only am I in big trouble, so is everyone else that lives here. The Reapses are already not happy with us existing as is."

"No!" Holly cried. "This is my fault. *I'm* the one who should be in trouble."

Genesis closed her eyes and took a breath. "Neither of us are going to be in trouble."

"Then what are we going to do?" Holly begged hysterically.

"You came here in a car, right?"

"Uh-huh."

"So we'll carry him down to your car, and we'll drop him off at his house."

"Oh yeah, that will be easy. 'Good evening, Mr. and Mrs. Reaps, can you sign for the delivery of your vegetable son?'"

"All right. Maybe we just leave him somewhere safe where he'll be found," Genesis reasoned. "Like outside the church. Or a hospital. I don't know where the closest one is. I've never been myself."

"Wherever it is, it's probably full of security cameras. They'll know it was us."

"And we can't just leave him lying outside alone. That would be so cruel," Genesis admitted. She was at a loss. This was demanding far too many real-world skills for someone who had spent most of her existence secluded from it. She tried to think of someone, anyone, on the outside who she could depend on in her time of need, besides God himself.

"Call Zoe," she said. "She'll probably know what to do."

Holly stood up, the panicked adrenaline finally letting her function instead of keeping her frozen to her knees, and pulled her phone out of her pocket and called.

Genesis placed her hands on Dustin's chest and closed her eyes again.

"What are you doing?" Holly hissed, the phone ringing in her ear. "Did he stop breathing?"

"No. I'm just laying hands on him and saying a prayer."

17

ZOE

The utilities were still out in Zoe's house, so she sat by the living room window next to a single lit candle, feeling like an old-timey woman waiting for her husband to return from war.

Her mother and brother had left for her aunt and uncle's house that morning, where they planned to stay until the bill situation resolved itself, which didn't look like soon. Marla had told Zoe she had to come with them as punishment for her outburst at church, but Zoe countered that she couldn't move somewhere an hour away from her job without a car. At a time like this, as Zoe was the only real breadwinner in the family, Marla couldn't argue with her logic. Plus, though Zoe wouldn't mind running water and central air-conditioning, having the house to herself was infinitely better than being trapped in her aunt Sharon and uncle Phil's, which was decorated nearly identically to a Bass Pro Shops, the bathrooms especially.

The glow of the Buick's headlights illuminated the street. Zoe jumped from her seat and out the back door as soon as Holly turned the car onto the driveway.

"He's not awake just yet, but the good news is he's been

mumbling incoherently," Holly said as she stepped out of the driver's seat.

"*Is* that good news?" Zoe begged. Holly shrugged her shoulders helplessly.

Zoe opened the back-seat door. Genesis was sitting with Dustin's incapacitated head in her lap, his limbs splayed across the seat.

"So this is his bad-boy outfit, huh?" Zoe noted. "The dirty sneakers are a nice touch. Here, I'll lift his arms, and you two get his feet." She stuck her hands underneath his armpits, getting a whiff of BO lightly masked by Axe body spray, and cringed. Zoe hated being within twenty feet of Dustin Reaps; she'd never imagined a scenario where she would have to be this close to him.

Dustin wasn't much taller than Zoe, who towered over the other girls at five foot eight, but from a horizontal angle, he felt enormous. "How did you guys get him through the woods?" Zoe said, her voice strained.

"Barely." Holly sighed. Zoe looked up and realized her hair was full of leaves and sticks, the beginnings of a nest. "This is the longest night of my life, and it's not even over."

Together they hoisted Dustin's body around the back of the house and through the door.

"Let's get him to the couch," Zoe said, then paused. "You know what, no, you might get blood and dirt on my mom's nice slipcover. Let's just put him on the kitchen floor."

They eased him down onto the linoleum, and his head landed with a *thud*.

"Should we get him a pillow?" Genesis asked.

"Nah." Zoe shrugged.

Genesis gave her a stern look, like a schoolteacher who knows you know the right answer when you've given the wrong one.

"Fine." Zoe went to her brother's room and grabbed one from his bed that looked like it'd seen a fair share of slobber.

Genesis took the pillow and gently propped it up beneath Dustin's head. Zoe closed the blinds above the kitchen sink and swept the living room curtains shut to block out any potential nosy neighbors. She collected an assortment of scented candles from around the house and brought them back to the kitchen, then lit them with a match, creating a dizzying aroma from a combination of baking sugar cookies, cucumber melon, lavender, and ocean breeze.

After a few minutes, Dustin suddenly inhaled, then groaned. The girls all froze in place like they were in the presence of a wild animal. "I don't want to wear the jacket," he mumbled, then rolled onto his side.

"Say that again?" Zoe asked.

"It's flashy. It's ugly. I don't want to wear the jacket, Mom! Okay?!" He jolted awake, his eyes going wide.

"Hi, Dustin," Zoe said calmly, putting herself in his line of vision.

"Hi," he responded flatly, squinting. "Where am I?"

"Wait, I thought your name was Orlando?" Holly asked.

"Oooh," Zoe said. "Good call, Holly."

Dustin's eyes went wide again, then ping-ponged back and

forth between Holly's and Zoe's faces. "I . . . I . . . don't know . . . my name," he stuttered. "I don't know where I am."

"You hit your head," Genesis explained patiently.

"I hit my head," Dustin echoed, reaching for his forehead. "Ow."

"You're in my kitchen. Me. Zoe Peters. We haven't acknowledged each other since probably Vacation Bible School a decade ago, but I know you know who I am." She knelt down to meet him at eye level and made a peace sign with her hand. "How many fingers am I holding up?"

He stared at them a few seconds too long, then looked to Holly, then back to the fingers. "Three."

"Dustin," Zoe said firmly. "*How many* fingers am I holding up?"

"Who's Dustin?" he groaned, and rolled onto his side.

Holly gestured for the girls to come closer to her. "What if he has amnesia?" she whispered.

"This isn't a soap opera! People don't just get bonked on the head once, then wake up an hour later not knowing who they are!" Zoe cried. "He's putting on an act."

Genesis scratched her neck. "He *does* seem very disoriented."

"All right. Well, if he has amnesia, I don't know what to do with him," Zoe said loudly. "I guess that means we just need to CALL. HIS. PARENTS. Sure, we'll probably have to explain ourselves, and we might just get in trouble, but if he has *amnesia*? I bet he needs some very serious medical attention."

Dustin rolled onto his back and faced the ceiling with his eyes still closed. "Do not call my parents."

"Hm. Interesting," Zoe said. "You don't know who you are, but you do know you have parents."

"Everyone has parents," he mumbled.

"I thought your parents were dead," Holly said, just as Zoe snapped, "Cut the crap, Dustin!"

"Fine." He sat up on his elbows. "Can I have some water, please?"

"You can have some water once you apologize for lying to Holly here about your entire identity."

Holly blushed and stared at the floor. "It's okay. That doesn't need to happen right this second."

"I didn't lie about my *entire* identity!" Dustin scoffed. "I just used a different name. Shuffled some things about myself around." Holly looked at him with wounded eyes.

"That's exactly what lying is! Don't gaslight her, Dustin," Zoe persisted. "We know how you really feel about the church and that you cheated on Heather and that you are certainly *not* treating your body like a temple. Soon, so will the rest of the world, because guess what: Holly's got it all on tape!"

"What?!" Dustin cried.

Holly tried to shake her head imperceptibly in Zoe's direction. "Well . . ."

"Yep," Zoe said, ignoring her. "She's got it all on her phone. And if you don't pay up, we'll post it online."

"Pay up?" Dustin scoffed. "Really? Okay. How much?"

"Ten thousand dollars," Zoe said without missing a beat. Dustin broke into uproarious laughter.

"What?" she pressed. "Is that pennies to you? Maybe you think that's not a lot, but that is a life-changing amount for—"

"You think *I* have ten thousand dollars?" He stabbed a finger to his chest.

"Yeah." Zoe shrugged. "Isn't your family loaded?"

"My *parents* are, but me? I've got . . ." He reached into his back pocket and pulled out a few crumpled bills. "However much that is."

"You're kidding me. Don't you have, like, an arcade in your house?" *And a walk-in closet, a subzero fridge devoted just to non-alcoholic beverages, a resort-size pool, and a movie theater,* Zoe thought but didn't want to reveal just how much she actually knew.

"Sure, but I had no say in that. I have no control over anything my parents do with their money. Believe me: if I did, things would look a lot different."

"How so?" Genesis asked.

Dustin squinted at her. "Who the heck are you?"

"Answer her question!" Zoe snapped.

"First can I *please* have some water?" Dustin begged. Zoe resigned herself and grabbed a bottle from the case next to the fridge, which she'd been rationing for cleaning and drinking. She knelt down and handed it to him. He frantically twisted off the cap and took a long gulp.

"Answer her question. How would things look different if you controlled the money?"

He gasped and wiped his mouth with the back of his hand. "I don't know. Everything would just be less over the top. Maybe we would do more stuff to actually help people. Less wasteful. Less perfect. You have no idea how exhausting it is to have everything be so goddamn *perfect* all the time. That's why I go for walks at night. I can just . . . relax." He glanced at Holly, then to the floor. "I know it sounds dark, but sometimes I just wish I could disappear. Not die or anything like that, but just be someone else. Someone who actually has control of their own destiny."

A heavy silence fell upon the whole kitchen. No matter how much they disagreed with his methods, all of the girls could relate exactly to the feeling Dustin described. Even Zoe didn't know what to say; she just stared solemnly at the peach Bellini candle on the kitchen table.

But then she snapped out of it: he was just playing up a sob story to get off the hook. For a second, she could see why Holly had been so easily seduced by him. He was a good actor; she'd give him that. So Dustin Reaps's perfect life wasn't so perfect? Boohoo! Poor little rich boy. At least he had a home with running water to return to. Dustin had no idea what it felt like to be truly misunderstood in this town; he had no idea what it really felt like to keep your true self hidden just to make other people comfortable. He didn't have to worry about how the rest of his life would fall into place; it was all tied up for him with a bow. This town— no, this whole world—was created with Dustins in mind and everyone else was just living in it.

Dustin cleared his throat and craned his neck to look into the living room. "There's not anyone else here, is there?"

"No," Zoe said. "My whole family's out of town."

"Then can we please just keep this between us and pretend it never happened?" he said, standing up uneasily with a palm to his head wound.

"Fine," Holly muttered.

Genesis nodded solemnly.

"No, no, no," Zoe said, shaking her hands. "You don't get off that easily. See, I don't like you, Dustin, but what I've just realized is that we have something in common: we are both miserable here. Neither of us like what the church is doing with their money, though *some of us* clearly benefit from said money. If you want me to keep quiet, then you have to form a sort of . . . alliance . . . with me."

"What does that even mean?" Dustin pressed.

"I need to think about it some more. All I know is I have brains, which—evidenced by your actions—you are clearly lacking. But you have access to the inside, which I definitely do not. Sure, you don't control the money, but you know a lot about the people who do."

Dustin studied her face. Zoe looked back at him with urgent eyes. "Well?"

He started to cackle.

"An alliance?! What is this, *The Hunger Games*? Are we sure that *you're* not the one who hit their head tonight?"

• • •

Zoe added up her tips for the third time in a row, hoping that this would be the time to prove she had made a counting error and didn't really only have sixteen dollars to show for a day's work. At this rate, she would be nearing retirement age by the time she could regain all the money her mother had blown on Ree Reaps's meal kits. That wouldn't be so bad, she tried to convince herself. She and Delia could escape to a senior citizen community in Arizona or something. At least it would be sunny there.

Maybe blackmailing Dustin Reaps wasn't the only fast way out of this hole. Maybe she could speed things up another way. Maybe Tom could finally sell his case of pre-ban Four Loko on eBay and lend her the profits as a no-interest loan? No, there was no way that stuff was worth anything, she reminded herself. She must have been losing her mind if her brother's delusions started to sound like a solution. Still, Tom was always yammering on about how cryptocurrency was the future. Zoe usually tuned him out, but what if there was a chance he was on to something? He could help her become an early adopter of the next Bitcoin and transform the cash in her hands into thousands, maybe millions. Though she probably had a greater chance of winning the lottery jackpot than cooperating with her brother long enough for that to actually happen.

She could tell Delia the truth, that her mom had spent the fund she was going to use to get them out of this town and now they had to start from nothing. Zoe knew Delia would respond with relentless positivity. *So we wait another year or two and save up,* she could almost hear her say. *What's another year? I'll get a job too. My parents can't stop me from working once I'm eighteen.* But Zoe could not wait another year or two. She felt like she was losing her mind, and perhaps there was no greater proof that she was than how she'd spent the past week seriously trying to blackmail

Dustin Reaps like it was the only thing that made sense.

Suddenly, the entry bell on the diner door dinged and threw off Zoe's count.

"Agh!" she groaned without looking up from the counter. "Did you not read the sign? We're closed."

"Hi," a low voice said.

Zoe looked up and froze. Dustin Reaps was standing behind a stool with his hands in his pockets. A quarter slipped from her fingers, but her face betrayed nothing. "What do you want?"

"I did some thinking," he said slowly. "About your alliance idea. I realized it's not as stupid as I originally thought it was."

"Well, gee, thank you," she said.

Dustin ignored her sarcasm and took a deep breath. "I think I've figured out a plan that could be beneficial to both of us. It would be a huge risk, of course, but the reward has the potential to be . . ." He glanced down at her pathetic pile of money. "Life changing."

Zoe crossed her arms and leaned back to assess him. Her face contorted itself through about six different emotions, ranging from delighted to disgusted.

"Welp. Never thought I'd say this, but . . . Dustin, I am all ears."

He glanced around the diner, then leaned across the counter to whisper in her ear.

"I want you to kidnap me."

18

GENESIS

Genesis loaded up pies into the delivery van as if everything were normal and she hadn't just experienced the worst yet most exhilarating week of her life. From the loss of her phone to the disastrous visit to Hope Harvest to spilling her heart out to Zoe and Holly at the diner to rescuing Dustin Reaps, it was as if she were watching a movie starring someone else playing herself. It was the longest she'd ever spent with people outside of the ranch. Now things had settled down, and the isolation of life without her phone set in.

She shut the doors and walked around to the passenger side of the van.

"What's going on, Beginning?" Sage asked, tapping a beat on the steering wheel and putting the keys into the ignition. "It feels like we haven't talked in so long."

"Nothing much," Genesis replied. "Just gearing up for rhubarb season."

Sage was her best friend, but Genesis couldn't really talk to him like he was. It was easy to bare her soul to some judgmental girl she hardly knew, but the thought of sharing her real self with Sage, who she'd known for her whole life and had never once hurt her feelings, gripped her with fear.

He gave her a goofy smile. "So we're going to talk about the harvest schedule?"

"I guess." She shrugged. "My life is pretty boring."

"Oh, I doubt that. I bet there's a lot going on behind those celestial eyes of yours that you're not telling anyone about."

Sage looked into his rearview mirror and backed the van out of the driveway. As they drove down the hill toward the ranch gates, a cluster of people came into view.

"What is all of this?" Sage wondered aloud.

Genesis's stomach sank. The 100 Days of Prayer for Hope Harvest Ranch had begun, and members of the congregation were gathered outside. Though she couldn't reveal why or how she knew that, or what it even was.

"No clue," she mumbled.

Sage idled the car into front of the gate. "Stay here," he said, reassuringly tapping her shoulder. He opened his door and stepped out. "Excuse me, folks," he called, unlocking the gate from inside. "Can I help you with something?"

They said nothing and solemnly closed their eyes.

"If not, do you mind moving aside?" Sage asked, raising his voice just a bit. "We have to exit out of here."

"Ephesians 6:10," the group yelled in unison, then recited every line of the Bible verse.

Sage let them finish, then lifted his palms in a peaceful gesture. "That sounds cool and all, but if you wouldn't mind just scooting over to make some room."

"All right, all right, everybody, let's give them some space. It's only our first day," one guy called, coming closer to the van. Genesis recognized him as the pastor who was unrelated to the Reapses, who led the congregation in prayer. Pastor Marcus, she recalled. "Hey, man," he said to Sage. "You know, it's never too late to break free from this lifestyle and accept Jesus as your Lord and Savior. No pressure. I'm just saying, we're here if you want to talk."

"I appreciate that." Sage nodded politely. "But right now we have some pies to deliver, so if you wouldn't mind . . ."

Pastor Marcus stiffened and motioned for the congregants to move behind him. Sage hoisted himself back up into the van and closed the door.

"What's happening?" Genesis asked as if she didn't know.

"A bunch of Jesus freaks or something," he muttered, shaking his head. "And people say *we're* the cult."

"Huh." Genesis sank into her seat, practically melting with shame. They drove through the gate and turned onto the road. "Do you think they're *all* freaks?" she asked after a moment of silence.

"All those people back there? Most definitely. If they weren't, I'd say they'd be doing something much more productive with their Wednesday morning."

"Not the people back there, exactly. I mean people who believe in God. Jesus. Whatever." She feigned nonchalance.

"No. But I don't think most people who believe in God are particularly passionate about it. They just do it because it's popular, and believing in anything else, or maybe nothing else, scares them."

"So you think people believe in God just because it's popular?" A lump formed in her throat. She tried to fight it back.

"I suppose so." Sage shrugged. "It's easy to go along with what everyone else believes in. It's comfortable, right? I think what we do is harder: we believe in something even when the rest of the world doubts us."

Genesis's cheeks went hot. He had it all wrong. Her life was so much easier back when she just believed what everyone else at the ranch did.

"Yeah, but I bet all of those people back there would argue the same thing. They all probably think the world is against them too." She stared out the passenger window as they turned onto Main Street. "Maybe that's the problem. Everyone spends so much time arguing about who's right that they never want to admit that none of us really know. That's why it's called 'believing' in something, not 'knowing.'" They sat in silence for a beat. "Right?"

"See!" Sage exclaimed, tapping on the steering wheel again. "This is what I'm saying, Gen. You're not boring; you're a genius! My mind is blown."

"Thanks," she said quietly, convinced he would never actually understand.

They pulled into the diner's gravel parking lot and went inside. Zoe was standing at a booth, topping off a couple's coffee mugs. She looked up as the door's bell dinged behind them.

"Genesis!" Zoe exclaimed, as if she were a world-famous pop star who had deigned to visit this little greasy spoon.

The customer cleared their throat, and Zoe turned. She'd gotten so excited to see Genesis that she'd overpoured, creating a small puddle of coffee in the middle of the table. "Oh! Sorry about that. I'll grab some napkins." She abruptly pivoted back toward the counter, the coffee sloshing over the edge of the pot and onto the floor. "And some more napkins!" The couple stared her down, unamused. She went behind the counter and grabbed a thick stack of white napkins, then came back around, dropping one half of them into a pile on the table and the other onto the floor, sloppily moving them around with her foot.

"Do you need some help, Zoe?" Sage asked.

"You know what, these are some crappy napkins. We need paper towels. Genesis, could you go into the ladies' room and grab a few paper towels? There are some really nice paper towels in there. Actually, you know what? I'll show you where they are."

"Uh. Okay," Genesis said. Zoe grabbed her by the arm and led her into the single-person bathroom at the other end of the restaurant. As soon as they were inside, Zoe slammed the door behind them, locked it, then slapped the hand dryer on the wall so it made a thunderous whooshing sound.

"Is everything all right?" Genesis asked.

"Yeah, everything's great," Zoe said, pulling out paper towels from the wall dispenser, three at a time. "Why?"

"You seem a little . . ."

"Jittery? On edge? Like I didn't sleep at all last night and in-

stead drank three Red Bulls this morning? Because you'd be correct. Anyway, I wanted to let you know: in the coming days you
might hear that a certain acquaintance of ours has gone on a bit
of a digital detox."

Genesis squinted. "What are you talking about?"

"How else do I put this . . ." She tented her hands and put them
to her mouth. "Soon I will be temporarily adopting a very large
son who is the same age as me, and he is going to come live in my
basement."

Genesis just stared at her with zero comprehension. The hand
dryer went quiet. Zoe slapped it again without breaking eye contact with Genesis.

"Okay, I'll just tell you," Zoe whispered. "I'm fake-kidnapping
Dustin. He's in on it. I mean, obviously, hence the 'fake' part. So is
Holly. The idea is that if I keep him in my house long enough, his
parents will offer reward money for whoever can find him. When
that happens, we'll dump him in the woods and Holly—who for
all intents and purposes is a stranger to Dustin—will pretend she's
discovered him. If that doesn't work out, we write a ransom letter.
I'm hoping it doesn't get to that point because I've only seen people
do it in movies using letters they cut out from magazines—"

Genesis held up her palm. "Why are you telling me all this?"

"Well, you're the only person besides Dustin and Holly who
was there the other night. I figured if you hear about his disappearance in the coming days, you might suspect it's us. So: in
exchange for your silence, we have agreed to give you a share of
the reward money."

Genesis's eyes darted around the tiny bathroom as she fully processed what Zoe was saying. "Oh no," she said at last. "Zoe. No more schemes. We should be grateful that the one we tried wasn't fatal."

Zoe scratched the back of her neck and looked to the ceiling. "But that whole thing was different. This one's more . . . collaborative!"

"I thought you hated Dustin."

"Well, you know what the Bible says: 'Keep your friends close and your enemies closer.' We're working together now for our common goal."

"I don't think the Bible says that, Zoe. I'm pretty sure it says, 'Love your enemies and pray for those who persecute you.'"

"Eh." She shrugged. "Same difference."

"I don't want any part of this," Genesis said, turning to the bathroom door.

"Wait!" Zoe said, reaching for her shoulder. "You could buy a new phone with the money, Genesis. Heck, you could even get out of Astralia for good."

Genesis paused and considered this. It would be so easy for her to keep silent; she barely even spoke to begin with. She wanted to get out of Astralia, but not this way. The whole thing was wrong. So very, *very* wrong.

"I won't tell anyone," she said. "But I don't want your money."

Zoe opened her mouth to speak, but Genesis had slipped back out of the bathroom before she could utter another word.

19

HOLLY

"Should we go look for him?" Holly asked, tapping her phone to check the time. It was 1:34 a.m. They were parked on the side of the road, near the wooded hill where Dustin and Holly had snuck into the ranch before. If he was moving at the same pace they had that night, he would've been back to the car by now.

Zoe quickly swatted Holly's phone down into her lap.

"What'd you do that for?" Holly exclaimed.

"Sorry. It was the glow from your screen. I just want to keep it as dark as possible in here," Zoe said, glancing at the back window. "And no. I'm sure he'll be back any minute."

Holly chewed on her thumbnail. "What if he got attacked by a bear or something? Or another beam fell on his head?"

"Well, then that's just natural selection at work." Zoe curled up into the passenger seat and hugged her knees, staring straight ahead. It was so silent that Holly could hear Zoe's teeth grinding over and over.

"You're nervous too, aren't you?" Holly asked quietly.

Zoe froze and looked at her. "No. I'm not nervous. Why would I be nervous?"

"You seem a little shaky."

"It's because this is my fourth Red Bull today," she said, gesturing to a can in the cupholder. Then she splayed out her fingers, counting. "Wait. No. Fifth."

"Jeez. Is that normal for you?"

"I don't know. Today was my first time having Red Bull. They've always sounded disgusting to me, but I couldn't sleep last night thinking about what we're about to do and then I got up and thought: my life has turned into the kind of life of someone who drinks a lot of Red Bull. They're surprisingly good. *Is* five in a day normal?"

Holly vehemently shook her head. "No."

Before she had resorted to the pills that were not prescribed to her, Holly would just bring Red Bull to the library. Two in a night had been enough to make her feel like her heart was going to burst out of her chest.

Suddenly, the back-seat door opened. Both girls jumped.

"Hey," Dustin grunted, sliding into his seat.

"You dumped it?" Zoe asked.

"Yep," he answered.

"And you definitely deleted your house's security camera footage from the app?"

"Uh-huh."

"And then you triple-checked that you deleted the footage?"

"*Yes,*" he said, rolling his eyes.

"Do not roll your eyes at me, Dustin," Zoe said, staring into the rearview mirror. "I'm just ensuring this is an airtight operation."

Holly reached for the keys in the ignition. "Wait," Zoe said, sticking out a finger. She leaned over and reached for a plastic shopping bag underneath her seat. "Put this on." She tossed the bag behind her, straight into Dustin's lap.

He opened it up, holding the bag to his face in darkness of the car. "A wig? Seriously?"

"There's a pair of my mom's old sunglasses in there too."

"Isn't this kind of overkill?" he asked.

"It's to be safe while we transport you," Zoe said. "No one will know it's you. That's the entire point."

"Fine," he said through a clenched jaw. Dustin reached into the bag, flipped his head over and back up, emerging with a shiny neon-pink bob.

"Glasses," Zoe commanded.

He pawed a lock of the plasticky hair out of his mouth. "You're enjoying this, aren't you?"

"Like I said, I'm just ensuring this is an airtight operation."

Dustin took the pair of black plastic cat-eye sunglasses out of the bag and slid them up his nose.

Holly started the car and turned back onto the road toward town.

"I feel like we should give you a code name, Dustin," Zoe mused.

Dustin scoffed. "That's . . ." he started, then went quiet. "Actually not the worst idea."

"Do you have a preference?

"I don't know. Maybe just, like, another normal name, to make it easy. Joe or something."

Holly snorted. Zoe looked to her. "What?"

"Nothing. It's just . . ." She glanced in the rearview mirror. "You seriously want to add a *third* name to your collection, *Or-lan-do*?"

Dustin pushed the sunglasses closer to his eyes. "Point taken."

. . .

When they got to Zoe's house, she unlocked the back door and led them inside, turning on a camping lantern she'd left on the kitchen counter.

"Okay, now *this* is a bit dramatic, no?" Dustin asked, pulling the sunglasses off his face. "If the curtains are closed, I think it's fine if you turn on the lights."

Holly stared at Zoe. "You didn't tell him?"

"I thought he knew." Zoe shrugged, dropping her house keys on the table and reaching for a pack of matches.

Dustin froze. "Knew what?"

"That my power is out indefinitely, and I—*we*—will be living by candlelight for the foreseeable future."

"What?!"

"Yeah. Didn't you notice that there were no lights on when you woke up here last time?"

"I was a little incapacitated," Dustin snapped. "I wasn't exactly my most observant self."

"Well, what did you think these dozens of candles were for?" Zoe asked, striking a match and lighting the remaining two inches of the ocean breeze–scented three-wick in the middle of the table.

"I don't know. I thought it was just some witchy ritual you were doing or something."

"Wow! You think I'm a witch?"

"What does it matter, Zoe?" Dustin exclaimed, his voice getting higher. "Why can't you just call the electricity company or whatever and get them to turn the power back on?"

"Because that would require money!" Zoe replied, her voice rising with his. "Which I do not have much of at the moment!"

"Stop!" Holly hissed, putting herself between them. "We've made it so far tonight. The last thing we want to do is wake the neighbors."

"Fine," Dustin said, rubbing his eyes. "Whatever. So where am I sleeping? The couch?"

"Absolutely not." Zoe dismissively shook her head. "For security reasons, you will be staying in the basement."

"Oh, good," he deadpanned. "Just like a real hostage. Should I sleep in the wig, too?"

"It wouldn't hurt," Zoe said.

Dustin sighed and reached into his back pocket, pulling out his pack of Marlboros. He took one out and stuck it in his mouth.

"What are you doing?" Zoe asked.

"What does it look like I'm doing?" Dustin shrugged.

"Nope. No smoking in my house."

"I thought you were cool, Zoe."

"I *am* cool. That's exactly why I recognize how pathetic you look, having the audacity to destroy your lungs in front of my mom's Bible-verse oven mitts. Give me those." She stuck her hand out. "You can have them back when this is all over. In fact, I do not care one bit what you do with yourself when this is all over, but you're not smoking under my roof, got it?"

Dustin rolled his eyes and slammed the pack into her palm. Zoe pointed to the remaining cigarette between his lips.

"C'mon . . ." he groaned.

Zoe promised Holly a share of her and Dustin's future earnings if she could discreetly transport him to the house and then surveil the place while Zoe was at work during the day. It occurred to Holly that she had fulfilled her end of the deal for the time being and that she could remove herself from this situation, leave now, and return to her cozy, drama-free bed.

"So, I'm gonna go." She gestured outside with her thumb, inching toward the door.

"What?!" Zoe and Dustin both asked, turning their heads.

"You have to stay and make sure she doesn't kill me in my sleep," Dustin said, pointing at Zoe.

"Yeah." Zoe nodded. "You have to make sure I don't murder him."

"She's not going to murder you." Holly pointed at Dustin with her car keys, then said to Zoe, "*You're* not going to murder him. If not out of the kindness of your own heart, Zoe, then at least for the sake of successfully pulling off this whole thing. Both of you just need to go to bed."

"Okay," Zoe said. "But if I do kill him, you're helping me bury the body."

Holly waved goodbye and unlocked the door, only 80 percent sure Zoe was joking.

. . .

The next morning, Holly awoke at the crack of dawn. She had to be back at Zoe's in time for Zoe's shift at the diner, which was tricky given that Danny had to be at the diner at the exact same time. She got dressed, and put a couple of books in her backpack, knowing that her entertainment options would be limited at Zoe's without electricity or Wi-Fi. The smell of coffee and the sound of local news wafted down the hallway into her bedroom.

"Our top story today is some disturbing news out of Violet," said the anchor's voice.

Holly's chest seized, and she burst out of her room and down the hall.

"A local gas station employee was attacked by a bear last night."

The footage on the TV cut to a bandaged man leaving a hospital in a wheelchair. Holly immediately recognized him: the balding guy with a soul patch who Dustin paid off for cigarettes. She exhaled with relief, but if all things went according to plan, it was only a matter of days, maybe hours, until Dustin was headline news.

"I was just taking the trash out to the dumpster, and next thing I know—" the gas station guy went on.

"Morning," Danny said, noticing her hovering at the end of the couch. "You're up early."

"Um, yeah, I thought I'd go for a hike today." She walked into the kitchen and filled her bag with an apple and granola bar.

"Alone?" Danny called.

"Yeah," she called back, reaching for her reusable water bottle from the dish rack and filling it up at the sink. "Is that okay?"

"It's not . . . ideal." He hesitated.

"Don't worry. I won't be carrying a juicy bag of rotting garbage like that guy on the news."

Danny got up and leaned against the kitchen threshold. "You know, I could take the day off and come with you. I'll call Arnold and Zoe, see if they can hold down the fort. I doubt it's going to get busy today. It never is."

"That's really nice of you to offer, Danny, but I don't want to inconvenience you." She tightened the cap on her bottle and threw it into her bag.

"All right." Danny nodded, sticking his hands in his pockets, clearly uncomfortable but absolutely clueless as to how to set his foot down and tell her that this hypothetical hike was a terrible idea. "Well, be safe. And, here." He opened the cabinet below the sink and pulled out an aerosol can. "Take the bear spray. You remember how to use this stuff?"

"Of course," she lied, and threw the spray into her backpack, then slung it over her shoulders and headed for the back door. She put her hand on the doorknob, then paused. "But maybe some other day you can join me?" she offered. "So we can plan ahead."

Danny's face lit up. "Yeah. Yeah, that would be good. We could make a day of it. Pack lunch. Nothing bears would want to eat, though."

"Guess we'll have to leave the honey sandwiches at home."

Danny chuckled. Then they stood in awkward silence. "Okay, well, see you later. I'll text you on my way back," Holly said, finally leaving.

When she got to Zoe's, Holly knocked on the back-door window. After a minute, the blinds opened an inch, and Zoe's eyes peeked through. She unlocked the door and cracked it open, allowing Holly to just barely slip inside.

"I'm running late," Zoe said, adjusting her bike helmet strap below her chin.

"If he gets hungry, there are some Ree Reaps meal kits and a case of water. Let him upstairs *only* if he has to use the bathroom. There's some hand sanitizer and baby wipes by the sink."

"And the diapers are where?" Holly asked.

Zoe froze. "Wait, the wha—You know, that's not the worst idea. Then he wouldn't have to come up here at all. The smell, though—"

"Oh my god, I was joking!"

"Oh. Ha. Okay, I'll be back like three thirty-ish. Text me if you need anything!" Zoe slammed the door behind herself, shaking the little house, leaving Holly alone in the dim morning light.

Holly slipped her backpack off and placed it on a kitchen chair, then walked over to the door leading to the basement. She took a deep breath, then opened it and tiptoed down the creaky wooden stairs. In the middle of a fortress of boxes, Dustin was curled up in a sleeping bag on the cement floor, clutching the pink wig from the night before to his rising and falling chest. A single beam of light glowed through the matchbox-sized window in the top corner of the basement, causing his long eyelashes to cast shadows on his cheeks. There was something so angelic-looking about him, it took Holly's breath away. And then a snore escaped from his nose, and she remembered the monster she was actually dealing with.

"Rise and shine, Orlando," she bellowed, standing over him.

Dustin jolted awake and widened his eyes at Holly, then seemed to remember where he was. "I feel like I got beaten up by a pack of gorillas in my sleep," he groaned, stretching his arms out like a cat. "What's going on?"

"This is just me ensuring you didn't die last night."

"Oh. Thanks, I guess."

"You don't have to thank me. This is purely out of my own self-interest. I just really do not want to be an accessory to murder. Anyway, I'll be upstairs keeping an eye out." Dustin nodded and rolled back over, resting his head on a caseless pillow.

Holly crept back upstairs, took her water bottle and the Iceland guidebook out of her backpack, then lay on the couch. She was picking her research up again. In the event that this plan worked, she would take her share of the reward money and use it to pay for her senior year of private school. So now she needed a believable tale of what she did over the summer.

As she read a paragraph about Iceland's famous hot springs, she closed her eyes for a second, imagining she was as relaxed as the couple pictured in the book, sitting arm and arm in a geo-thermal pool and staring at the northern lights. Before she knew it, she had drifted off to sleep and she *was* in the hot spring. Holly nuzzled herself into the chiseled chest of the man, then looked up to stare into his eyes only to realize it wasn't a man; he was techni-cally a boy, because it was Dustin.

She startled awake, the book lying on her chest. The smell of something burning filled her nostrils. She sat up and looked over the back of the couch, through the small dining room, to see Dustin, the real-life version, hunched over the counter, stirring something with a disgusted look on his face.

Holly stood up and stumbled into the kitchen, rubbing the nap out of her eyes. "What is that?"

"My rations," Dustin said darkly without looking up. Upon closer inspection, Holly realized he was stirring a small metal pot full of what looked like creamy dog food atop a portable Sterno burner, like someone would use on a camping trip. An open box sat next to the burner. Holly picked it up for a closer look: the front was printed with a photo of Dustin's mom holding a plate of breakfast between two gingham pot holders. *Ree's Country Biscuits and Gravy Casserole.*

"Is this one your favorite?" she quipped.

Dustin cringed. "Never tried it before."

"Never?"

"Nope. I wouldn't go near these if I had the choice."

"That's not very supportive of your mom, is it?"

Dustin pulled the pot off the flame and reached for a serving spoon from the crock next to the stove. "A little fun fact about these so-called meal kits," he said, dumping the slop into a bowl. "They were originally manufactured for some other big pastor as survivalist food for end times. You know, so when the world is burning, you and your family are taken care of because you have enough freeze-dried soup to last through the whole rapture? But then that pastor went bankrupt, so my parents bought out his whole factory's worth of food—which doesn't expire till 2035—

for super cheap and rebranded it. Fearmongering isn't really their thing, you know? They're all about selling Christianity as an aspirational lifestyle."

He took a bite and swallowed it down like it was cough medicine. "Want some?" he taunted, holding up the spoon.

"No thanks," Holly said, grimacing. "I'll let you eat in peace." She walked back over to the living room, but Dustin followed her, taking a seat in the recliner opposite the couch.

"So did you really not know who I was?" he asked. "When you first picked me up on the side of the road?"

"I don't think Zoe wants you to take your meals up here."

Dustin lowered his head. "I'm not sure what I'm eating counts as an actual meal, so . . ."

"Nope. No idea." Holly shook her head, answering his original question. "I'd heard of your parents before, but that was it."

"That's wild."

"Maybe this is hard for you to understand, Dustin, but the whole world does not revolve around you."

Dustin laughed once, putting his bowl of foodlike substance down on the coffee table. "But when did you realize? That night when I woke up here, Zoe said you'd recorded me. You guys tried to blackmail me. You knew."

Holly looked away from him and at the carpet. "The day before that night. Sunday. Zoe invited me with her to church for the first time ever, and you got pulled onto the stage. All the times before that, I thought your name was Orlando. I believed everything you told me."

Dustin stared at her like he was figuring out an equation on her forehead.

"So that night we snuck onto the ranch and went into that cabin, you knew who I really was?"

She nodded.

A smile danced on his lips. "Yet you still kissed me?"

Holly's face went hot. "Well . . . I mean . . ."

Dustin sat back, cupping the back of his head with his hands and leaning into the recliner. "So finding out that I was really some spoiled pastor's kid didn't completely ruin your attraction to me, did it?"

"No," she said firmly, staring back up at him. "That wasn't it. It was that you lied. And then you got caught and showed zero remorse." Dustin's face fell. "Especially after all that stuff you said about my friends not being my real friends because I thought they'd completely change their opinion of me if I told them a basic fact about myself," Holly went on. "When all along you were keeping this enormous secret from *me*. Meaning you never thought of me as a real friend, someone you could confide in like I did with you. You thought I was just some gullible idiot you could hook up with for the summer."

Hurt flashed across Dustin's face. "That's not true."

"You told me your parents died in a tragic accident," Holly said. "One that killed actual people."

"Okay, fine, that was pretty bad, but I was panicking! Being with you was like escaping into a fantasy. I didn't want to spoil it with my real life."

Holly grabbed a throw pillow that said FAITH and hugged it to her chest. "I'm a real person, though. I have thoughts and feelings. And so does *Heather*! Your girlfriend, since it seems you forgot all about her."

Dustin sat up and raked a hand through his hair. "Heather is not my girlfriend."

"So what is she, then? Your friend that you hold hands with at church? That seems pretty scandalous for—"

"We've never even hung out without a chaperone!" Dustin snapped. "I'm not allowed to date unless it's with someone I intend to marry. And in that case, it has to be a girl I can run the church with someday. My parents want that girl to be Heather. She's a nice person, but we can't even hold a conversation with each other, and it's not just because Pastor Marcus is breathing down our necks the whole time we're together. She just agrees with everything I say and never challenges me. It's so predictable, there's no . . . excitement."

He blushed and quickly looked away from Holly.

She clutched the pillow tighter. Being with Dustin sure had been exciting, but it had been a lie. "Then you should probably tell your parents all that. Before they start making you shop for promise rings."

"It's not just Heather, though. I don't want any part of anything they've ever worked for. How do I even begin to tell them that? I'm supposed to be their golden boy. If I try to tell them the truth, I know they won't listen. That's why I'm doing this," he said, gesturing vaguely around Zoe's living room. "I need the money so I don't have to depend on them anymore and I can go live my own life."

"Well, either way, it will still be their money you're depending on. They're the ones who will have to pay the ransom."

"Why are you being so hard on me, Holly? You'll get a piece of it too."

"Zoe asked me if I would help her out because she needed my car and someone to keep watch here while she's at work. I'm helping *her*. And yeah, if this works by some miracle, I'll split the reward with you two. Everything will go back to normal, and I can pretend that I never met you."

"Is that what you really want?" Dustin sneered at her. "To just go back to your fake friends and your humanly impossible GPA?"

"You can't always get everything you want. That's not how the world works!" Holly snatched his dirty bowl from the coffee table. "I think it's time for you to go back into the basement."

20

GENESIS

Genesis was on an atonement mission.

With a roll of barbed wire in her arms and a pair of pliers in her pocket, she walked up the hillside to the spot where Dustin and Holly had snuck in the other night. She was going to repair the hole in the fence to ensure no one else could ever sneak in again and, more importantly, that *she* could never sneak *out*. Of course, she did not want to be stuck in Astralia, but right now it felt like the rest of the world was full of even greater temptations.

As she got the top of the hill, she heard a persistent buzzing sound. Then when she reached the fence, she noticed something just barely rustling in the leaves. Upon closer inspection, it was an iPhone.

Instinctively, she dropped the barbed wire and reached for it. The screen lit up from top to bottom with notifications.

> **Mama Reaps:** Where are you?
> ???
> HELLO?

Mama Reaps
— Missed Call (6) —

Mama Reaps
— Voice Mail (2) —

Mama Reaps
— Missed Call —

Papa Reaps: D, give your mama a call. She's going crazy over here lol.

Papa Reaps
— Missed Call (2) —

Mama Reaps
— Voice Mail —

Behind the messages, the phone's lock screen was a selfie of Dustin making a goofy face next to a little girl who looked a lot like him. It had to be his phone, but how did it get here? Maybe it fell out of his pocket the night he snuck onto the ranch, Genesis reasoned. Yet how had it stayed alive all these days later?

Her hand shook as she realized the power that sat between her fingers: she was a few mere taps away from her now former idol Ree Reaps.

She steadied the phone in her left hand and tapped a random assortment of passcode numbers with her right. Of course, the phone shook with rejection. Then she tried 1-2-3-4. That also failed. Genesis closed her eyes and tried to envision the Instagram post Ree had posted last year for Dustin's birthday: him bashfully hiding behind two big Mylar balloons spelling out the number seventeen. That would mean he was born in 2003. She tried 2-0-0-3.

It worked.

A pop-up for a voice mail appeared and she tapped it with right pointer finger, then placed the phone to her ear.

"Hey, Dustin, it's Mama. Just wondering where the heck you are. If you stayed over at Marcus's, that's fine, but you got to let me know next time! Call me when you get this."

Genesis played the next voice mail. "All right, Dustin, now you got me worried. If you lost your phone again, there are going to be big consequences, okay, mister? I'm calling Marcus now."

And the next one. "Sweetie? It's me again. Now you're scaring me. Marcus said he hasn't seen you since Sunday. Neither has Heather. Your car is in the garage." Ree's voice caught. "I know you'll just say I'm being dramatic, but please, please call me when you get this."

The desperation in Ree's voice made Genesis feel sick. Sure, Ree had disappointed her, and the Reapses were liars, but it didn't mean she wished this kind of pain upon them.

A thought crossed her mind: she could just call Ree Reaps right then and there and tell her Dustin was up to no good. That he was hurting inside and acting out as a result. Maybe Ree would even see Genesis as a good Samaritan. Take her to her favorite hair salon to get matching highlights as a thank-you gift. Invite her to church and adopt her into her own family, even though Genesis was nearly a full-grown adult.

No, Genesis told herself, she had to snap out of it. That was all just a fantasy, one that clearly was never going to happen. Even if she called the Reapses, how would she even explain herself? They would never believe she had just happened upon Dustin's phone in the woods.

It buzzed again. Genesis jumped and the phone fell to the ground.

She let it ring until it went to voice mail again, then picked it back up, opened Dustin's contacts, and scrolled all the way down to the end. There was no one named Zoe listed. So she opened the internet browser and googled "Violet diner Montana" and clicked on the first phone number that came up.

"Hello?" Danny answered after a couple of rings.

"Uh, hi, may I please speak to Zoe?"

"Sure, who's calling?"

Genesis panicked. Danny probably didn't recognize her voice, but he definitely knew her name. "This is her mother," she blurted out.

"Hey, Marla. How are you?"

Genesis coughed twice. "Good," she said in a raspier tone, trying to sound something like Zoe, and failing. "Sorry. Getting over a cold."

"Oh, well, hope you're feeling better. Give me one second. I'll grab Zoe for you."

It sounded like he placed the receiver on a countertop. Pots and pans clanged in the background until Zoe picked up. "Mama?" she said. "Is everything okay?"

"Sorry, this isn't your mom. It's Genesis. I found Dustin's phone outside the ranch."

Zoe was quiet on the other end. "Put it back," she said finally.

"Dustin's parents won't stop calling," Genesis went on.

"Are you talking to them?" Zoe asked.

"No! I haven't picked up. I haven't said a word, but his mom keeps leaving these messages, and she sounds really upset."

Zoe was silent for a beat. "So what do you want from me, Genesis?"

The thought crossed Genesis's mind that she could ask if she could keep Dustin's phone. She really did miss hers. But she knew that simply replacing it with this one was not enough. A phone was just a ticking time bomb, really. Eventually, it would break or get confiscated by Grace, just like the original one. She couldn't google her way out of the ranch, at least not practically speaking. Genesis could research the rest of the world all she wanted, but it would take actual *money* to get there. Where exactly she'd go with the money, or with whom, that was still unknown.

"Hey, um, Mama, I've got to get back to work," Zoe said quickly. "But I know how forgetful you can get, so just remember, my cell is listed in your phone under 'Bible Study Bros' all caps."

"What?" Genesis asked.

"Yeah. You remember that little inside joke we had? Anyway, if you need anything, if you are having *second thoughts*, you can call me there. Okay? Bye! Love you!" Genesis could hear her slam the phone into its receiver.

She knew Zoe was just saying it for show, but Genesis realized that was the first time anyone had said they loved her in her entire life.

21

ZOE

"What are you doing here?" Zoe asked as Delia sat down on a stool in front of the diner counter.

"It's so nice to see you too," Delia said, sarcastically raising her eyebrows.

"I'm sorry. This is a nice surprise. Just unexpected. Do you want anything?" Zoe gestured toward the kitchen.

"Nah, I'm not hungry. I'm actually here to tell you in person some weird news I just heard from my mom. I know I could've texted you, but, selfishly, I really want to see your live reaction."

Zoe leaned on the counter and tilted her head. "Weird news as in good news or weird news as in bad news?"

"Mmm, it depends." Delia put her knuckles to her mouth, suppressing a grin.

"What is it?"

Delia glanced around the diner. "Okay, so, something happened to Dustin Reaps?" She whispered so low, it was as if she was just mouthing the words. "I don't know what, but no one's seen him since last night, and his family can't find him."

Zoe blinked once and frowned in a manner that she hoped

read as nonchalant yet concerned. She had practiced this reaction in her head what felt like thousands of times over the last few nights when she couldn't sleep from the anxiety of what she was planning. "Whoa."

Delia's face fell. "I thought I was going to delight you with this morsel of gossip."

"I mean, you *did*. It's just, like, that's really unsettling."

"Oh, c'mon, Zo." Delia rolled her eyes. "I bet he's just lost in that giant house of theirs. He probably got locked into, like, their ninth powder room that they forgot they had. It's funny!"

"What if he ran away?" Zoe pressed.

"What would *he* have to run away from?"

"Maybe Dustin is fighting some demons. He for sure has always struck *me* as a little bit demonic. Or I don't know. Maybe he got kidnapped?"

Delia scoffed. "No. Why would someone take *him*?"

Zoe shrugged. "Why does anyone kidnap anyone? For money? Who really knows?"

"But his little sisters are all fine."

Zoe knit her eyebrows together. "What does that have to do with anything?"

"Well, if you're going to kidnap one of the Reapses to get money, wouldn't it make sense to take the toddler who can't defend herself and not the one who's basically a full-grown man?"

Zoe swallowed hard. She couldn't believe neither she nor Dustin had realized this major flaw of believability in their plot before. "Well, jeez," she said after a few seconds. "It sounds like *someone's* thought a lot about how they would commit a kidnapping."

Delia blushed. "I'm just saying!"

"So what are the Reapses going to do?"

"My guess is they're talking to the police, but my parents got invited to some emergency all-hands church staff meeting tonight, so I'll probably find out more from them after. Hey, you know, while they're out, you should come over." Delia discreetly brushed the back of Zoe's arm with her knuckles. "I feel like we haven't hung out in forever."

"What do you mean?" Zoe said, gesturing between them. "This is hanging out."

"I wouldn't exactly call it that. You're on the clock," Delia said. She warily eyed a trucker slurping a cup of soup at the other end of the counter. "And the ambience isn't exactly ideal."

"Yeah, I told Danny we should mix it up around here. Try out some fresh flowers and white tablecloths," Zoe quipped.

Delia sighed. "I just don't get why you're being so avoidant. I thought things were good between us."

"They are!"

"Then why don't you want to come over? Is it because everything went south last time you did?"

Zoe so desperately wanted to just eat pizza bites with Delia and watch *The Great British Bake Off* while taking intermittent make-out breaks like any normal couple would on a random Thursday evening, to feel utterly and completely relaxed, but relaxation was privilege. When you were hiding another human being in your

basement, relaxation was off limits. Her sacrifice was an investment toward a lifetime of comfort for her and Delia later, but
there was no way she could explain that to her girlfriend at this
moment.

"Yeah. That's exactly it," Zoe said quietly. She wasn't *totally* lying; she never felt 100 percent comfortable at the Johnsons' house.
But she would've compromised under normal circumstances.

"Okay," Delia said, looking away. "I get that."

"But you should come over to my place," Zoe quickly blurted
without thinking.

"What?"

"Yeah. Mom and Tom are at my aunt's house for a little while. I
have the house all to myself."

Delia lowered her head skeptically. "You have the whole place
to yourself and you didn't tell me?"

"Well, that's the thing. They went away because our power is
out and, well, you know my mom can't live without all her gadgets."

"Why didn't you mention it? That sounds awful."

"I didn't want to bore you with the details. The county's doing
some weird electrical work on my block? Something got messed
up with the grid because of all the new construction happening in
town or something like that." She dismissively waved her hand. "So
yeah, just be forewarned, if you come over, there will be no lights,
no TV—nothing. We'll have to get creative and figure out some
way to entertain ourselves in the dark." Zoe gave her an earnest,
apologetic look, hoping this information would truly persuade her.

Delia smiled and burst out laughing. "Oh, I'm sure we'll think of *something* creative we can do together in the dark."

Zoe smiled back, but it didn't reach her eyes. She hated how the constant lying seemed to strip her of her personality, making her humorless out of fear of saying too much. She reminded herself that she was in charge; Dustin was a guest in *her* house, not the other way around.

She bit down on her lip and peered up at Delia. "Yeah. I'm sure we'll think of something."

.   .   .

"Hey, Orlando!" Zoe called, lighting her way down the basement stairs with a flashlight.

Dustin was sitting cross-legged on the floor, carefully arranging a stack of boxes with the camping lantern next to him. "So we're really committing to the code name thing, huh?" he asked without looking up.

She stopped at the bottom step. "What are you doing?"

"I noticed all your, uh, merchandise was all mixed up, so I started organizing it by brand. Then when I got done with that, I organized each brand by category. That became less fun when I got to the essential oils because they're, well, all oils. So currently, I'm breaking them down by general vibe." He gestured to a few small piles next to his angles. "We've got the calming section, so, you know, you've got your lavender, cedarwood, chamomile. That sort of thing. Energizing: orange, lemongrass. And finally, for focus: eucalyptus and peppermint."

Zoe was absolutely speechless.

"What?" Dustin asked, looking up at her and raising an eyebrow. "Are you mad I touched your stuff?"

"N-n-no," she said finally. "It's fine. That's not my stuff. I don't care. It's just not what I expected."

"You left me trapped in your basement with nothing to do all day. I had to make my own fun. If you come down here tomorrow and see me drawing a face on a box and introducing you to my new girlfriend, Mary Kay, don't say I didn't warn you."

In spite of her profound hatred for Dustin, Zoe had to laugh.

"Hey, so . . ." she said, leaning against the rickety stair railing. "I'm having a friend over tonight. *Not* Holly. They don't know about you being here. Just thought I should give you a heads-up."

"What?" Dustin said, accidentally knocking over one of his piles with his elbow. "Are you nuts?"

"Well, it's *my* house! As long as you stay put down here and don't make any noise, it will be fine. If anything, it will give me an alibi if anyone suspects you're here. Worst-case scenario, my friend can speak to the fact that I was home alone, all by myself."

"Still seems like a risk."

"This is a person who is *very* important to me, Orlando. We don't get to spend a lot of time together alone."

Dustin lifted an eyebrow and assessed her face. "So it's a guy, huh?"

"What does it matter?" Zoe sputtered. "You don't need to know anything about who's coming because you won't have to interact with them at all."

He smiled, satisfied. "So it *is* a guy. You know what?" He raised his hands in surrender. "This is fine. Maybe if you get laid tonight, you'll stop being so paranoid and uptight."

Zoe gave him a disgusted look. She couldn't believe she'd actually found him funny just a few minutes before.

"I'm a lesbian, you freaking worms-for-brains idiot! Not that it's any of your business."

Dustin's eyes went wide, then quickly relaxed. He opened his mouth to speak, then closed it again, then opened it. "Oh," he finally said. "That . . . that makes sense. That's cool. Um."

"Yeah. And regardless," Zoe continued, "the idea that having sex would, like, cure me into being a calmer person is some deeply sexist, retrograde nonsense. I am paranoid and uptight because I am currently trying to successfully pull off a fraudulent scheme. Sorry that I can't be more *chill*." She shook her head and scoffed. "Anyway, this is all pretty ironic coming from you, Mr. Purity Ring."

Dustin looked down at the simple silver ring on his left hand and twisted it, blushing in the glow of the outdoor lantern. Zoe could remember the ceremony they'd had at youth group, committing themselves to no premarital sex the year they'd both turned thirteen. Zoe couldn't afford a real ring, so Marla had gotten her a rubber bracelet that said TRUE LOVE WAITS instead. She'd lost it somewhere in the mess of her room just a few months later.

"Sorry," Dustin said quietly. "I shouldn't have assumed. You know, I'm not like everyone else at church. I don't have a problem with gay people or . . . anyone else who's not like me. I don't think it's cool how passive-aggressive they are toward anyone who doesn't fit into their idea of the perfect heteronormative family."

"Wow," Zoe said, completely underwhelmed. "*Heteronormative.* Nice to know that in additional to a Bible, you own a dictionary."

"Seriously. That's one of the main reasons I want to get out of here."

"Well, how would I ever know that? You've never once shown that you're any different from the rest of them."

"It's complicated," he sighed.

Zoe narrowed her eyes. "Is it?"

"My parents never listen to me. Or they say they're listening, but they're really just listening for sound bites they can use in their sermons, you know? Everything's just material for this big performance. They never actually want to think critically about their lives or challenge their faith. It would terrify them."

Zoe knew the feeling well. How all the adults in her life seemed to brush off her concerns with positive sayings, like she was a clueless child, instead of really digging in deep with her about why she felt the way that she did.

"Maybe you're just not being loud enough," she said. "I'm sure they'd listen to you more than a lot of people. More than someone like me, that's for sure."

"Yeah, well, I don't know if you have the best technique," Dustin said, smiling to himself. "Physically attacking my dad at the pulpit isn't really the way to set yourself up to be heard."

"Okay, sure, was that a little out of line? Yes. But you don't know anything about what it's like to see your mom throw away all of your family's security—your entire future—for the sake of some false promises. It makes you do things you would never predict. Like somehow ending up here, in a bad dream come to life where I'm having a heart-to-heart with Dustin Reaps in my basement while he organizes my mom's essential oils by vibe."

"You mean a heart-to-heart with *Orlando*," he corrected. "And is that what this is? A heart-to-heart?"

Zoe flushed. "No, I'm just k—"

"I think it is."

She rolled her eyes. Suddenly, the sound of cartoon birds chirping over and over traveled down the stairs.

"What's that noise?" Dustin asked.

Zoe froze. "My mom's novelty doorbell." Then came a persistent knocking.

"Is that your special guest?"

"If it is, they're early. Shut off the lantern and be quiet," she hissed.

Zoe stomped back up the stairs and locked the basement door behind her. She walked across the living room to the front door and peeked through the blinds, catching a glimpse of someone wearing head-to-toe purple, then unlocked the door and opened it an inch.

22

GENESIS

"Hi," Genesis said, sheepishly sticking her hands in her pockets.

Zoe's eyes darted up and down the street. "So were you just in the neighborhood, or . . . ?"

"I walked here. To see you."

Zoe opened the door another two inches and nodded for Genesis to come in.

Genesis was startled by the sheer amount of things inside the tiny house—dusty angel figurines and plaques with sayings on them. Technically, this was the second time she'd been in another person's house in her whole life, the first time being when she was here helping to save Dustin. Genesis hadn't noticed the details then; she had been too distracted by Dustin's lack of consciousness. While the ranch was all unfinished flooring and exposed electrical wires like the whole thing was an ongoing construction project with no definite end date, everything in Zoe's house seemed warm and comforting, although a little bit suffocating, like living in the middle of a cinnamon bun. The couch had so many throw pillows that Genesis wondered how anyone could comfortably sit on it.

She pulled her eyes away from the distractions, squared her shoulders, and stared into Zoe's eyes.

"I changed my mind. I had an epiphany today." Genesis started to pace back and forth in front of the door. "When we were on the phone, you said 'Love you!' And I know you were just saying it so it sounded like you were talking to your mom, you weren't actually saying it to me. But I realized no one has ever said 'I love you' to me in my whole life. Not one person at the ranch. They just don't say it as a custom. And hearing Ree get so emotional over her son on the voice mails . . . No one cares about me like that. I can't go through the motions anymore. I need to leave. I don't know where I'm going to go, but I need money. And I know it's wrong, getting it this way, but I don't really see any other options. Maybe God put you in my life for this reason. Zoe, this is me blinking twice."

Zoe sat down on the couch and blew a gust of air out of her mouth. "This is a lot."

"I know," Genesis agreed.

"Wait, do you still have Dustin's phone?" Zoe asked.

"No. I left it where I found it."

"Okay. I'll have to check in with my, um, business partners."

Genesis took a deep breath, squaring her shoulders again. "I am not going back to the ranch, and I am not going to take no for an answer."

Zoe stared at her in disbelief. "Well, damn."

She turned away from Genesis and scratched the space between her eyebrows for a long moment, weighing her options. Part of her knew if she sent the girl away, she could be a loose cannon and blab the little she knew to the Reapses. But an even bigger part of her saw herself in Genesis: Zoe knew exactly what it was like to feel so trapped, so desperate. Of course she couldn't give her no for an answer.

. . .

In the middle of the basement floor, Dustin lay still, the sleeping bag zipped all the way up, partially obscuring his head like he was a molting caterpillar.

"It's okay, Orlando, you don't have to hide," Zoe said.

Dustin tentatively opened one eye, then the other. He looked at Genesis where she stood on the bottom of the rickety staircase, then quickly rolled around. "*She's* your special guest?"

"No," Zoe sighed. "Genesis has surprised us with an unexpected visit."

"Might as well invite the whole neighborhood over," Dustin muttered.

Zoe rolled her eyes. "I'll be right back. I have to go cancel my plans."

She stomped up the stairs and slammed the door shut, leaving Dustin and Genesis to stare at each other in awkward silence. Genesis sat down on the bottom step, facing away from Dustin as if they were just two strangers in a waiting room.

Dustin unzipped the sleeping bag from inside and sat up. "So what's it like?" he asked in a whisper. "Being an Astralian?"

"I can't say," she said to the cement bricks in front of her.

"You're not allowed to?"

"No. I'm not an Astralian anymore."

Dustin snorted through his nose. "What?"

"I left today. Forever."

"Wooow," Dustin said. "You're blowing it."

"What?!"

"You don't know how good you have it."

"*You* don't know how good you have it," she mumbled. Genesis's eyes quickly darted to him and back to the wall.

"Excuse me?"

"What about being a member of my community is so appealing to you?" Genesis asked.

"Uhhh . . ." Dustin raked a hand through his hair. "Well, you guys are self-sustaining. You don't have to depend on industrial agriculture to survive. That's pretty cool."

"It's a lot of hard work."

"Yeah, but you get to reap the benefits of it all, without caring about money. Just living off the grid, enjoying the feeling of being alive. No gods. No masters. It sounds pretty sweet. I don't know anywhere else where people are living like that. It's pretty wild that you guys manage to do it right here."

"You wouldn't last a day," Genesis said, startling herself with her own sharpness. She was dehydrated and tired, trapped in a basement with some stranger explaining to her how grateful she should be for the life she was so exhausted by. "We're not 'self-sustaining,' we're barely surviving. You think your life would be so much easier if you were just freed from the burden of all your worldly objects, just like all of those people who followed Jimmy

Joe James here twenty years ago, but that's only because you have a choice."

Dustin scoffed. "I *don't* have a choice."

Genesis closed her eyes. "I've never been to school. I mostly taught myself how to read. I've never been to the dentist. I've never been to the movies. I've never been in a swimming pool. All of my clothes are hand-me-downs. I'm not allowed to use computers or modern technology. I have no idea who my father is, but apparently lots of other people have *theories*. I don't know what I'm going to do with the rest of my life." She opened her eyes and turned to Dustin. "I don't say all that to make you feel sorry for me. At the same time, I am blessed with fresh air and clean water and nourishing food. And we do have television, but I prefer not to watch it."

"'Blessed'?" Dustin asked, raising his fingers in air quotes. "I thought you guys didn't believe in God."

"They don't. I do." She got up from the step and sat down cross-legged at the end of his sleeping bag. "Dustin, I think we both have a lot to be thankful for but don't realize it. As Psalm 23 says, with the Lord as your shepherd, you shall not be in want."

Dustin flinched away from her. "Did my parents put you up to this? First Zoe coming down here and lecturing me, now you coming in and quoting scripture? How would *you* know what I have to be thankful for? You don't even know me."

Genesis couldn't tell Dustin that she knew enough about him from his mother's social media to write a small novel. Like that his birthday was July 30. Or how his favorite food was French fries dipped in ranch dressing; his least favorite, cucumbers (she knew this because Ree once posted a recipe for cucumber salad: "I even caught my biggest cucumber-hater, Dustin, sneaking a bite!"). Or how as a toddler he used to carry around a plastic dinosaur toy he affectionately called Ted everywhere he went until he lost it and cried for three days straight afterward. Or that he actually liked to help clean the house and loved the satisfaction of creating lines in the carpet with each push of the vacuum. But these were all just fun facts, like a pile of decorative seashells, when to really know a person was to know an entire ocean.

"I suppose I don't," Genesis admitted.

Dustin lay back down on the sleeping bag and rested his head in his hands. Genesis turned away from him, staring back at the wall.

A moment of silence passed. "Since we're stuck down here, do you want to take a quiz?" Dustin whispered.

"What?" Genesis asked.

Dustin sat up and pulled out a beat-up-looking book from behind one of the piles of boxes. "I found this earlier when I was trying to organize all this stuff. I think Zoe's mom is a hoarder. Not even joking."

Color Me Beautiful, the cover said. *Discover your natural beauty through shades that make you look great and feel fabulous! Whatever your style or mood, this quiz will help you find the special colors that will make you glow.*

"You answer a few questions and it tells you what colors you should wear based on a season." Dustin scratched the back of his neck and cleared his throat. "Apparently I'm a 'summer.' It's extremely stupid, um—"

"Okay," Genesis agreed. "Ask me the questions."

Dustin opened the book. "How would you describe your eye color?"

"Brown."

He narrowed his eyes at her in the dim light. "Really? I'm getting more of a hazel."

"Hazel, then."

"Would you say your hair is light or dark?"

Genesis pulled her long braid around her shoulder and concentrated on the ends. "What if it's kind of in between?"

Dustin pursed his lips. "Um. Yeah. Medium-dark is an option on here. Would you say you have warm or cool undertones?"

"I have no idea."

"Uh, okay, according to this, if you look at the veins in your inner arm and they look greenish, you probably have warm undertones. If your veins are blue or purplish looking, that means cool undertones."

Genesis squinted at her wrist. "Warm. I think."

"Great," Dustin said flatly. "So here we have it." He turned the page. "You're an . . . autumn." He dramatically cleared his throat. "'The autumn palette is easy to remember if you think about a beautiful autumn landscape. You can wear both muted and rich, warm colors like the autumn foliage or that of spices such as paprika and turmeric. You receive compliments most when you wear shades of the autumn season, like moss, rust, and terra-cotta.' Huh. Congrats."

Genesis stared down at her purple overalls. Tears welled up at the corners of her eyes.

"Hey," Dustin whispered softly. "It's just a stupid quiz. She told *me* I need to start 'embracing pastels in a big way.' I'm pretty sure this book was written in, like, 1984."

She looked up at him and smiled, tears pouring down her face. "No, no, it's just: all this time I've only been wearing purple."

23

HOLLY

Holly's phone lit up just as she was drifting to sleep, casting a blue shadow on the wall above her bed. She told herself to ignore it until the morning; sleep was hard to come by these days. First her internal clock had been thrown off by her habit of sneaking out in the middle of the night until just before dawn, then by waking up *at* dawn to get to Zoe's house in time to keep watch. Combined with her persistent anxiety over getting caught, this gave her the feeling that she was napping on a roller coaster all day long. But the blue light persisted, so she rolled over and gave in to it.

Zoe: !!!!

LOL

I'M DYING

Following the texts, Zoe sent a link to an Instagram video by Ree Reaps. The thumbnail showed a close-up of her face stained with mascara-laced tears.

"Whewww," Ree exhaled as Holly pressed play. "This is not an easy announcement to make. But I thought y'all better hear it from me, before the rumor mills start spinning. My son, my eldest, our only son, my baby boy, my sweet, sweet Dustin has—" She paused and sobbed, wiping the tears from her face with the pads of her fingertips. "He's gone missing." Her voice cracked at the end of *missing*. "We don't know where he's gone. We don't know *how* he's gone. This is a mother's worst nightmare come to life, as I'm sure you can all imagine. The local authorities are looking into it. And we just ask for your prayers. That God will give them the guidance to bring our boy home safely. That's all we can ask for. And if anyone has seen Dustin or has any information at all, please let us know. I've posted a graphic to my feed with his photo and identifying information; share it far and wide. Hold your babies tight tonight. That's all I can say. God bless you all."

Holly quickly flipped the phone facedown on her bed. Until now, the whole scheme had felt like a joke. And it *was*, she reminded herself; Dustin wasn't actually in danger. He was safe and sound at Zoe's house by his own admission. The only risk to his life was a vitamin deficiency from the lack of sunlight in the basement and nutrients in the meal kits. But his mother's pain was very real, or at least it looked that way. Holly imagined how Courtney would react if she were to suddenly disappear herself, and it wasn't so different.

She rolled over and tried to fall back asleep, but her mind was racing at the thought of Dustin's family also lying wide awake across town, their imaginations running wild with the dark possibilities of where he'd gone. Eventually she drifted off, only to have a nightmare in which Ree's crying face melted into a puddle that then transformed into an oozing bowl of congealed country biscuits and gravy casserole.

Holly got up before Danny, made a pot of coffee, and switched on the local news.

"Well, Pam, it looks like we've got more disturbing news out of Violet this morning," a middle-aged male cohost with spiky hair said.

The woman across the desk from him nodded. "That's right, Ed. Local celebrity pastors Jay and Ree Reaps have come forward to say their teenage son, Dustin, has gone missing." A cropped photo of Dustin smiling unnaturally wide flashed across the screen. Holly gripped her mug of coffee tight. "He was last seen at their family home on Wednesday evening. According to county police, a block of private surveillance footage from the Reaps home is missing, leading investigators to believe that his disappearance may be the result of some kind of coordinated effort. Anyone with information regarding his disappearance is encouraged to call local authorities."

"Jesus," Danny muttered quietly. Holly turned to see him leaning against the living room threshold with his arms crossed.

"I hope that boy is okay," she said. "Do you know him?"

"Nah. The Reapses used to come by the diner years ago, but not since they started building up that little empire of theirs. I'll tell you what, we haven't had anything like this happen around town since you were a kid. Maybe you brought the chaos back with you," he joked.

Holly sipped her coffee, her cheeks flushing. "Maybe."

"I'm just kidding. Poor kid probably just ran away. I know I would've done the same if those wackos were my parents."

He eyed her backpack sitting next to the couch. "Are you going on a hike again?"

"Oh, uh, no. Today I'm going to an estate sale. It's a couple hours away. I'll be back by dinner."

Holly had to keep her excuses for leaving the house so early somewhat believable. It just wasn't plausible that she'd go from zero physical activity to hiking nearly every day. She had to mix things up.

Danny looked at her skeptically. "Since when are you into antiques?"

"I'm not planning on buying anything. Mostly observing. I just think it's so fascinating," she lied. "A person's whole life boiled down to all their stuff."

"Sure, sure," he said, though he didn't seem to understand at all.

. . .

When she got to Zoe's house, Zoe cracked open the back door and glanced warily at a neighbor mowing their tiny lawn across the street. "Can we talk in your car for a minute?"

Inside the Buick, Zoe explained how Genesis had left the Astralians and wanted in on the plan. "She slept over last night, but I still haven't given her an answer. I wanted to make sure you're okay with it first."

"Well, she needs the money more than I do, and it's safer this way. Now everyone who knows anything about this is right under your roof. But is Orlando okay with it?"

"He wasn't exactly thrilled about sharing the money even more. But I basically told him the same thing: Genesis is our only other witness. There's no way anyone will find out about him until we want them to know."

So Zoe left for work, and Holly went inside, where Genesis was sitting at the kitchen table, reading the Bible by candlelight.

"Morning," Holly said.

Genesis looked up and gave her a small smile. Holly almost felt bad for intruding; there was something about her that looked so at peace.

She pointed to the Bible. "Is that any good?" she joked.

"Yeah." Genesis laughed uncomfortably. "Um, oddly enough, this is my first time reading a physical copy. I'm so used to just reading it on my phone."

"Genesis is a book in the Bible, right?" Holly asked, slipping off her backpack and taking a seat across from her. "But that's not where your name comes from?"

"I'm not sure. I think my parents picked it as a general reference to the creation of man, but I doubt they took it from here specifically."

"Haven't they told you your name origin story?"

"What's that?"

"Like, my name is Holly because I was supposed to be born on Christmas. I came a few days late, though, but my mom was still really attached to the name anyway."

Genesis gave her a blank look. "I don't get it."

"Like 'Deck the halls with boughs of holly, fa-la-la-la'? The Christmas carol?"

"We don't celebrate Christmas on the ranch. I know a little bit about it, from seeing all the decorations around town that time of year, and, you know, reading Jesus's birth story." She looked down at the Bible.

"Do you celebrate *any* holidays?" Holly asked.

"Well, we celebrate the autumnal equinox every year. Kind of like Thanksgiving, I guess. But instead of feasting, we fast for two days, then break it by sharing a loaf of nine-grain bread at the same time."

Holly cocked her head to the side, studying Genesis's face. "How about birthdays?"

"Nope. They're big on horoscopes, though, so everyone knows their sign and birthday. We just don't celebrate it. I'm a Pisces. February twenty-fourth."

"And that makes you how old?"

"Seventeen."

Suddenly, Dustin emerged from the door to the basement, his hair sticking up in multiple places, a blanket wrapped around his shoulders.

"Hey," he grunted at the girls, opening a kitchen cabinet.

"You're front-page news this morning," Holly said without looking at him.

Dustin snorted through his nose. "I've been gone, like, not even two days."

Holly pulled her phone out from her pocket and googled his

name. The top result was a web story from the same station she had watched earlier. She walked over to the counter and showed him.

He glanced at the phone, then did a double take and grabbed it from her hands. "Holy crap."

Dustin scrolled down and paused. The article had linked to his mother's teary plea. He clicked on it and watched the first ten seconds, then burst into uncontrollable laughter. "*My sweet, sweet Dustin,*" he mimicked in his mother's Texan accent. "Oh, I'm sure she's loving every second of this. Just couldn't wait to share the news with all her followers. It's perfect publicity for her new little TV show." He handed the phone back to Holly and turned to the cabinet, slamming it shut, then opening another one. "Doesn't Zoe have any, like, candy or cookies or anything?"

"It's not even nine," Holly sneered.

"I woke up craving sugar." Dustin sighed. "And my whole body hurts again. I don't know what's happening to me."

She studied his face. The bags under his eyes were more pronounced than ever. He looked nothing like the smiling boy they showed on the news. "You're having nicotine withdrawals. It makes you want to snack."

"What? No. I barely smoke."

She gave him a sideways glance. "My mom quit when I was little. The same thing happened to her. For months she just ate a handful of Skittles anytime she wanted to smoke. I don't know if a doctor would approve, but eventually it worked."

"Well, great," Dustin snapped. "I don't suppose you have a bag of Skittles on you, do you?" He flipped open another cabinet and pulled out one of the boxed meal kits. "Otherwise it's Hickory Smoked Salmon with Ree's Garden Salsa for me."

Holly crossed her arms. "That doesn't sound so bad."

Dustin looked into her eyes and opened the box without breaking eye contact. He pulled out the inner sealed pouch, tore it open, then held it out near her nose. "You want a whiff?"

She leaned away and shook her head. Even from a distance it smelled like a bad cocktail of sour milk and canned tuna.

"I thought so," Dustin said. "Genesis, you hungry?"

Genesis looked up from the Bible and shook her head. "No, thank you. I'll have something else later."

"Well, this crap is all we've got."

"Um," Genesis said, brushing a strand of hair behind her ear. "Zoe told me if I get hungry, I should walk to the diner and she'll get me whatever I want."

Dustin swung the packet of food onto the counter, leaving a trail of multicolored dust. "Of course she did. Never extended that offer to me, the whole reason we're able to do this thing."

"Unbelievable," Holly said, crossing the kitchen back to her chair. "I show you that you're headline news and your mom is posting videos of herself crying out for you, and your first inclination is to throw a temper tantrum over breakfast?"

"What do you want me to say?" Dustin asked, throwing up his hands, the blanket falling from his shoulders. "'Oh, that's so horrible'? It just means the plan is working! None of that is real. Hopefully, it means they'll start offering up a reward soon and then I'm closer to not having to live like a captive anymore."

"And then what will happen?" Genesis asked, closing the Bible shut. The cover had roses on it and said *Women's Devotional Bible.*

"What do you mean?" Dustin asked, reaching for the blanket from the floor.

"Say this all goes according to plan. Your parents offer money to whoever finds you." She paused and looked meaningfully at Holly. "They get the money and give you some. Then what will you do?"

"I'll leave town." He shrugged. "Probably use some of it to buy a cheap car. Or all of it. Who knows how much that will actually be? But I can figure it out as I go."

"So you'll leave your family again?" Genesis asked plainly, without judgment in her voice. "Without saying goodbye?"

Holly realized that he would finally be living his life as Orlando the drifter, for real. She felt a pang of sadness thinking about him driving through the night alone, without her.

"Yeah, I guess," Dustin admitted. "Seems easiest that way. Isn't that what you just did to everyone back there at your ranch?"

Genesis looked down solemnly at the table. "That's different. I'm not news like you. There are no search parties for me. Other members of the Astralians have left, and no one went looking for them. It's just how our community is. They're used to people leaving." She stared back up at him. "When you get home, your parents will probably throw a big celebration. Everyone will be so glad to have you back. Then when you leave forever, it will feel like they've lost you twice."

Dustin rubbed his jaw, and his eyes glazed over, then he cleared his throat and looked back at Genesis. "Well, they'll just have to get over it. By then, I'll be an adult. My birthday's in a few weeks, and I'll be legally able to do whatever I want. Anyway, speaking of doing what you want . . . did you ask Holly about the . . . ?" He touched a lock of his hair and waved it back and forth.

"I don't know," Genesis said. "I slept on it, and maybe it's not the best idea."

"Oh, c'mon! Don't chicken out, Gen."

Gen? Holly looked between them. Since when were they such pals? "What is it?"

"She was wondering if you knew how to cut hair," Dustin explained. "I definitely don't. We'd ask Zoe, but she seems to have her hands full right now."

Genesis threw her heavy braid over her right shoulder. "Last night we were looking at this old book of beauty advice that Zoe's mom kept in the basement."

Again, Holly felt that pang in her chest. She realized it wasn't sadness she was feeling, but jealousy. She was *jealous* that Genesis and Dustin were hanging out. Holly wanted to hate him for all he did, but a part of her missed when Dustin was Orlando, a person she could confide in—a friend.

"Most of it was pretty strange," Genesis continued. "But one part stuck with me: it said that changing your appearance when you start a new path in life, like a new job or getting back on the dating scene—whatever that is—can boost your confidence. The whole reason I have this big, long braid is because Jimmy Joe James believed women shouldn't cut their hair because it would interfere with their childbearing chakras—whatever *those* are. I thought maybe if I'm going to have a new life, outside of Astralia, I should have a new look." She fingered the ends of her hair and shrugged. "But it's silly. I shouldn't be so vain at a time like this."

"It's not silly," Holly said, grateful for a distraction. This was the kind of thing she was *supposed* to be spending her summer thinking about: haircuts, TV shows, memes, crushes—or at least crushes on boys who weren't compulsive liars. Mindless stuff, not the existence of a God or the logistics of fake kidnapping or the moral weight of abandoning one's own family. "My mom always cuts my hair, but I've watched her do other people's hair for years, so I can give it a try. How much do you want cut off?"

"Maybe to my shoulders. Or shorter." She paused and bit her lip. "And dye it? I don't know. I'm getting carried away."

"No. You should do it. What color were you thinking?"

"I have no clue. Just something different."

"Blue," Dustin said. Genesis eyed him nervously.

"It would be so badass!" he continued. "Nothing says 'I just escaped a cult and I'm looking for adventure' like dyeing your hair blue."

"I don't think that's what I want to communicate to the world. At all."

"Well then, what *do* you want to communicate?" he asked. "According to our new leader, Carole of *Color Me Beautiful*, your hair is the eye to your soul. Besides your actual eyes."

"I would like hair that says . . . I'm a well-adjusted, normal person who has definitely not just escaped a cult."

"How about we just start with a cut, then?" Holly suggested, giving her a reassuring smile. "I can go slow."

Genesis looked down at her braid one more time, then released it from her hands. "Okay. I'm ready."

And so Holly went in search of scissors and did something that many women before her had done for generations: threw all of her energy and attention into a haircut instead of confronting her feelings.

24

ZOE

"**I**s that my T-shirt?" Zoe asked as Genesis sidled up to the diner counter. It took her a moment to realize that the shirt, her most prized item of clothing—a piece of bootleg *Twilight* movie merch featuring an airbrushed image of Kristen Stewart as Bella, Zoe's first real crush—was the second most newsworthy thing about Genesis's appearance. "And where the heck did your braid go?"

Genesis tucked her hair, now cut into a chin-length bob, behind her ears with both hands. "Holly cut it off for me. What do you think?"

"You look hot!" Zoe exclaimed, pretend-fanning herself with her order pad.

"Oh no." Genesis crumbled her face in her hands. "What have I done?"

"No, that's a good thing! It looks great. I didn't mean to make you feel self-conscious. This style really suits you."

Genesis looked up. "Are you sure?"

"Yes. The T-shirt, however, only looks good on me. Don't take it personally. It's just, that's my future family heirloom."

"Sorry. I just grabbed whatever I could find from your room. I thought it would look too conspicuous if I was walking around town in my purple overalls."

"I think you managed to pick the only article of clothing slightly more conspicuous than those. Don't worry about it, though." Zoe shrugged. "I'll find you something else to wear. You hungry?"

"Starving," Genesis said.

"Chocolate milkshake?"

"Yes, please. And French fries. And . . . a cheeseburger."

Zoe raised an eyebrow. "Aren't you vegetarian?"

"I was. Until now."

Zoe glanced over her shoulder, then leaned in conspiratorially. "I'm just warning you, this really isn't the place to lose your meat virginity," she said through her teeth. "The burgers are not good."

Genesis furrowed her brows like she was going to cry. "Please don't say that."

"I mean, they're not. It's just a fact."

"No, I understand. I mean please don't say the words *meat* and *virginity* next to each other."

"Okay. Yes. Fair. You know what? You're in charge today, Genesis. Let's get you that cheeseburger."

Zoe went back into the kitchen and placed the order, then filled a metal milkshake cup with ice cream and brought it back behind the counter. There were few things she felt like she had complete control over in her life, but the milkshake machine was Zoe's domain. Anytime she got to flick on the ancient robot that drowned out any sounds within a ten-foot radius, she felt a fleeting sense of power that said, "Yep, I'm the one who gets to control this ole thing."

The machine was so loud that she didn't hear the bell on the doorway ding. So she was surprised when she turned to retrieve the Reddi-wip from the fridge and saw that Sage was standing against the counter broodingly and Genesis was nowhere to be found.

"Hi, Zoe," he said. His eyes were rimmed in red.

"H-hey," she stammered. "Sorry, I didn't know we were expecting a delivery today. I'll go tell Danny you're here."

"That's okay. Um, I'm not here for a delivery."

Out of the corner of her eye, Zoe spotted a customer at the very end of the counter, holding up a plastic menu, obscuring their face. They quickly lowered the menu just beneath their chin. It was Genesis. She placed a single finger over her lips, then lifted the menu back up.

Zoe quickly looked back to Sage and forced a smile. "Well then, what's up? Can I get you anything?"

"I know this is kind of a long shot, but have you seen Genesis, the girl who comes with me sometimes to make the deliveries? She helped you." He thumbed toward the bathroom. "With the paper towels last week."

"Right. Ummm." She pretended to wrack her memory. "No, not since then. Why?"

"I just haven't seen her all day and can't seem to find her."

Zoe frowned. "That's weird. Well, I'll call you if I see her. I'm sure we have the number for the ranch around here somewhere."

"Thanks. I'm probably overreacting, but this morning some police came by saying that they wanted to search the ranch. They didn't have a warrant, so they didn't. It freaked me out, though. Apparently some pastor's kid is missing. My head started spiraling. What if something like that happened to Genesis?" He shook his head, as if to erase some darker scenario in his imagination. "She's probably just in the barn and I missed her."

"I hope that's the case, but I'll keep an eye out," Zoe said.

"Thanks, Zoe," Sage said. "I appreciate it."

"Anytime," she said. He gave her a sad smile and waved goodbye. "Stay safe out there," she added. Zoe wasn't sure if she had gotten so good at lying that it came naturally or if she was overcompensating for being terrible at it.

When Sage was gone, she grabbed Genesis's meal from the kitchen and brought it over to her spot on the other end of the counter. "All clear," she said.

Genesis lowered the menu from her face and exhaled deeply. "Thanks."

Zoe rested her elbows on the counter. "So what's the deal between you two?" She flicked her head toward the parking spot where Sage's van had just been parked.

Genesis peeled the paper off a plastic straw. "We're, uh, family."

"Like, he's your brother?"

"No," she said, sticking the straw in the milkshake and stirring it around. "Well, I'm not entirely sure."

"Wait." Zoe placed a palm up. "What makes you unsure?"

Genesis stared down at her burger, cheeks reddening. "At the ranch, they don't believe in parents," she said. "Everyone gets raised together by the group. No one is one hundred percent certain who their biological parents are."

Zoe tried to keep her face neutral, but inside she felt disgusted that her initial snarky comment about Genesis and Sage being so beautiful as the result of inbreeding maybe wasn't just a joke after all.

"It's not like it's a secret," Genesis continued. "Most of us know who our moms are because they had to nurse us and watch over us when we were very little, but we don't call them Mom. And dads . . . some people can figure out from resemblance, but that's still a mystery for me." Genesis breathed through her nose and scowled out the window.

"Does it get . . . How do I put this?" Zoe furrowed her brows and tented her fingers together. "Weird? Like, um, relationship-wise?"

"No," Genesis said quickly, looking back at her. "I know what you're thinking, but no one's had children on the ranch since I was born. And none of us who were born on the ranch are . . . involved . . . with each other."

"Okay . . ." Zoe said.

"You sound unconvinced."

"It's just, I've seen the way Sage looks at you. My brother would never look at me like that. Because, for one thing, we can't stand each other, but also, it'd be creepy."

"The way he looks at me?" Genesis finally took a sip of her milkshake.

"Like you are the sun. The air he breathes. Other assorted nature metaphors about being in love with someone."

Suddenly Genesis choked and coughed. "Sage looks at everyone like that. That's just who he is."

"But you hiding from him just now—and leaving the ranch in general—it makes me wonder if you don't *like* how he looks at you. Maybe I'm letting my imagination get the best of me, but I know that in . . . communities like yours, relationship dynamics between men and women can be really problematic. Genesis, you can tell me if you've ever been uncomfortable or he's ever done anything—"

"You've got it all wrong!" Genesis sputtered.

Zoe stood up straight and put her hands on her hips. "Then tell me what I'm missing."

Genesis sat in silence for a beat, then swallowed hard. "I'm the one who's in love with him, not the other way around," she said.

"Huh." Zoe opened her mouth wide and put her hand to her chin. "You're full of surprises, Gen. I'll give you that."

"It's one of the main reasons I had to remove myself from that place. Lust is a sin. Especially lusting after someone you're related to. I had to take myself out of temptation's way."

"But you just said you're in *love* with him, not lust. Love isn't a sin."

"*Incest,*" Genesis whispered, "is definitely a sin."

"Well, you don't one hundred percent know if you're related. I'm sure you could do some kind of digging around. Even you guys have birth certificates, right?"

"I don't know if we do. I've never seen mine," Genesis admitted. "Even if we're not blood relatives, it still feels wrong. We've grown up together. Besides, we hold completely different belief systems. A relationship between us would never work." She glumly picked up three fries at once and stuffed them in her mouth.

"Does he know about your thing with God?" Zoe asked.

Genesis winced and swallowed her food. "My 'thing'? As in my deeply personal connection with my Lord and Savior Jesus Christ? No."

"Sorry, I didn't mean to make it sound unimportant."

"It's okay. You don't have to pretend to respect my beliefs, Zoe. I'm sure you think I'm crazy."

Zoe shook her head. "I don't think you're crazy. Unpredictable? For sure. But definitely not crazy. You know, I get it. I used to love church. Sometimes I even miss it."

Genesis leaned back and scrutinized Zoe's face. "Really?"

"Well, I don't miss Hope Harvest or Pastor Marcus's cringy jokes or Jay Reaps's obnoxious voice—at all—but . . ." Zoe looked down and started to pick a fleck of purple polish off her thumbnail.

"Sometimes I miss God," she went on. "The idea of God. When I believed, I used to be less anxious all the time. Prayer made me feel so calm. Life felt so certain, you know? But maybe it only felt that way because I didn't really know myself. Now when I think about my life ahead of me, I feel scared, honestly; there's no reassurance that someone has a plan for me or that good will always win over evil. Especially when you realize all the things you thought were good might actually *be* the evil. But at least now I really know who I am, and I know that being a good person doesn't mean I have to sacrifice being myself or loving who I love. For you, it might seem like the opposite situation, but it's really the same. You were raised to believe some things, but now you're testing the waters elsewhere and figuring out what you believe for yourself. I respect that a lot, Gen."

Genesis peered up at Zoe, her eyes like two moons. "You don't think I'm just jumping from one cult to the next?"

"Nah." Zoe waved a hand. "You have a mind of your own. The way you didn't just ignorantly follow the Reapses proves that. There are all kinds of ways to interpret the Bible and God and not just the super-specific ones some guys decided were true. Just because you have faith doesn't mean you're just some follower."

Genesis smiled. "Thanks. You know, you're really wise, Zoe."

She laughed once and clutched her chest in mock humility. "You're the only one around here who seems to notice that."

"Do you think you'll ever go back? To church?"

Zoe crinkled her nose. Figuring out what she really believed in felt like a problem for Adult Zoe, something she pushed into a drawer until the time was right. And now she was too busy fighting to make sure Adult Zoe would have a chance to exist.

"Definitely not here. Maybe when I'm older and finally out of this place, I can find one of those socially aware churches with a gay priest who always wears, like, a rainbow sash around his neck and believes that burning fossil fuels destroys God's beautiful green Earth. But even then . . . we'll see." She sighed. "Anyway, we got sidetracked. I want to know more about you and Sage."

Genesis rolled her eyes. "There's nothing more to know."

"Won't you miss him?"

"Of course I will, but he loves it on the ranch. I know he'll be okay without me."

"Well, maybe you're the reason he loves it there."

Genesis rolled her eyes again. Under Zoe's guardianship, it was like she was growing into a regular, non-sheltered teenage girl with each passing day. "I don't understand why you're so invested in this. Just a few minutes ago you implied you were concerned I was being held in a sex cult again my will."

"Whoa, whoa! Your words, not mine. I'm just saying," Zoe said. "He seemed pretty broken up at the thought of you missing."

"Well, wouldn't your brother care if you went missing?"

Zoe pursed her lips and shook her head. "He wouldn't notice for weeks. Tom's noise-canceling headphones are basically glued to his ears. Besides, Sage isn't your brother."

"But I told you, he very well might be." Finally, Genesis picked up her burger and put it to her lips.

"I just have a gut feeling now," Zoe said. "The more I'm learning about this situation, the more I feel confident the test is not a match."

Genesis plopped the burger back down before she could even take a bite. "So say he's not my brother. Then what am I supposed to do?"

"Tell him everything! Tell him about your beliefs. Tell him that you love him. Just put it all out there and see what happens."

"That's much easier said than done, Zoe. It's better this way. I'm making a clean break."

"Or maybe—just maybe—you're running from your feelings . . ."

"So what if I am? All possible outcomes seem bad. If he feels the same way about me, then what? I stay at the ranch, living a lifestyle that I don't believe in. Or . . ." She looked up and out the window. "He totally rejects me, and I leave here with a broken heart. The way it is now, I don't have to worry about either of those things."

"Orrrr . . ." Zoe raised a finger. "Potential third scenario: he reciprocates your feelings and wants to leave with you. The rest of the world seems a whole lot less scary when you have someone to share it with. That's what keeps me going, at least."

"That would never happen. He thinks nothing in the world compares to the ranch."

"But like I said, maybe it would lose its sparkle without you there."

Genesis ignored her and picked up the burger again, took a bite, and cringed. "Ugh," she groaned, and spit the food into her napkin. "You were right. This is horrible."

"See?" Zoe raised her eyebrows and tapped Genesis on the shoulder. "I *am* wise. Listening to me always pays off."

The entry bell on the diner door dinged again, and Zoe turned her head to see Delia standing by it, clutching a stack of paper to her chest.

"Hey!" Zoe called over her shoulder.

Delia puckered her forehead at Zoe and Genesis for a few seconds, then half smiled and waved.

"What's up?" Zoe asked, walking over to the middle of the counter.

Delia placed the stack of papers down. "You're feeling better?"

Zoe gently clutched her stomach. She had lied the night before and said she was sick from eating diner chili as a last-minute excuse to cancel their date. "Kind of."

"My mom sent me over with a favor to ask of you."

"Me? Faith Johnson wants a favor from a mere peasant such as myself?"

"She wants to know if your boss would be willing to hang up some of these flyers around the diner." She slid one across to Zoe. It had the same picture of Dustin that had been on the news, printed out in black and white with big bold letters asking HAVE YOU SEEN THIS BOY? "In her words, some of the 'seedier elements of Violet' hang out here, and they might know some tips on where to find him."

Zoe smiled to herself. Faith Johnson was correct that the exact type of person who would kidnap Dustin Reaps did, in fact, hang out here. Nearly every day of the week.

"Yeah, why not? I'm sure Danny won't mind. We'll do *anything* to help bring our boy home." She clutched her heart in fake sadness, then winked at Delia.

"I don't know, Zo," Delia sighed. "The more time that passes, the more I think you might be right that something really bad happened. It's freaking me out."

"Oh no." Zoe frowned. She felt a pang of guilt, not for hiding Dustin, but for inadvertently doing something that would cause

Delia so much distress. "I didn't mean to scare you. I'm sure he'll turn up. Seriously, do not lose any sleep over this."

"The Reapses are organizing a prayer vigil for Dustin tonight. I thought maybe we could go together?"

"Uhhh . . ." Zoe scratched the back of her neck. "Maybe."

"What is it?" Delia quickly glanced down the bar at Genesis, then back at Zoe. "Do you have plans?"

"No, I'm just still feeling kind of blah."

"Well, what if you or I went missing? You would hope people wouldn't just sit out because they were 'feeling kind of blah.'"

Zoe snorted once. "If either of us were missing, Dustin Reaps definitely wouldn't lift a finger. Well, maybe for you, because your moms are best friends. But *me*?" She pointed to her chest. "He wouldn't care or even know, because no one in this town would organize a vigil. If anything, they'd throw a party in celebration."

"I would organize a vigil for you!" Delia protested. She glanced down at the stack of papers. "*And* I'd design a much more compelling flyer and print it out on neon-colored paper. Much more eye-grabbing than this rush job."

"That's reassuring, but I'd hope if I were missing, you'd also be missing because we ran away together for good."

Delia's tense shoulders relaxed, and she smiled up at Zoe. "True." Then quickly she frowned again. "But you know, it shouldn't be a one-for-one transactional thing. We should go not because he'd do the same for us but because we're good people and it's the right thing to do."

Zoe considered Delia an undoubtedly good person and, to her, the kindest, most honest person in the whole wide world. But she was increasingly unsure about herself. She knew what she was doing with Dustin wasn't exactly good, but it wasn't necessarily bad either. It was extreme, definitely, but it felt like the only way she could possibly right the wrong that plagued her life. It was this new habit of constantly lying to Delia about the whole thing, and how easily it came to her, that made Zoe question whether she was really a good person after all.

"All right," she sighed. "I'll come."

Delia raised her brows. "Really?"

"Sure. Though I think we should really reconsider your initial thought that he's just locked into one of the Reapses' many bathrooms. Maybe we should tip his family off tonight."

She smirked. "I'll meet you outside Hope Harvest Market at seven."

Zoe nodded, and Delia leaned in across the counter, toward her ear. "That girl over there who you were talking to has the same Bella shirt as you," she whispered. "What are the chances?"

Zoe glanced at Genesis, who had been watching them but now looked down with sudden interest at her fries.

"Oh my god, I know," Zoe said in a low whisper, turning back to Delia. "Isn't that amazing? I was just asking her about it when you came in."

"Do you know her? I've never seen her in my life."

Zoe pressed her lips together and shook her head. "Nope. Apparently she's just passing through town."

It was just another lie in her ever-increasing collection.

25

HOLLY

"So it's no Skittles," Holly said, walking down the basement stairs, "but I found this pack of sugar-free gum between the couch cushions that must belong to Zoe's mom, and I thought you might want some—" She paused at the bottom step. Dustin was lying flat on his back, gloomily staring straight at the ceiling.

"You can just leave it there," he said without looking at Holly.

She placed the gum on the concrete floor, turned to go back upstairs, then paused. "Are you okay?"

"To be honest, no, but I'm sure you're the last person who wants to hear about it."

Holly sat down on the step. "Well, I've got nothing else going on."

Dustin was quiet for a minute, then rolled over onto his side and looked at her. "I'm just thinking about what Genesis said earlier. That when this is all said and done, my family is going to feel like they've lost me twice."

"So why do you care? Don't you hate them?"

"I don't *hate* them. I just hate being a member of my family. It's . . . different. I won't miss being a Reaps as a whole, but I'll miss parts of it."

Holly rested her elbows on her thighs and her chin on her hands. "Like what?"

"Like . . . I'll miss seeing my little sisters grow up," Dustin said. "Ella can't stand me. Gabriella and Eden are at the age where they'll do whatever Ella tells them. So they'll do these stupid little kid pranks, like they brought a plate of Oreos to my bedroom door, but they'd swapped the cream filling for toothpaste." He smiled to himself. "As if I wouldn't think it was sus enough that they'd be bringing me a snack out of the blue. But Chloe, the littlest one, she's my buddy."

"And these are all actual people?" Holly asked coldly. "Unlike your . . . Gammy."

"Yes," he said through his teeth. "They are one hundred percent real." Dustin looked back up at the ceiling. His eyes started to glisten in the glow of the camping lantern.

Holly didn't want to show Dustin any sympathy. She wasn't sure if this sudden burst of affection for his sisters was all just a part of his act. Still, she wanted to keep talking to him. "I've always wondered what it's like to have siblings," she said.

"Well, you'll find out soon, right? When's your mom due, again?"

She was struck that he remembered, as if him remembering something she told him when he was Orlando was proof that their time together hadn't just been some game.

"September."

"Hmmm," he mused. "Seventeen years is a pretty big age gap. You know this can only go two ways for you."

Holly pushed herself to the edge of the step, closer to him. "What do you mean?"

"You either get to be the cool older sister who drives them places and buys them beer, or you get to be the second-mom sister, the one who helps with their homework and lectures them on making good decisions."

"Maybe I can be both."

Dustin sat up and grinned at her. "No, you don't get to be both. It doesn't work that way."

"How would *you* know?"

"Let's just say I've seen my fair share of youth pastors who've tried to be both and failed."

Holly grimaced at the thought of someone like Pastor Marcus driving her to a liquor store on the way to a party.

"Seriously, this is completely new for me," she said. "Maybe I'm too old to be feeling this way, but when your parents started having your siblings, did you ever feel like you were being replaced? Because that's how I'm feeling this summer. Shipped off to the junkyard while they get a new model installed."

"And in this scenario, Violet is the junkyard?" Dustin pressed.

Reluctantly, Holly smiled. "Exactly."

"Well, yeah, I've definitely felt that way," Dustin said. "My parents' attention got stretched thinner each time a new kid was born, but I'd say the bigger problem for me was that I'm also sharing them with the several thousand members of their congregation, not to mention their hundreds of thousands of social media followers around the world. Then there's the product lines or the book deals or some sponsored content opportunity or freaking reality show for the sake of 'furthering God's mission'—"

"Wait, wait, wait—reality show?"

"Oh yeah. If this plan doesn't work out, you're looking at the TLC network's next heartthrob." Dustin pointed at himself and grinned a wide, cheesy smile like the one on his missing flyers. "Don't tell Zoe that. She'll have a field day."

"I'm not making any promises."

They smiled at each other for a long moment, then Holly quickly turned away.

"Anyone would be lucky to have you as an older sister," Dustin went on after a beat of silence. "I mean, imagine just being born and then getting the privilege of knowing you their whole life? Your parents don't know how good they have it."

"You're full of it," Holly said to the ceiling.

"I'm serious, Holly. I've been doing a lot of thinking down here." He scooted over, closing the space between them, and peered into her eyes. "I'm sorry that I lied to you. And I'm sorry that I didn't apologize sooner. I know you think I take some sick pleasure from pretending I'm someone else and sneaking around at night, but do you know how much I wish I never had to lie to you? How much I wish I could've just asked you on a date, in public, like I was some average guy? That first night we met and you told me you had been lying about everything in your life, I felt so relieved and so terrible at the same time. You of all people would understand exactly why someone would lie about themselves even when it seems totally irrational from the outside. I finally found someone who would understand. Yet I didn't confide in you—I just kept going with my own lie. Holly, you deserve so much better than someone who has to lie to you."

Even though he was wearing three-day-old clothes and his breath reeked of freeze-dried stew, Holly suddenly felt the urge to reach out and touch Dustin's jaw, where a blanket of stubble had grown and surprisingly suited him.

"Yeah, I think she *knows* she deserves better than that," Zoe called out from the top of the stairs. "You don't need to tell her."

Zoe's voice was like a splash of ice-cold water to Holly's face. She leaned away from Dustin and looked up to the open door at the top of the steps. "Hey. Didn't hear you come in."

"You're supposed to be keeping an eye out!" Zoe moaned, clomping down the steps.

"My fault," Dustin said quickly, holding up the packet of sugar-free gum. "She was bringing me this."

"I need you to stay here tonight, Holly," Zoe said. "Tell your dad we're having a sleepover."

"Why?" Holly asked.

"Well, I need you to keep watch a few hours longer. I told Delia I would go with her to . . . Dustin Reaps's prayer vigil." An evil grin broke out across Zoe's face.

Holly looked to Dustin. He was frozen, staring at Zoe in disbelief, the opposite of how delighted he'd seemed that morning when he first saw the video of his mom crying on Instagram. "*A vigil?*" he asked. "Already?"

Zoe pulled a folded-up HAVE YOU SEEN THIS BOY? flyer out of

her cutoffs. "I know! They're taking it seriously. We won't have to keep this up much longer. I bet you your parents will be offering a reward by this weekend!"

"Don't you think that *you* going to the vigil is kind of . . . overdoing it?" Holly asked.

"No," Zoe scoffed. "If anything, it makes me look innocent."

"Or it makes you look like you're trying to hide something. Realistically, would you have gone to a prayer vigil for him in any other universe?"

"Yes! Because I'm a good person!" Zoe said a little too forcefully.

"Just please, *please* don't draw any attention to yourself while you're there," Holly begged.

Zoe mimed a halo around her head with a finger and rolled her eyes. "I'll be on my best behavior." She started back up the steps and waved for Holly to join her.

Dustin opened his mouth to speak, then closed it, then opened it again. Holly raised an eyebrow.

"Thanks for the gum," he said quietly.

. . .

"You two looked pretty chummy down there," Zoe said as Holly shut the basement door behind them.

Holly blushed. "We weren't. He was just apologizing to me for . . . everything."

"Don't buy it for a second. I bet he's just trying to make his life in the dungeon a little less miserable. Win you over again and get your attention, maybe convince you to bring him some solid food or something. He's still our enemy, Holly."

"But what if he's not? What if he's really not that bad? Maybe he just felt like he was losing his mind and made some really stupid choices to cope? You know, I've been there."

Zoe's face softened for a few seconds, but then she stood up straight and tightened her fists at her sides. "It's better to be safe than sorry. I've got to get changed for this vigil. Are you supposed to wear all black to these things or is that just funerals?"

"I have no idea." Holly glanced in the direction of the kitchen. "Hey, by the way, we're running low on supplies. Almost all the candles have burned out and half the batteries in the flashlights are dead and there's only a few water bottles left. If we're going to keep this up, one of us needs to go to the store. We shouldn't have to make ourselves suffer, let alone have Orlando die down there from dehydration."

Zoe's eyes went blank, and she appeared to be calculating something in her head. "Can't the human body go for a month without water?" she asked after a few seconds. "Or is that food?"

Holly glared at her.

"Okay, fine," Zoe sighed. "Why don't you make a Walmart run before I head out? I have some cash. For once, I made over twenty dollars in tips today, though I'm pretty sure it only happened because someone gave me two fives that were accidentally stuck together, not because they were being generous."

"Perfect. Also, . . ." Holly started, glancing at the kitchen again. The idea she'd been formulating in her head all day as a distraction felt ridiculous as she prepared to finally speak it out loud. "I think we should have a birthday party."

Zoe looked at her like she had sprouted multiple heads.

"For Genesis. I can chip in too. Not like a birthday party *party*. It's just . . . she told me she's never celebrated a single birthday. It made me really sad. And I think we all deserve a little break. I'm feeling on edge; I'm sure you are too, but we should be proud of ourselves in a weird, kind of messed-up way." She gestured at the flyer on the table. "We've successfully convinced the town that D—Orlando is missing. That's huge."

Zoe stared at the ceiling for a long moment. "Some birthday cake *would* really boost my morale right about now."

"Is that a yes?" Holly asked.

"Yeah. What the heck? We're going to be rich soon." She reached into her back pocket and pulled out a pile of crumpled bills. "Spring for the finest sheet cake that twenty dollars can buy. Make sure they write something nice on it."

Holly smiled and took the cash, then gathered her backpack.

"I'll see you later, Genesis," she said as she walked through the kitchen.

Genesis looked up from her Bible and gave Holly a small smile. "See you tomorrow."

"Actually, I'm staying over tonight," Holly said over her shoulder as she unlocked the back door. "Just running to Walmart right now."

"Oh. Wait!"

Holly paused with her door on the handle and looked back. "Yeah?"

"Can I come with you?" Genesis asked quietly.

Holly hesitated. How was she supposed to communicate *No, you can't come because I'm supposed to surprise you with a cake to celebrate all of your combined birthdays out of some deep pity I feel for you that I hope doesn't come off as condescending* without spoiling the surprise?

"I've never been inside a store before," Genesis said, louder this time.

Holly blinked twice. "Ever?"

Genesis shook her head. "It's an experience I've always wanted to try."

Holly considered just how small Genesis's world really was. Never stepping foot inside of a superstore was just the tip of the iceberg. She imagined all the music and books and movies she'd never listened to or read or watched. All the foods she'd never tried. Suddenly, Holly, who berated herself for watching too much reality TV and eating Cheetos for dinner, felt like the most cultured person alive.

"Well, let's go, then," she said.

Genesis grinned and jumped up from her chair.

"I feel like I need to curb your expectations, though," Holly said. "We are going to a poorly stocked Walmart in the middle of Montana. It's no Disneyland."

Genesis looked at her blankly. "What's Disneyland?"

26

GENESIS

The automatic doors snapped shut behind Genesis, and there she was, inside a hermetically sealed oasis of fluorescent light, cool air, and low, low prices.

"Wow," she said with reverence.

Holly grabbed a shopping cart. "I'm curious: If you've never been inside a store, then where do the Astralians get supplies?"

"We make most things ourselves, but we buy the essentials we can't. I'm not sure where from, though. I've never been involved with that. I only started leaving the property to help with the deliveries last year. Sometimes the elders use this thing called Amazon Prime. Have you heard of that?"

Holly made a funny face as if she were trying to suppress a laugh. "Yeah. I've heard of it." She pushed the cart ahead, then paused for a second. "Wait, if they can use that, then how come you're not allowed to use the internet?"

"Exactly. That kind of hypocrisy is why I needed to get out."

They walked through the supermarket area of the store, and all of Genesis's senses were on edge, the way she felt when she went to the service at Hope Harvest. Everything felt too bright, too loud, even the objectively low-volume canned music coming out of the store speakers.

Ocean's assessment of grocery stores had been correct: everything looked like it was made of wax. Piles of tomatoes and bell peppers looked like they could melt in your hands with a single touch. Genesis pointed to a pyramid of something yellow in the center of the produce section. It looked to her like a religious altar compared to the way the rest of the fruit was displayed. "What are those?"

Holly froze and stared at her with alarm. "Bananas," she said slowly.

"Oh. Are they grown domestically?"

"Ummm . . ." Holly hesitated, then picked up a piece of fruit and studied it. "The sticker says 'Product of Costa Rica.' So, no, these ones aren't."

"That would make sense." Genesis nodded sagely. "I'm only familiar with crops we harvest on the ranch. We've never tried to grow bananas. Not really the climate for it, I guess."

Holly turned to put the banana back and paused. "Would you want to try one?"

Genesis shook her hands. "I don't have any money."

"It's on me."

"Oh, no, I couldn't possibly—"

"Something you should know, for your new life, is that bananas are one of the cheapest foods you can buy. If you're ever in a pinch, you can almost always afford a banana. My mom used to say that. And she would ring up other items at self-check as bananas, but that's neither here nor there." Holly pointed to the sign that said $0.58/lb. "That's not even for one banana. One pound is, like, three bananas."

Genesis smiled bashfully. "Okay, I suppose I should try it, then. Thank you."

Holly placed the lone piece of fruit into the front of the enormous cart as if it were a very important scientific specimen they came to collect for research purposes, and then she pushed along, toward the bakery counter.

"Genesis, I don't want to spoil the surprise, but since you came with me, this is kind of awkward. So I'll just tell you. And you can say that I'm being completely weird and that this is a bad idea and it's, like, no big deal if you think so and—"

Holly gestured to the fridge of half sheet cakes in plastic shells in front of them. "I thought we should get you a birthday cake. To make up for all of the birthdays you haven't celebrated."

"Oh." Genesis blushed and stared down at the monstrosities before her with their messy neon piping and plastic figurines in the shape of unicorns and yellow cylindrical cartoon creatures with goggles, which she couldn't identify. They were marked $18.99. "That's so kind of you, but really not necessary."

Holly twisted the end of her ponytail between her fingers and looked away. "I made it weird, didn't I?"

"No. It's just . . . the banana is enough. Really. I'm touched by the generosity that you and Zoe have shown me. If anything, it's you two who deserve a cake."

"Yeah, well, that's another thing: Zoe's definitely expecting to eat some cake tonight after I told her I was doing this."

"Then we should get a cake to celebrate all of us, not just me." She stared down at her options. "What about that one?" Genesis pointed to a cake with a frosting sun, flowers, and bumblebees, not drawn to scale and all wearing smiley faces. Next to them, someone had piped just the word *Awesome!*, officially making it the most ambiguous cake ever.

"Cute, but also kind of a little scary if you look at it too hard," Holly said. "Imagine a bee the same size as the sun."

"Well, everything we're doing right now is a little scary if you think about it too hard," Genesis countered. "So maybe it's the most appropriate for the situation."

"True." Holly shrugged and reached into the refrigerator case to grab the cake.

They found their way to the bottled-water aisle and loaded up the cart with generic-brand gallons, then wandered through the endless aisles until they came upon shelves and shelves of scented candles.

"Hmm," Holly said, eyes panning the rainbow assortment. "Maybe we should see if they have unscented candles somewhere else."

"What's wrong with these?" Genesis asked.

"It's just—I don't know about you, but Zoe's house has put me off scented candles for a lifetime. It's nothing personal, but we have to light so many at once, and I don't think the human brain was designed to process the smell of fresh-cut peonies, pumpkin spice waffles, and pine trees all together. Gives me a headache."

Now that she thought about it, the odor in Zoe's house was particularly unpleasant, but Genesis had assumed that's just what regular people's houses smelled like and she needed to get used to it.

"And plain candles will probably be a lot cheap—" Holly added, turning the cart out of the aisle, then stopping in her tracks. Genesis followed her eyes to the back wall of the store, where Dustin's face flashed across a dozen flat-screen TVs in various sizes.

CULT SUSPECTED IN DISAPPEARANCE OF PASTOR'S SON; CELL PHONE RECOVERED NEAR ASTRALIA RANCH read the chyron at the bottom of the screen.

Genesis put her palm to her lips, suppressing a gasp. The photo of Dustin smiling switched to live overhead footage of the ranch from a helicopter, the roof of her old cabin just a tiny blip in the landscape.

"Oh my god, that's not the local news," Holly mumbled. "It's CNN."

"What's CNN?" Genesis asked.

"National news. Meaning that people all over the country, even the world, might be watching this."

Holly pushed the cart closer to the back of the store, and Genesis followed. The sound on the televisions was off, but the closed captioning was on, moving in chunks of text that were too fast to fully comprehend.

. . . Violet was the site of national attention in the early 2000s . . .

. . . cult leader found guilty of fraud . . .

. . . unclear if related to Dustin Reaps's disappearance . . .

. . . authorities trying to obtain warrant to search the ranch . . .

Genesis put her head in her hands. She hadn't considered the possibility that her involvement in the kidnapping might put anyone at the ranch in danger. "This is all my fault."

"Shhh," Holly whispered, putting an arm around her shoulders and furtively glancing around to make sure no one was listening. "No, it's not. It's fine." Though Genesis could feel Holly's hand tremble against her. "Let's just grab those candles we saw back there and check out, okay?"

Back in the Buick, Genesis sat in the passenger seat with the sheet cake on her lap.

"I'm sorry your first time at Walmart got cut tragically short," Holly said, putting the keys into the ignition. "I just had to get out of there."

"This is why I found Dustin's phone right outside of the ranch, isn't it?"

Holly stared straight ahead. "What do you mean?"

"You all planted it there, didn't you? To throw the police off and make them think the Astralians did this."

Holly opened her mouth and closed it again.

"You did, didn't you?"

"Well, it was fairly obvious, no?"

"No! Not to me! I have no idea how something like this works," Genesis cried, her face getting hot. "I'm not stupid, but I might as well have grown up on a different planet. I don't even know what a banana or CNN is. Of course it wouldn't have been obvious to me."

"It's okay, Gen. The good thing is you left. They won't know this had anything to do with you."

"Well, what if I hadn't left? What if they have tracked down the phone and assumed that *I* did something to Dustin? How would that make you feel?"

Holly winced. "I don't think it would've gone that far. We were just trying to throw the authorities off our trail. It's not like the Astralians actually have anything to hide."

She stared down at the frosting sun on her lap. "This is why you wanted to get me a cake, isn't it? Out of guilt?"

"No!" Holly said vehemently, tears pooling at the corners of her eyes. "I wanted to get you a cake because I think you deserve to feel special. I thought it was unfair that no one's done that for you. I know what it's like to feel completely unseen and misunderstood, and it sucks. Honestly, I'm surprised you're concerned about the safety of the Astralians after how they treated you your whole life."

Suddenly, the donuts Sage set aside for her that morning she cried behind the barn crossed Genesis's mind. It clicked for her: he *was trying to make her feel special.* All those times he saved breakfast for her. She wasn't really as neglected as Holly thought she was.

"Even if I don't want to be a part of their community anymore, I still care about the people I left behind. What if they get into real trouble?"

"They said they found the phone *near* the ranch, not on it. And the police still don't have a warrant to search it. So they should all be okay. This is all okay. It's all going according to plan. We know where Dustin is. He is safe and sound. This is all fake, and it's all going to be okay." Though Holly sounded more like she was saying these words to convince herself than because she actually believed in them.

27

ZOE

"Is it just me, or does it feel like everyone's a little too happy to be here?" Zoe whispered into Delia's ear. She certainly wasn't a stickler for tradition, but Zoe felt that the vibe of Dustin's vigil was, well, offensive to actual missing and kidnapped people everywhere.

The space behind Hope Harvest Market, the former gum factory parking lot, which had been converted into an unnaturally green lawn where the church held family-friendly events and concerts, was bursting with people. Zoe was one of only a few people wearing all black. Nearly everyone else, including Delia, was clad in a tie-dyed T-shirt with Dustin's face printed on it and #PRAYERSFORDUSTIN stamped across the back. Some of the girls from youth group had their arms linked around a weeping Heather as one of their moms snapped a picture of them from behind, their backs blending into one endless hashtag. As the sun set, volunteers handed out small LED candles with color-changing plastic flames. The same DJ who opened up Sunday service was stationed at the front, hyping up the crowd. It felt like they were waiting for a music festival in which Dustin was the headliner to start, not preparing to solemnly pray for his safe return.

Delia warily eyed a news anchor standing in front of a camera at the edge of the crowd, who was fanning herself with a paper fan in the shape of Dustin's head. "Oh, yeah, but would you expect anything less from the Reapses?"

Zoe knew she should've been laughing at the spectacle around her, basking in her own power that simply hiding Dustin in her basement had generated something so predictably over the top. What a waste of time and energy and custom T-shirt ink! Yet all she could think of was how disgusted Dustin would be if he could see the whole thing with his own eyes. How it validated everything he had complained about to her: his family's shallowness and their inability to listen to him. She wanted to delight in how it was his worst nightmare come to life, but somehow all Zoe could feel was . . . sorry for him.

Suddenly, the music lowered and the sound of microphone feedback echoed throughout the crowd.

"Good evening, everybody," Pastor Marcus bellowed. "On behalf of the Reapses, I would like to thank you all for coming out tonight. This is a scary situation right now. I'm not going to sugarcoat it. I'm worried. Boy, I have barely slept a wink these last few nights. But the thing that gives me peace is knowing we've been here before. Did you know that? We all have. Now, I don't know if this will sound familiar to you all, but . . . amazing grace?" He paused and smirked at the crowd. "How sweet the sound. That saved. A wretch. Like me. I once was lost, but now I'm what?" He pointed the microphone toward the crowd.

"Found!" they shouted back.

"That's right. Dustin may be lost right now, but he *will* be found. And we ask God to give our law-enforcement officers the power to not be blind, but to . . . what?"

"See!"

"You got it. So let's begin tonight by joining together and sending up one massive prayer for our friend and brother in Christ tonight." Pastor Marcus bowed his head and closed his eyes, then the crowd followed suit. "Lord, we just ask you to bring Dustin home. You are our great, all-knowing God, all-powerful creator of the universe. And you know that Dustin is somewhere out there, needing to be touched by the Holy Spirit to find his way back home. If, for some reason, Lord, he is being held against his will, we command the abductors to release him unharmed, in the name of Jesus Christ! And let's say it together, everybody . . . Amen! Talk to you later, big guy. Now let's bring Dustin's parents, our leaders in faith, Jay and Ree Reaps, onto the stage."

The Reapses were wearing jeans and the same T-shirts as everyone else in the crowd, much less elaborate than the normal getups they'd wear in front of a crowd this size; Zoe had never seen Ree wear anything so casual. Sure, she had her country-chic outfits for horseback riding and volunteer photo ops, but those were all a little too well accessorized. This at least looked like proof she had actually been emotionally affected by their son's disappearance and this wasn't all for show.

"Thank you, Pastor Marcus, and thank you all so much for coming out tonight," Pastor Reaps said, grabbing the mic. Ree leaned into his side as if she didn't have the strength to stand on her own. "These past few days have been a true test of faith for our family. I've been angry like I never have before. I've felt more helpless than I ever have in my life, like everything I thought was certain is spinning out of control right before my eyes. I've felt like giving up. But thankfully, I know I can turn to the One"—he pointed to the sky—"who is fully in control and perfectly able to help in our time of need. This is not the time to give up; this is just the beginning. As Galatians says, 'Let us not become weary in doing good, for at the proper time, we will reap a harvest if we do not give up.' And, well, tonight, we've decided to share our own harvest for the sake of bringing Dustin home and ensure that none of you give up in this fight."

Pastor Reaps paused and looked meaningfully at Ree, who gave him a small nod.

"Tonight, we are announcing a one-hundred-thousand-dollar reward for information leading to the return of Dustin."

In an instant, Zoe's legs were Jell-O. The dozens of people around her went blurry. Without thinking, she was clutching on to Delia's arm for support.

One hundred thousand dollars.

Six figures.

Even split between Zoe and the others, she'd walk away with

twenty-five thousand, more than she thought they'd even have to share in the first place.

"Are you okay?" Delia whispered.

Zoe swallowed back the wave of bile traveling up her throat. "Yeah. I'm fine. Never been better."

28

HOLLY

"Ladies!" Zoe breathlessly exclaimed, bursting into the kitchen and slamming the door behind herself. "It is time to pop the champagne."

Holly was slumped against one end of the couch looking like she had been crying, and Genesis sat on the other with her arms crossed, staring at the wall. An untouched sheet cake sat on the coffee table before them.

Zoe's face fell. "What's wrong?"

"I know that you all dumped Dustin's phone," Genesis said. "You wanted to cast suspicion on the ranch and distract everyone from where he really was, didn't you?"

"No. I mean, yes. Well, I just figured . . . nothing bad would actually happen. It was a win-win. Keeps the cops off his trail. Nobody gets hurt. Honestly, I would've told you, Gen, but I forgot by the time you came over here. These past few days have been a whirlwind. Why does it matter now?"

"On the news," Holly explained quietly. "They were saying the police recovered Dustin's phone near the ranch, so now they're trying to get a search warrant."

"Well, they're not going to have a reason to search the ranch for long. Dustin will be home soon. The Reapses announced a reward tonight: one hundred thousand American *doll-hairs* for information leading to the return of their beloved baby boy." Zoe unclipped her bike helmet from beneath her chin and took it off, shaking out her bangs victoriously.

Holly sat up straight. "No way."

"Is that a normal amount for this kind of thing?" Genesis asked breathlessly.

"It's more than I expected." Zoe shrugged. "So let's celebrate." She walked into the living room and glanced down at the cake. Condensation had started to creep up the sides of its plastic case. "Jeez, could you guys not find a less depressing option? This is like the cake equivalent of a participation trophy."

"Wait!" Holly raised her palms. "We can't get ahead of ourselves. There's still so many logistics to work out. When are we going to sneak *Orlando* out? Where are we going to take him? And say this all works out . . . do we have to pay taxes on the one hundred thousand dollars?"

"These are all very valid questions," Zoe said, turning back to the kitchen and foraging in a drawer. "Which I will be better equipped to answer once I have some of this hideous cake in my system." She returned with a plastic cake cutter and some paper plates. "Wait. Where are my manners? We need to light some birthday candles and sing to you, Genesis!"

Genesis shook her head. "I'm not in the mood. Besides, we decided this is more of a group cake, not my birthday cake. I already celebrated privately with a banana earlier."

Zoe blinked rapidly. "Excuse me?"

"It was her first time having a banana," Holly clarified.

"I don't think I would call it my favorite fruit, but I'm grateful to have experienced it," Genesis said. "It wasn't long, but my first trip to Walmart was educational."

Zoe knit her eyebrows together and thoughtfully put the cake cutter to her lips. "Holly and I are making this an awfully boring rumspringa for you, aren't we?"

"What's *rumspringa*?" Genesis asked.

"It's . . . you know . . ." She looked to Holly for help. "The Amish spring break thing."

"It's when young people who are a part of this kind of strict religion where the members live together off the land without modern technology—sort of like the Astralians, but also not at all—are allowed to leave their communities for a time to experience the outside world, then they decide whether they want to stay a part of it or not," Holly explained.

"What sort of things do they do to experience the outside world?" Genesis asked, sitting up in the recliner.

"My mom and I watched a reality show about it once. All I remember is they made a really big deal out of wearing jeans for the first time, then one of them got arrested for drunk driving. It was actually a pretty depressing show, to be honest."

Genesis's face fell.

"Oh, but haircuts were a really important plot point too!" Holly's eyes widened hopefully, and she pointed to Genesis's freshly cut bob. "The girls had short hair for the first time. So I would say this is actually a pretty successful rumspringa, thank you very much, Zoe."

"You know what? Let me make the whole phone thing up to you, Gen," Zoe said. "I'm sorry. I should have been more honest with you about that. It wasn't fair. How about we celebrate tonight by doing something you've never done before? Your choice."

Genesis bit down on her lip and stared intently at the floor. "I want to do something *normal*. What do normal people do to have fun?"

Suddenly, Zoe got a wild look in her eyes.

"What?" Holly pressed.

"I was joking about popping the champagne, because obviously we cannot afford nor procure champagne, but . . . alcohol could be a good idea," Zoe said. "*We* should get drunk!"

Genesis stared at Zoe like she'd just suggested they slaughter a kitten.

"That's what you're taking away from my review of *Breaking Amish*?" Holly asked. "I don't know if that's the best idea."

Back in LA, Holly had nervously gulped down too many vodka sodas at house parties to break out of her shell, only to wake up the next day replaying every drunken thing she'd said over and over again, wanting to slide down her shower drain and live as a blob in a sewer forevermore.

"Genesis has had a lot of firsts today," she added. "We shouldn't overwhelm her."

"That's the thing," Zoe said. "It would be my first time drinking too. You're not alone, Gen. This could be rumspringa for the both of us!"

"What?!" Holly and Genesis said simultaneously.

"I know, I know, you guys think I'm the official bad girl of Violet because this life of crime comes so naturally, but I'm just a big homebody. I've told you that. Now, though, I have a good reason to experiment."

"This is an absurd idea, Zoe. Where would we even get alcohol?" Holly asked. "None of us have fake IDs, and besides, we spent all of our money on supplies and this freaking cake."

A slow smile spread across Zoe's face. "Follow me."

. . .

"Banned Four Loko?" Holly sputtered. They were gathered in a corner of the basement around a shrink-wrapped case of drink cans. "Do you want us to *die*?"

"What's Four Loko?" Genesis asked. "And why was it banned?"

"Poison," Holly answered flatly. "It was banned because it's poison. Why do you even have this?"

"It's my brother's safety net. Or something. I'm sure he won't miss a few cans."

Dustin poked his head out from behind his fortress of boxes. "I was wondering about those," he said lazily, then raised an eyebrow. "Wait, you guys are going to actually drink them?"

"Yeah. Tonight we are raising a glass—er, can—to one hundred thousand dollars."

Dustin cocked his head. "What?"

"Your parents announced the reward. I've got to hand it to

you, Orlando, I was started to get a little nervous it wasn't going to go as you'd predicted."

His eyes widened in amazement. "No way." He started to laugh without smiling, his whole chest convulsing up and down.

Zoe joined him, throwing her head back and cackling like a cartoon villain. "It's crazy, right? We actually did it!"

"Hold on a second." Holly raised her voice. "We are by no means finished. Like I said earlier, Zoe, we need to figure out the rest of the logistics before we get too comfortable."

"We will, Holly! C'mon!" Zoe playfully begged, holding up one of the tallboys of Four Loko in the ominously named Blue Hurricane flavor. "It's better if we take our time figuring it out. It will look suspicious if you were to say you stumbled upon Dustin just hours after they announced the reward. But give it a few days of people looking for him, then it'll be so convincing!"

Holly sighed and crossed her arms. "Fair enough. Though I'm still not convinced why taking our time and drinking go hand in hand."

"They don't! This is for Genesis. And allowing ourselves to relax. For once."

"Why do I feel like I'm in one of those low-budget videos about the dangers of peer pressure that they play you in health class?"

"You don't have to do anything you don't want to do. None of us do," Zoe said, looking at Genesis. She started to put down the can. "Okay, I get it, you guys aren't into my rumspringa idea. Let's just go back upstairs and eat some ca—"

"No!" Genesis blurted out. "I want to try it."

Zoe paused and gave her a crooked smile, wiggling her eyebrows up and down. "We love to see it."

"Are you sure, Gen?" Holly asked. "Isn't it, like, against the word of God to drink alcohol?"

Genesis squared her shoulders. "I believe it just says not to do it in excess. One time won't hurt. For research."

"Besides, if you never sin," Zoe said, "then there will be nothing God can forgive you for, you know?"

"Exactly!" Dustin bellowed from the floor.

Zoe turned and glared at him. "Did I say we were sharing with you?"

"Let him have some," Genesis said, then turned to Holly. "My rumspringa wish is that all of us try it together."

"There's no such thing as a rumspringa wish, as far as I know," Holly said. Genesis just stared at her imploringly.

"But if that's what you want . . ." she relented. "We will share a single can of Four Loko, and *that is it.*"

Zoe bounded up the stairs. "I'll get some cups!" she called behind her.

A moment later she returned with a stack of paper Dixie cups. "I'm trying to conserve on dirty dishes because of the water situation, so I took these from the bathroom."

She laid them out on the concrete floor, then grabbed the Four Loko and pulled on its metal tab. "It's stuck," she said through strained teeth.

"Let me try," Dustin said, standing up from his fortress. He placed the can on the ground, squatted to his knees, and gripped the tab with one hand and the can with another, his biceps straining against his dirty black T-shirt. Holly swallowed hard.

Suddenly, a loud popping sound came from the can, more characteristic to a bottle of champagne than a cheap, terrifying malt liquor–energy drink hybrid. Zoe held the paper cups steady, and Dustin poured some of the shockingly blue liquid into each one.

"All right. Let's do this," she said with hungry eyes, though her voice was shaky. They each picked up a cup. "Genesis, do you want to make a toast?"

Genesis stared thoughtfully into the drink, then raised her cup. "To blessings," she said. "To each of you. I know you might not realize it, but you've all been a blessing to me. And to the many, many blessings we have to come."

"TO BLESSINGS!" they all called out in unison.

Holly took a deep breath and tipped her cup back. At first, it tasted like candy. Then, as it traveled down her mouth, it felt as if someone was gagging her with a hot curling iron. This stuff had not aged like a fine wine, as Tom claimed it would.

"Holy fu—I—No—Aghhhhh!" She couldn't form coherent words, and neither could the rest of them. Zoe's eyes seemed to have turned to the back of her head, and Dustin was coughing like a bone was lodged in his throat.

Somehow, Genesis was the most composed. She just blinked hard and shook her head. "Honestly, this doesn't taste that different from the kombucha they serve on the ranch."

* * *

Holly felt warm inside. It was a wholly different kind of drunk than she'd ever experienced back home. Maybe it was the three-fourths of the sheet cake they had collectively gobbled down or the multiple pine-tree-scented candles or that, despite her protests, they had all shared four more cans of Four Loko, but it was a kind of drunk that felt like Christmas in the middle of July.

The four of them had migrated back up to the living room to eat the cake, and now they were all strewn across the room like discarded rags: Holly on the floor, Zoe sitting sideways across the recliner, and Genesis and Dustin on the linoleum floor.

"I just want to say you guys are so amazing," Holly slurred, staring at the ceiling. "Zoe, you're so brave. You're just so smart and powerful and so much better than this godforsaken place, but it's kind of impressive in its own special way. You're like a flower growing out of concrete. Both of you are. It's really beautiful."

"Awww. Holly, really?" Zoe asked.

"Uh-huh." Holly sniffled, tears beginning to form in her eyes. "And you too, Genesis. *You're* so brave and kind and pure of heart and I just feel like people like you don't exist anymore and I don't want to see the world tarnish your shine, you know?"

Genesis smiled serenely. "Thanks, Holly."

"I've never felt like I could talk honestly about my feelings with people before all this. You know, my friends back home, they don't even know about my real life. They don't know that I got sent away this summer for stealing money from my mom to buy pills."

"You what?!" Zoe slurred.

"So even though this whole situation is so messed up and I'm totally freaked out," Holly went on, "I just want to say . . . I'm really glad I met you guys this summer and I hope we can be best friends for life, if that's not too much to ask."

Dustin sat up on his elbows and squinted at her. "Does that include me?"

"You? No. I wish I never met you," she mumbled. "You're just a demon with beautiful flaxen hair." Holly rolled over, turning her back to him. "I feel like we should drink some water. Do you guys think we should drink some water?"

"Noooo," Zoe mumbled, her chin falling to her chest.

Holly had never felt so awake, but then suddenly the urge to sleep came upon her like an asteroid from the sky. She let it hit her, then sank into the pile of inspirational throw pillows.

.   .   .

Suddenly alert to the sensation of what felt like dozens of fuzzy caterpillars crawling in her mouth, Holly awoke. She sat up and woozily walked to the kitchen, then struggled to pull the plastic seal off an unopened gallon of bottled water. When she finally succeeded, she desperately brought the bottle to her face, half of the water actually making it inside her mouth, the other half down the front of her shirt.

When she had successfully drank enough to feel like she was only 90 percent dying instead of completely, she paused and wiped her face with the back of her hand, glancing back at the living room. All of the candles had burned out by now, and she could see Zoe and Genesis sleeping peacefully in the faint glow of the rising sun coming in from behind the closed curtains.

She was about to crawl back onto the couch, when she realized that Dustin, who had been lying on the floor when she fell asleep, was now nowhere to be seen. Her chest started to pound in rhythm with her already-pounding headache.

She rushed to the basement door, grabbing a flashlight along the way, and bolted down the stairs.

Relief overcame her as she raised the light in the direction of his sleeping back and it stirred.

"Ow." He squinted as he looked directly into the bulb. "What's going on?"

"Nothing," Holly said, turning away. "Just checking that you're still here. Ignore me. I'm going back to sleep for a million years."

"Where would I even go?" he mumbled.

"I was confused when I woke up and you weren't upstairs. I thought maybe you would cherish the rare occasion Zoe would let you sleep on the carpet floor instead of the concrete."

"While that certainly is a hell of an upgrade, I know when I'm not wanted."

She froze in front of the stairs. "What do you mean?"

"You wish you never met me? I'm *just a demon*?"

The words Holly said hours earlier came flooding back to her, and her face went hot. "I was just drunk and saying stuff. It doesn't mean anything."

"A drunk mind speaks for a sober heart," Dustin said.

Holly cringed. "Please don't quote Bibles verses right now."

"It's not a Bible verse, it's just a saying. Anyway, I'm not upset. Everything you said is true. Including the fact that I *do* have beautiful flaxen hair." He grinned crookedly in the dark, then his face turned serious. "I know I said before that maybe we can be friends, but if you don't want to ever talk to me again after you fake-find me in the woods or whatever and this is all over, I one hundred percent understand. My parents will probably beg you to go on *Good Morning America* with us to recall your harrowing discovery, and you can tell them to go to hell."

Holly turned around and walked over to the edge of Dustin's sleeping bag. "You know what? Do you want to hear another thought from my 'sober heart'?"

He swallowed and nodded once.

"I miss how it was before all of this. When it was just me and you driving around at night. Part of me wishes I never found out who you really are so I could've just stayed in that perfect bubble all summer. Even if it was all a lie." She knelt down and crawled next to him. "And, yeah, I won't want to be your friend after this is all over, Dustin. Because we were not meant to be friends."

Maybe it was the remaining Four Loko flowing through her system that compelled her to do it, but then she leaned in and kissed him.

29

ZOE

Zoe woke up feeling certain that she'd died and gone to hell, which, no surprise to her, was decorated just like her mother's living room. Her body felt like it was anchored to the recliner with sandbags, and her head like someone was inside of it, shaking a pair of maracas right up against her skull.

"Answer the phone already!" Genesis groaned in an uncharacteristically whiny way, covering her own face with a throw pillow.

After a few seconds, Zoe realized it wasn't the world's tiniest pair of maracas shaking inside her head, but the ancient landline in Zoe's kitchen that was making all the noise. She was surprised that someone would be calling this early, let alone at all; no one but telemarketers or bill collectors called the Peterses' house number anymore.

She stood up too fast, stars blurring her vision, and stumbled over to where the phone hung next to the refrigerator, planning to just hang up on whichever kind of money vulture was calling within seconds of answering.

"Hello?" she croaked.

"Zoe? Oh, praise Jesus," Marla said on the other end. "Your

phone was going straight to voice mail, so I figured you were busy at the diner, but I called over there and Danny said you hadn't showed up today, which is just so unlike you."

Zoe looked to the clock hanging on the wall, with its decorative background that said TRUST GOD. HIS TIMING IS PERFECT! in a big curly font. Like most of the inspirational knickknacks in her house, she'd grown numb to its message, but right now she wanted to punch the clock: it showed the time was half past noon; she was supposed to be at work hours ago.

Her head continued to throb, and her stomach churned. "Yeah, I'm not feeling super well, so I accidentally overslept," she said, almost proud of herself for telling a complete truth for once.

"Oh, well, your brother and I are on our way home, sweetie. I'll be there soon to take care of you!"

"What?" Zoe cried, her mouth going even drier than it already was.

"Yeah, I decided we couldn't just sit around while that poor Dustin Reaps is missing. We're coming home to join the search party!"

"NO!" Zoe exclaimed. Genesis rustled from her spot on the carpet in agony. "I mean," she corrected herself quietly, "why would you do that? The utilities are still busted over here. Aunt Sharon and Uncle Phil's house is so . . . comfortable."

"Well, how am I supposed to be comfortable when the Reapses are suffering and their son could be out there starving in the wild? It's a small sacrifice for the safety of that fine young man."

"This sudden interest in Dustin Reaps doesn't have anything

to do with the enormous monetary reward his parents are offering, does it?"

"Oh, Zoe," Marla sighed. "Why are you always trying to look for the worst in people? I'm just trying to help. Well, I won't keep you. Go get some more rest. We'll be home in about a half hour."

"Maybe you guys should stop for lunch. Since we obviously have nothing here."

"Oh, we had a late breakfast, and besides, I heard the Reapses are catering the search party later this afternoon."

"Of course," Zoe mumbled. "Okay, bye, Mom." She slammed the phone down and collapsed onto the linoleum floor, sticking her head between her thighs.

"Genesis?" she called. "I need your help."

Genesis rolled over and lazily made her way to the kitchen, a throw blanket around her shoulders. "I think I may be dying," she said quietly.

"Me too," Zoe said, her chest heaving up and down.

. . .

"Are you *kidding* me right now?" Zoe groaned as she made it to the bottom of the basement stairs.

The small strip of sunlight from the tiny window in the top corner of the basement was shining directly onto Dustin and Holly, asleep with their arms intertwined. Holly stirred and pried her eyes open, looking to Zoe, then back at where she was lying underneath the unzipped sleeping bag turned blanket for two.

"This isn't what it looks like," she grumbled, then smiled to herself. "Okay, yeah, it's totally what it looks like."

Zoe stared up at the ceiling and blew a stream of air out of her mouth. "You two need to get out of my house ASAP."

"Seriously?" Holly clutched the sleeping bag to her chest. "Are you mad at me?"

"Yes. I mean, no." Zoe shook her head and pinched the bridge of her nose. "I mean, yes. I mean—yes, you need to leave, but I'm not mad at you. Though, I am definitely judging you hard for whatever is happening here." She grimaced at them like they were two bags of leaking garbage. Though her reaction wasn't totally unwarranted given that Dustin hadn't showered in days. "My mom is coming home any minute now."

Holly just stared at her, still too groggy to fully comprehend what was happening.

"IT'S TIME!" Zoe yelled, shaking her fists.

Suddenly, recognition dawned on Holly's face, and she jumped up off the floor. "Oh. Oh no, no, no. We still don't have a discovery strategy in place! Where am I going to drive him? I told you we should've figured out the logistics first! This is a mess." She put her head in her hands. "God, *why* did we drink expired Four Loko last night? Why did I just give up and go along with what everyone else wanted?"

Dustin finally stirred awake next to her and rubbed his eyes. "Go away, Zoe."

Zoe snorted once. "*You* go away. I hope you've enjoyed your stay here at Chateau de Multilevel Marketing, Dustin, but shit is seriously hitting the fan."

"What are you even saying?" He squinted.

"Her mom is coming home," Holly translated. "You have to leave, or else we're going to get caught."

Dusted glanced at the small window. "Right now? In daylight?"

"There's no other choice. C'mon, keep it moving!" Zoe waved for him to get up.

"Someone in town will see me."

"So ride in Holly's trunk!"

"Are you joking?"

"I am as serious as one hundred thousand dollars right now."

"The wig!" Holly interjected.

Zoe snapped her fingers together. "Yes! See, you laughed at the wig the first time, but I told you guys—airtight plan."

Dustin fumbled around until he found the pink bob wedged between boxes of flat-tummy tea. He turned his head down and flipped it onto his head; the wig was never supposed to look natural, but it looked even worse for wear.

"Where are the sunglasses?" Holly asked.

Dustin shrugged. "No clue."

"WHERE ARE THE SUNGLASSES, ORLANDO?!" Zoe cried.

"I don't know!" Dustin said, shaking, tears starting to form at the corners of his eyes.

Zoe took a deep breath. "It's okay. There are more in my mom's dresser upstairs. Let's go!"

"Wait," Holly said. "His outfit. It's too identifiable."

"But I need to be wearing this when you find me, or else it

won't add up," Dustin said. "This is what my family last saw me wearing."

"So I'll find you something else to wear on top! Then take it off when it's time for Holly to fake-find you," Zoe said. "We need to move, people!"

And so that's how after approximately three days of isolation, Dustin Reaps emerged from Zoe Peters's basement in a pink wig, sunglasses, and an oversize nightgown that said I MAY NOT BE PERFECT, BUT JESUS THINKS I'M TO DIE FOR in rhinestones.

30

GENESIS

"I tried my best to tidy up," Genesis said as Zoe shut the back door behind her. "I felt bad throwing out the rest of the cake. But I'd say it looks like no one was here."

"Don't do too good of a job," Zoe said, rushing over to the living room and opening the blinds for the first time in days. "My mom will actually get suspicious if it looks like I really cleaned the place."

"So where should I hide?" Genesis asked. "Basement?"

"Oh." Zoe froze with her hands on the curtains and cringed. "Um, I'm sorry, Gen, but you have to go."

"But I don't have anywhere *to* go."

Zoe scrunched her eyes closed. "Right. Um. Okay." She sighed and opened her eyes. "Walk over to the diner for now, and I'll meet you there in a little bit."

"After that, though? I don't have anywhere else to stay."

"Well, I don't know what to tell you!" Zoe snapped. "Does it look like I run a hotel?"

Genesis stared down at the floor, and a lump began to form in the back of her throat. "No. Of course not. That's okay. I shouldn't have been so entitled," she said quietly. "It's not your responsibility."

"I'm sorry," Zoe breathed, closing her eyes again. "It's just, my mom is going to be home any minute and my head is killing me and I am really, really hoping Holly doesn't get caught. Or that she *does* get caught, but at the right moment. Everything is just becoming a lot and it feels like it's all crashing down at once. But, hey, this will all work itself out. It has to. We've come too far for it to not." She gave Genesis a small, unconvincing smile.

The sunlight streamed through the freshly open blinds onto Zoe's face; her dark eye makeup had worn off in the night, her freckles were more pronounced, and her greasy bangs sat flat against the sides of her face, making her look startlingly young. Not that she ever looked old, but she carried herself to be. That's when Genesis realized that Zoe was not some experienced wise woman of the world, but, just like her, she was a kid trapped in a place with no real clue on how to get out. And she hadn't done anything to deceive Genesis. Rather, Genesis had deceived herself into believing that somehow this girl would be her ticket to a different life.

Genesis smiled back her, just as unconvincingly. "We sure have."

31

HOLLY

"Where am I going?" Holly begged, her hands vibrating on the steering wheel. She had made it to the end of Zoe's street, but the rest of her route was a mystery.

"It has to be somewhat close to Astralia, right?" Dustin asked. "Not too far from where they found my phone. I know a trail a couple of miles from there. We used to go there when I was a kid."

"Right. You decided to go on an early morning hike and got lost. For a couple of days."

"I hit my head and passed out," Dustin said quietly, touching the bruise on his forehead that he sustained the night they snuck onto the ranch that had mostly faded.

"Exactly!" Holly said shakily. "See. We have our story straight. This will be easy."

They turned a corner where a group of people were gathered in their #PRAYERSFORDUSTIN T-shirts.

"Agh!" she exclaimed, jerking the car down the next street. "Or not."

Dustin slunk down into his seat and grabbed the dashboard for support. "I can't do this."

"You *can*," Holly said as encouragingly as she could even though her own driving was making her hangover-induced nausea even more intense.

"No, I mean," Dustin said through labored breaths, "I don't want to do this, Holly. I don't *want* to be found. I can't go back to being Dustin Reaps, even if it's just for a little while longer. What if it's impossible for me to leave a second time? I can't go back to my family just to get sucked back into the whole machine. I want to start over." He swallowed and peered up at her. "With you. Last night, you said you wished we could go back to how it was before you knew who I really was. Remember what I said about living for ourselves? Well, now we can."

Holly studied his face; his eyes were completely sincere. "How?"

"To start? We drive as far away from here as possible. All the way to the Pacific Northwest, to the coast, like you said you wanted to that second night we met up."

"What about Zoe? And Genesis? They're going to be so—What am I going to tell my dad? And the money? I don't—"

"Holly. When are you going to stop living your life for other people and start living for yourself?" Dustin begged.

Holly weighed her options, two lives flashing before her eyes: She could go through with the plan. Pretend that she'd stumbled upon Dustin in a patch of woods. Collect the reward money. Go home at the end of the summer. Return to school and not tell anyone a word about what she had done. Conjure up more lies about her fake summer in Iceland that no one would want to hear. Graduate high school without any long-lasting friendships. Go to college. Study something practical but soul-sucking. Probably lie some more about herself, then graduate without any long-lasting friendships again. Settle down a few years later with the type of guy whose only personality was posing with large fish in his on-line dating profiles. Have two children. Get divorced. Die. And that was if everything went according to plan, if she was actually able to uphold the cracks in her story and not be sniffed out as a conspiring criminal by the Reapses.

Or she could drive away with Dustin right now. What happened after that was one big question mark. It could mean stargazing and singing along to the crackly radio in the middle of the night and falling in love. It could mean bed bug–infested motels and petty theft and crappy jobs and Dustin having to shave his eyebrows off and singe away his fingerprints to never be discovered. This option scared her, but in a way that made her heart race instead of slowing it to a dull, dead thud.

So Holly jerked the car once again and made a sharp turn in the direction of the highway entry ramp, driving away from Violet as fast as she could.

32

GENESIS

"Can I help you?" a police officer asked Genesis, poking his head out of the front window of the patrol car.

He was parked horizontally in front of the gate to Astralia, blocking any other cars from entering or existing. A group of Hope Harvest members were off to the side in quiet prayer. The sky had turned gray, a storm on the horizon.

"No, thank you," she said, not making eye contact with the cop and proceeding around the vehicle to the small, faulty buzzer at the gate door.

"Young lady, nobody's allowed in or out," the officer persisted, craning his neck.

"I live here," she sighed.

He gave her a once-over, taking in her decidedly un-Astralian outfit of airbrushed *Twilight* T-shirt and denim cutoffs. "Yeah, right," he scoffed.

"This is my home," Genesis insisted, wishing that her words were as false as the officer thought they were.

"We've been monitoring the area for over forty-eight hours and I haven't seen you once. Nice try, sweetheart, but you don't want to get involved with these freaks. I've seen your kind. One of those Jimmy Joe James fangirls. Listens to a little podcast about the Astralians and thinks they've become ever so enlightened. These people are sick. Turn around and go back to your mom and dad, honey, okay?"

Genesis stared at the police officer with his condescending grin and the patch on his uniform that had a small embroidered landscape of a sun shining over a mountain. It reminded her of that freaking sheet cake, the yellow 5 dye from the frosting still moving through her digestive system.

Then she used her voice in a way she had never before, letting out a guttural scream that could be heard for miles.

"AAAAAAAAAAAAAAAAAAAHHHHHHHHHH!"

The Hope Harvest members looked up and stared at her from their prayer circle in horror.

"This is Officer Crane," the man said into his handheld radio. "Still down here at Astralia. I'm going to need backup regarding a disturbed female outside of the gate."

Genesis leaned over, bracing her hands against her knees for support. The scream felt good, therapeutic, even.

"That won't be necessary," she said, then picked herself up and jogged away.

. . .

Climbing up the hill that led to the secret entrance to the ranch started out easy enough. Dozens of people were congregated among the trees, scouring every inch for Dustin, and Genesis blended in seamlessly. It struck her that she should be concerned they were still looking for him; if all had gone according to plan, Holly should have "found" Dustin by now. Raindrops began to trickle down from the sky, and as the others descended the hill, racing to their cars as the drizzle intensified into a storm, Genesis continued up to the top, mud splashing against her calves and seeping into her dog-eared Birkenstocks. By the time she made it over the hill and had snuck onto the ranch and back to the main house, her T-shirt was soaked through to her bones.

Genesis slipped into the main gathering room, where all of the Astralians were congregated, with Grace presiding at the front. Her shoes squeaked against the wood floor, giving her away, and everyone's heads turned. She made eye contact with Sage from where he sat in the middle of the room, then quickly looked away.

"Thank you for joining us today. You're just in time," Grace said calmly, as if Genesis had just come in late from a morning of kale harvesting and had not been missing for days. She turned back to the room at large. "As I'm sure you've all been made aware by now, there is an ongoing investigation of our community to see if we had anything to do with the disappearance of Dustin Reaps. Of course, I know none of us have even heard of this person, let alone seen him. But for the sake of transparency, I am letting you all know that last night I met with his parents. After much deliberation, they told me they are willing to ask the authorities to drop any sort of investigation into our community if we comply with one condition: we sell them the ranch. And . . . I told them we would consider the idea."

The room broke into murmurs and gasps. Grace raised her

palms to ask for silence. "My friends, the reality is this: we are already struggling to survive. If these monsters continue to try to smear us for the disappearance of their son, we cannot afford the legal protections to defend ourselves."

"Why would we need some fancy lawyers?" Sage called out, rising to his feet. "There's nothing to hide."

"Of course there isn't, but until that boy is home safe, the Reapses will do whatever is in their power to build a case against us. Because of our history in Violet, we're just an easy target. To be honest with you all, I think they're taking advantage of a very terrible situation. I wouldn't be surprised if, given the choice, they would pick us leaving town over their son being found alive."

Genesis was shocked by Grace's words; she knew the Reapses were greedy liars, but she wasn't so sure they'd be willing to sacrifice their own flesh and blood for some real estate. Would they?

"If we take the money," Grace continued, "we can quietly relocate somewhere else, where these people can no longer infringe upon our peace." The idea was the same one Genesis had presented to her just weeks ago, sparking outrage in her birth mother, but now Grace shared it with everyone like it was the most reasonable choice on the planet.

"And just give up on everything we've built here for decades over something we didn't even do?" Sage said. He turned away from Grace and addressed the entire crowd. "Sometimes I feel like we've forgotten who we are. We have grown complacent and weak; we've filled our brains with distractions from the television and the internet instead of enlightenment. And now our community is not prepared for this attack. Astralia was created as a place to be free of the shackles of materialism. And now? We will just relent so these opportunistic pigs can build some kind of Christian propaganda–filled theme park on our hallowed grounds. Then we can walk away with a few dollars to avoid . . . what? A fight?" Sage scoffed. "I know we're stronger than that. Aren't we?"

Some of the Astralians began to nod and murmur in agreement, then someone burst into applause.

"We're stronger than that!" Sage echoed, his voice louder now, the clapping gaining momentum. It was as if Grace's authority over the group had melted away and Sage had instantly become their new spokesperson.

A chill ran up Genesis's soaking-wet spine as she realized that Sage reminded her of someone else in that moment. A person she'd never met but had encountered in his writing and audio recordings. A person who, according to the internet, was her father.

33

ZOE

"I'm so sorry I'm late! It will never happen again," Zoe called, bursting into the diner. Danny was behind the counter, his forehead dripping with sweat and two loaded serving trays in his hands.

"Oh, thank God you're here." He staggered back in relief, an omelet almost sliding off the tray and onto the floor. "We're swamped."

She stopped in her tracks and looked around. Never in her two years of gainful employment had the place been "swamped," but now people were sitting elbow to elbow at the counter, and the booths were packed. As it began to rain outside, the windows fogged up from the sheer amount of people breathing inside.

"Well, just call me Shrek," she muttered, pulling an apron from behind the counter. The hum of voices in the air did nothing to help her post–Four Loko migraine. "No offense, but why are so many people eating here?"

"Sounds like everywhere else is packed. These people are coming from out of town to look for Dustin Reaps," Danny called over his shoulder.

She reached for a pot of coffee and poured herself a mug before even attempting to help anyone. "*Or* they're coming from out of town for a chance to win one hundred thousand dollars." She took a sip and rolled her eyes.

"How could you say something like that?" a woman dressed in a #PRAYERSFORDUSTIN T-shirt sitting at the counter in front of her asked. "This is a tragedy, and we're just here to do our part."

"I'm sure he'll be found before you know it," Zoe said with a smug smile. In fact, if all was going according to plan, Dustin would be found within the hour.

The large lunch rush persisted for the rest of the afternoon, even as the storm outside intensified. While the many milkshakes she had to make would've usually come as a welcome distraction to her numbingly slow shift on any normal day, today they were an annoyance. With each moment that passed and every order she took, Zoe was increasingly aware of the lack of mood change within the diner. No one was gasping at a headline they read on their phone. The only thing coming out of the radio in the kitchen was soft rock; no breaking-news announcements that Dustin Reaps had been found alive. The visitors wiped their hands and tipped badly, then went back on their merry way to search for him.

When she finally had some down time, Zoe checked her phone where it had been charging beneath the counter, hoping for an explanatory text from Holly. There were a couple from Delia, first asking if Zoe wanted to come look for Dustin after her shift, followed by links to several videos and tweets. Apparently, Dustin's disappearance was trending across the country and people had started creating elaborate conspiracy theories as to how exactly he went missing. None of them were remotely correct. There were no updates from Holly, so Zoe dialed her number. It rang and rang, continually taking her to voice mail.

"Hey, Danny," she called into the kitchen. "Have you heard from Holly by any chance?"

He slung a dish rag over her shoulder. "No. Not since last night when she told me she was staying over at your place. Why? Is she okay?"

"I guess so. She left early for a hike this morning," Zoe lied, planting a necessary seed to corroborate what would hopefully be Holly's success story. "Hope she's okay out there in the rain."

"That girl and her hikes," Danny said, shaking his head.

Zoe returned to her phone and left Holly a voice mail. "Heyyyy," she said at the beep. "Just wondering what you're up to. How your day's going. Thought we could catch up and just dish, you know? Girl talk. That kind of thing. No big deal. Well, call me back as soon as you get this. Byeee!"

She hung up and took a deep breath, then tried to brainstorm reassuring reasons why it could be taking Dustin and Holly so long. Maybe they got a flat tire. Maybe one of them sprained an ankle while climbing the mountain in the rain. Maybe Holly had to pull over and throw up after the previous night's festivities. Maybe they got hit by a meteor.

The more she thought about it, the more a sinking feeling settled into Zoe's gut.

Something was wrong.

Then, like remembering you left the iron on as you're falling into a pit of quicksand, something else scratched at the edges of Zoe's brain.

Genesis! Where was Genesis? She told her to meet her here.

Zoe peered around the crowded restaurant, looking for her, and came up empty. God, she wondered, why had she snapped at her like that with the hotel comment? Zoe was one of a few people she knew on the outside, and the other two were AWOL. Genesis was just a helpless kid with no place to go.

But so was she! She was tired of everyone else always thinking she had all the answers. Was it because she was actually a natural-born leader or that she just had to pretend to be confident in order to survive? And why did her own mother think it was okay to leave her in a house without power to fend for herself? She wanted someone else to tell her what to do for once.

As if by conjuring, Delia walked through the doors of the dinner, beads of rain dripping down her hair like she was a beautiful mermaid emerging from the sea. The sight of her made Zoe's heart hurt; Delia deserved someone less messy, less of a constant magnet for chaos, she thought.

Zoe plastered a smile on her face. "What are you doing here?" she said, her voice shaky.

"You know, I feel like a creepy stalker boyfriend in some bad TV show for showing up at your place of work for the second time to ask why you never answer my texts, but . . . why does it feel like you never answer my texts anymore?" Delia asked, slinking into a stool.

"I'm sorry. I was going to. We're just . . ." She gestured around. "It's so freakishly busy today. Are you seeing this?"

"I don't just mean today, though. Something's been off for the last couple of weeks. I just feel like we're on different wavelengths or something."

Suddenly, Zoe's phone lit up beneath the counter, and she instinctively reached for it, looking away from Delia.

"Like, for example . . ." Delia muttered.

It was just Marla calling. Zoe threw her phone back down. "Sorry. What were you saying?"

Delia stared at her hard. "Is everything okay?"

"Yeah, of course!" Zoe said a little too emphatically. "Why?"

"Maybe I'm being paranoid, but I just get this nagging feeling that you're hiding something from me."

A nervous cackle escaped from Zoe's mouth. "What?"

"And then . . . No, never mind . . . now I'm really being paranoid . . ." Delia raked her fingers over her face.

"*What?*" Zoe pressed, her pulse racing.

"Fine, I'll just tell you," Delia said. "You conveniently forgot to tell me your family was out of town and you were living alone. Then you canceled our plans at the last minute. The next day I came to see you here at the diner, right? I saw through the window that you were laughing and talking closely with that girl you said was just passing through town. And I thought, 'Oh my gosh, Zoe's flirting with another girl. This beautiful girl I've never seen before in my life! Well, guess it was only a matter of time until someone as cool as Zoe came around and she realized that I'm this boring loser that she'll grow out of eventually.'"

"That's not—"

Delia raised a palm. "Well, then earlier today, I saw the same girl walking alone on the side of the road. And no, I wasn't imagining it, because she had the same outfit. The same exact Bella T-shirt. You lied. She wasn't just 'passing through,' was she?"

"Where did you see her?! Was she okay?" Zoe blurted out. "I mean, I don't think you're a boring loser. Not at all. You're my best—"

"So I'm not paranoid." Delia stared at her incredulously.

"No," Zoe sighed. "But it's nothing at all like you think. I would never do that to you. She's my friend. Yes, we've been spending a lot of time together, but it's because she's stuck in a sort of . . . bad living situation, and I've been giving her advice."

"The thing is that seems like something you would normally tell me about! That's a big deal, Zo. You never make new friends. You hate everyone."

"I don't hate everyone," Zoe said, indignant. "Everyone hates me first, that's all." Her phone lit up again, and her eyes flicked over to it.

"Sorry, I can see I'm keeping you from something really important," Delia said sarcastically, lifting herself up from the stool.

Zoe picked the phone up. Again, the source of its light wasn't Holly; it was just Marla texting to ask where the matches were.

"No, Delia, wait!" Zoe said, looking up and realizing her girlfriend had made it all the way out the door.

She rushed outside into the pouring rain and followed her.

"I know I'm being awful right now!" Zoe called. "But I can't tell you why. You're just going to have to trust me that there's a good reason for it."

It wasn't that Zoe worried Delia would hear the plan and go running to the Reapses to tell on her; it was the fear that Delia would be *so* utterly disappointed in her. Delia was always trying to tell her that she was more than the delinquent the congregation at Hope Harvest made her feel like. That she was special and good, no matter what they said. To do something like this only gave into their basest expectations of her.

Delia froze and turned around to face her. "That's not how this works. Relationships are supposed to be about honesty. We're not supposed to keep secrets from each other."

"Well, what if, in this instance only, I'm not telling you everything only to protect the future of our relationship? Like, the way you don't tell anyone else about us. It's not because you're ashamed of me. I know that. It's for your safety, right? Well, what if the thing I'm keeping from you is . . . for *our* safety?"

"What could you possibly be hiding from me that's on the same level as that?" Delia asked.

"Look, I'll tell you one day, okay? But just not now. And when that day finally comes, you have to promise you won't freak out."

"This is a lot of *trusting* and *promising* you're asking of me. I can't do those things unless we're going to be honest with each other." Delia flailed her arms wide, then paused and studied Zoe's face for a moment. "You're not doing anything illegal, are you?"

Zoe gave a humorless laugh. "I guess that would make sense

for me, wouldn't it? Since everyone thinks I'm such a terrible in-fluence. Now including you, I guess."

"I don't think that. It just seemed like a logical reason for some-one to start acting really erratic and saying things like they have to keep a secret from me for my 'safety.'"

"Oh, so, what, me not answering like three texts and making a friend all of a sudden makes me 'erratic'?" Zoe felt disgusted with herself as the words came out of her mouth. Delia's suspicion that something was amiss was completely correct, and now she was turning it into a petty argument.

"You *know* that's not what I mean!" Delia exclaimed. "I don't want to stand out here in the pouring rain arguing in circles with you. Maybe we should just take a break for a little while. When you're ready to tell me what's going on, I'll be there. But until then . . ."

She squinted into the distance and walked over to her car.

Zoe didn't move. She just stood there, letting the rain fall down her face and blend in with her tears.

34

HOLLY

"We need to make a pit stop," Holly said, eyeing the gas gauge on her dashboard; the little E had been flashing for the last forty-five minutes, and now she was speeding down the interstate on fumes.

Dustin shook his head, plastic hair flopping against his face. "It's too soon."

"Either we stop now or we're forced to stop because the car won't move anymore."

"Fine," he relented.

They had been driving west for about four hours when they finally crossed the state line into Idaho. The energy between Holly and Dustin had been less electric than it used to be when they'd drive around together at night, and the adrenaline of their decision to run away had worn off about a hundred miles back. Now feelings were crashing onto Holly in suffocating waves. Panic and fear underscored by the fact that she was hungover and hadn't eaten anything besides cake in almost twenty-four hours.

Holly made an exit at the next sign she saw for a rest stop, then pulled up to a pump at the gas station.

"You don't have any money, do you," she asked Dustin, though it was more of a statement than a question.

"Not on me. No."

Holly reached for her backpack on the floor of the passenger seat and took out her wallet. Inside was fifty-three dollars in cash, remnants from birthdays and Christmases, and a credit card Courtney had instructed her to use on essentials and emergencies only. In a way, this was an emergency, wasn't it? An emergency of her own making. She considered charging the tank of gas to the card but knew her accountant stepdad was vigilant about checking the balance daily and would no doubt question who the heck was using their card all the way in Idaho. If he called and asked her, she could lie and say she had no idea. Then of course he'd probably notify the credit card company about fraudulent activity, resulting in the card getting shut off, leaving Holly and Dustin truly stranded with nothing when the cash ran out.

"So are you going to fill 'er up, or do you want me to?" Dustin asked, breaking her thought spiral.

"No, no, I've got it," she said.

Holly got out of the Buick, and with unsteady hands, she pulled the nozzle out of the pump and pressed it into the tank, narrowly avoiding splashing gas on the side of the car. By the time it was full, the price gauge had risen to the painfully high number of thirty-four dollars and seventy-two cents.

She leaned down and tapped on Dustin's window. "I'm going inside to pay. Do you want anything?"

"Oh, yeah, that would be amazing. Um, can you get me a bottle of water? And a coffee, if they have it? Some snacks too. Cheetos. I'm starving." He gave her a tired smile.

"Sure," Holly said, knowing full well that would mean the last of her money. Still, she turned toward the mini-mart because they had to eat.

"Oh, wait, Holly!" Dustin called.

"Yeah?"

"Can you get me a pack of Marlboros?"

She narrowed her eyes at him and snorted through her nose. "No!"

"Seriously? I'm so anxious about everything right now. It would calm me down."

"Unless you want to cough up some cash, you should start learning some deep-breathing techniques to relieve that anxiety instead."

His face fell. "Right. Whatever." Dustin poked his head out the window and looked around, pushing his sunglasses up high on his nose. "I'll go to the restroom back there while you pay."

Inside the mini-mart, Holly quickly gathered up their haul, a small feast that lacked any nutrients. As she waited in line to check out, her eyes settled on a wire basket of fruit sitting at the register, a depressing attempt by whoever ran this place to encourage the drifters passing through to at least, for the love of God, consider a vitamin. A fly settled on one of the brown-spotted bananas, and suddenly Holly was overcome with sadness as she remembered Genesis trying one for the first time, her eyes filled with wonder. She realized she would probably never see Genesis again, would never be able to offer her other, even more valuable advice on how to navigate the outside world, would never know if she'd make it out here on her own.

At least Genesis still had Zoe as a connection, Holly reminded herself. Zoe and her dream of leaving town forever with the person she loved, dependent on the money that she would now never see all thanks to her and Dustin.

And then Holly realized how what she was doing could not compare to something like Zoe's dream, no matter how hard she tried to convince herself it did. She couldn't love Dustin the way Zoe loved Delia. Maybe in another life, where they hadn't gotten off to such a rocky start. If the only way to be with him was through a life on the run, maybe it wasn't worth it. Maybe his plan had never been to split the money with her and the other girls. Maybe his plan all along was to use them as his pawns on his path to disappear. Or maybe, just like her, he was confused about what he really wanted.

So yes, she felt a little guilty as she got back into her car and drove away while Dustin was still urinating in the filthy gas station bathroom. But Dustin had wanted to fade away, and she had helped him do exactly that. How else would he have gotten a ride without being recognized? Besides, he had been the one to ask her when she was going to stop living her life for other people and start living for herself.

Now she was.

When she reached a stretch of empty highway, she dialed her supposed best friend Marissa's number. It went to voice mail.

"Hey, M, it's Holly. I just wanted to let you know I'm not in Iceland. I never was. I'm actually in Montana. Well, right now I'm in the middle of Idaho, but that's neither here nor there. I'm not coming back to school next year because I lost my scholarship. Yeah, I was on a scholarship. I don't know why I kept that from you. It's nothing to be ashamed of. Probably because you're only friends with rich people, and that one time you joked that I was poor because I was eating generic-brand chips for lunch. That really stung. You actually kind of are a terrible person, and I don't even know why I tried so hard to impress you or any of our other friends. I'm done with lying over stupid stuff! I have nothing to be ashamed of! I'm smart and I am my own person. Well, maybe not just yet, but I'm getting there. Starting today." Holly paused and realized she was out of breath. "Okay, uh . . . this is embarrassing, but that doesn't matter because I'll probably see you never . . . yikes. Bye!"

35

GENESIS

Night fell and Genesis could still see the police car parked in the distance at the bottom of the hill, monitoring the ranch, along with a group of Hope Harvest members huddled in prayer, heads bowed and rainbow LED candles in their hands. This could only mean one thing: Dustin was still missing. The plan had backfired, and somehow he had not returned home safely.

She longed for her iPhone. If only she could quickly google Dustin's name and read the latest updates on his disappearance. But she remembered she had access to something more powerful than a phone: prayer.

Dear God, she said to herself. *I am confused and scared. Please grant me the understanding to know how I can help repair this situation. I thought that getting myself into trouble was the only way out of the darkness and into your light, but perhaps I was just trying to convince myself that what I wanted was right when really it was wrong. And please bring Dustin home safe, Lord. I think, like me, he feels lost and stuck. He has turned away from you, but can anyone judge him when his idea of you is so caught up in his parents' greedy ways? Grant him guidance, God.*

For both of us. And Holly and Zoe too. Amen.

"Don't think I didn't notice the makeover!" Ocean said from her bunk when Genesis returned to their cabin. "Nice haircut."

Instinctively, Genesis touched the wet ends of her bob. "Was anyone upset that I was gone?"

"Sage was asking around for you, and then some of the elders noticed, but don't worry—I covered for ya." Ocean winked.

"You did?"

"Oh yeah. Told them you weren't feeling well. I figured something was up. You were asking me more questions about the outside than usual, and then I heard that Grace took your phone away. Of course you were going to snap and up and leave. You know, I've been there. That's the problem with this place. They don't understand that for us younger generation, we need a taste of the outside to really appreciate it."

"Like rumspringa," Genesis said sadly, day-old memories of sheet cake and Four Loko coming back to her.

"Ha! Exactly," Ocean said, then peered up at her seriously. "But I'm glad you're back, dude. I missed you."

"Really?"

"Of course. You're, like, part of the furniture around here. It's not the same without you. Everything's changing too much already. First, there was talk of turning this place into a wellness retreat, and now everyone is all hyped up for some big confrontation against Hope Harvest. And it's like, uh, hello, I came back here for some peace and quiet, you know? Life on the range. You weren't alive for all the crap that went down with the FBI, but

believe me, it was terrible. I don't think any of us can handle something like that again, no matter what Sage says."

"But we haven't done anything wrong!" Genesis protested,
though by "we" she meant the rest of the Astralians, not herself.

Even though she was one of the few who knew the truth about
Dustin, Genesis felt completely helpless. No one would ever believe her if she even tried to explain. She crawled up to her bed,
pulled back the sheets, and a small fragment of paper flew out.

ith Johnson

tate Agent

ope Harvest Church

On the back was half a phone number. Frantically, she felt
around the threadbare linen until she found the paper's matching
half.

She climbed back down and walked to the door.

"Where are you going?" Ocean asked.

"I have to make a call."

36

ZOE

Zoe mopped the diner floor, reflecting on how she would give anything just to trade places with one of the stale fries she found lurking beneath the tables; to be a piece of a potato, no longer having to live with the burden of a brain. Mentally and physically, this was the worst she'd ever felt in her life, and she could not imagine anything that could ease the pain. Maybe crying herself to sleep, then staying asleep for the next seventy-two hours straight could do something, but the effect would only be temporary.

She had hauled the portable radio out from the kitchen and to the front counter to give a soundtrack to her one-woman pity party. Almost too on the nose, the local station began playing a cover of "All by Myself" by Céline Dion. She clutched the mop handle but didn't move it around, just swayed back and forth, using it as support to keep her from collapsing into a ball on the ground.

Behind, her the entry bell dinged. "Again, we're closed," she groaned, without looking up.

"It's just me," Holly said meekly.

Zoe raised her head, and the mop slipped from her hands, its handle dropping to the floor with a smack. "Why didn't you answer my calls? Is everything all right?" Her eyes darted around the diner and out the window. "Where's Orlando?!"

"Um, Idaho," Holly mumbled, staring down at her feet.

Zoe glared at her, waiting for more.

"As of about four hours ago. Can't say for sure where he is now."

"Why in the *hell* did you drive to Idaho?"

Holly slumped into a booth and rested her cheek against the table. "He wasn't ready to go through with it. He told me he wanted to disappear instead. Start a new life. With me."

Zoe reached her hands out and strangled the air. "Oh, Holly, *no*. Never *that*."

"I know. I ruined the plan."

Zoe sighed and sat down across from her. "No. *He* ruined the plan. I'm mad at *him* for not holding up his end of the deal. But then again, I don't know why I'm surprised."

"You don't think I'm a big stupid idiot for falling for him over and over?"

"If anyone's the idiot, it's me for going into business with the devil himself. For a second there, I felt like maybe he and I had more in common than I could've ever imagined. I guess he even charmed *me*."

"That's why I drove off while he was still in the gas station bathroom," Holly said, her eyes glazing over. "I knew if I tried to explain myself, he'd find some way to reason with me and pull me back in."

"You left him in a gas station bathroom?!" Zoe gasped.

"Yeah."

"Stranded? With no money, no phone, no food, no water?"

Holly nodded once, ashamed.

A slow, sad smile spread across Zoe's face. "At least now I have that visual to cherish. It's nowhere in the same arena as twenty-five thousand dollars, but definitely not the worst consolation prize."

They just sat with the radio, more sad ballads playing as their mutual exhaustion from the day set in. Apparently, tonight's DJ was going through it just as much as they were.

"Besides. The money's useless to me now," Zoe said after a few moments. "Delia broke up with me today."

Holly looked up at her from her place on the table. "Oh no. I'm so sorry."

"She totally suspected that something's up. I got greedy. I put the money before her. I thought I was so in control of the situation and—"

"Some breaking news tonight," the velvety woman's voice purred from the radio as a song faded out. "For those of you who've been following this Dustin Reaps case out of Violet, apparently an arrest had been made in connection to his disappearance."

Zoe and Holly widened their eyes at each other and bolted up, hovering close around the radio.

"Details are just trickling in," the host continued as Zoe turned up the dial. "But apparently a *minor*, yes, as in a child under the age of eighteen, folks, described as a member of the Astralian community—that's right, you remember them from back in the day—has been taken into custody. This story is developing, and I'll share more as we have it. My thoughts and prayers are with the Reaps family tonight. Here's 'Every Rose Has Its Thorn' by Poison. This one goes out to you, Dustin, wherever you may be."

37

HOLLY

"They've got to be talking about Genesis, right?" Holly said. "Who else would fit that description? She told us she's the youngest person at the ranch."

Zoe stared out the front of the diner, as if searching for something. "If they've arrested her, then they must be coming for us next."

"Gah!" Zoe stood up and yanked off her apron. "We have to find him. Bring him home before they get to us."

"It's been hours since I left him, Zoe. He probably hitchhiked away from the gas station. By now, he could be in . . . I don't know . . . he could be anywhere. Things are out of our control."

"We can't just give up! I can't just sit back and wait for the other shoe to drop while Genesis is stuck in the county jail! Can you?"

Holly frowned at the table. "No, but—"

"No buts!" Zoe protested.

"I don't think I can safely drive another eight-plus hours, Zoe. I'm exhausted."

"Maybe you should've thought about that before joining Clyde on your little road trip, Bonnie."

Holly rolled her eyes, both at Zoe and herself, for helping to create this mess. "Well, do you know how to drive?"

"Yes—"

"Great." Holly stood up. Let's go."

"—in an unofficial capacity."

"What does that mean, exactly?"

Zoe avoided eye contact. "It means I know how to drive, it's just the state refuses to recognize me because I won't adhere to their precious little rules."

Holly glared at her.

"It means I don't have my license," Zoe blurted out quickly.

"Do you guys have any coffee left back there?"

Zoe knotted her eyebrows together and glanced behind the counter. "Uh, yeah. It's cold. And six hours old. I was actually supposed to dump it out and—"

"Well, pour it over ice in a to-go cup for me and call it a cold brew, because I guess I'm not sleeping tonight."

38

GENESIS

"Your mother's here to see you," an officer announced from behind the door of the metal jail cell.

Genesis sat up from the concrete slab where she'd been lying peacefully. "*Mother?*"

Grace came forward from behind the officer. "Five minutes," he said, glancing at her warily.

"Genesis," Grace said, her eyes wild, gripping the cell bars. "What have you done?"

"I told the truth. I'd been hiding it for some time, but I couldn't stand by any longer and watch history repeat itself. I know the ranch is too important to you. It's our only home."

Grace studied Genesis's face, and her eyes softened. "And the truth is?" she asked.

"Dustin Reaps and I met when he was talking a walk near the ranch at night." Genesis stood up from the slab and walked over to the door. "We struck up a friendship. I was curious about his way of life; he was curious about mine. He started visiting me a few times a week. We would talk to each other over the fence for hours. Then it got more intense, you could say. Finally, one night, I invited him to the abandoned stretch of cabins and, well, you know how they're in such bad shape. We were just about to exit one of them when the ceiling fell in, and he hit his head. Hard. He wouldn't wake up. I was too scared of what would happen if anyone found out about us, so I carried him off our property and into the woods. Left him there, all alone." She paused and cringed at the ceiling. "After that, I don't know what happened to him, but he was gone. I had assumed he woke up and went home, but . . . I guess he didn't."

It wasn't a complete lie, Genesis reasoned. Sure, she subbed in herself for Holly, but she had struck up a brief friendship with Dustin during their time at Zoe's house. This was just a blending together of facts into a more digestible smoothie that let the rest of the Astralians off the hook. The more she told it—first to Faith Johnson on the phone, then to the cops who came for her, and now to Grace—the easier it was to share. She was scared about what this lie would mean for the rest of her life, but the rest of her life was already a mystery anyway. Being a martyr was better than being nobody, fading away into the background of the ranch.

Grace put her hand to her lips. "Why didn't you tell me?"

Maybe it was the jail cell door between them, the fact that the worst that could happen had happened, but Genesis was emboldened. "You don't listen to me. I knew I would just get in trouble before I could even be heard."

Grace winced. "Well, I'm here. I'm listening now. Is this what you were doing with that phone I found you with? Talking to Dustin Reaps?"

Genesis laughed once. "No. I can see why you'd think that, but I was actually using the phone to learn more about God. I'm a born-again Christian now."

Grace gasped as if Genesis had just kicked her in the chest. "Genesis, please don't tell me you changed your beliefs for some boy."

"This has nothing to do with Dustin. My faith was sparked before I even knew him. I've felt different from our community for a long time, but there's never been a chance for me to explore or question anything. I knew you wouldn't accept me like this."

"I've failed you, haven't I?" Grace said, swatting at the tears forming in the corners of her eyes. "I moved here when I was just a few years older than you because I wanted a totally different life from my buttoned-up parents, and now look what I've done! Isolated you from making your own choices and finding your own beliefs. I thought I was protecting you, but . . . now I see I'm just the same kind of monster in a different outfit."

"Oh, yeah. I know about you being an heiress," Genesis said calmly. "I know it's you who bought the ranch, not Jimmy Joe James. And I know that he's my father."

Grace snorted back tears. "He's not your father."

"What?"

"Yeah, your father left when things got bad. Coward. His name was Matt . . . something or other. I don't even remember. Who knows where he is now."

"Then why do people on the internet say Jimmy Joe James is my father?"

Grace shrugged. "Because it made for a good headline, I guess. *'American Candy Heiress Procreates with Spiritual Madman.'* Of course, you know, it wasn't as if we were never intimate, but . . ."

Genesis scrunched up her nose in disgust, then started to laugh.

"What?" Grace pressed.

"It's just . . . you're worried about me changing my beliefs for a boy, but you bought a whole fifty-acre ranch for one."

Grace half smiled, and sighed. "Yeah. I guess you got me there." She glanced over to where the officer stood at the other end of the hall. "It looks like they're going to kick me out soon. I need to go contact your maternal grandparents for the first time in over twenty years to see if they can help us out with a lawyer. We'll get you out of here." She peered into Genesis's eyes. "I won't fail you again. I know I haven't always shown it, but . . . I love you, Genesis."

Genesis smiled. "I love you too, Grace."

Grace turned to walk away.

"Wait!" Genesis called.

"Yeah?"

"This Matt person . . . was he Sage's father as well?"

Grace looked at her blankly. "No. Why?"

"No reason. Just curious."

39

ZOE

"I told you he'd be long gone," Holly said.

It was the middle of the night. She and Zoe had scoured the mostly deserted rest stop from end to end five times in total—twice from the Buick, three times on foot—with no Dustin in sight.

"Why do you sound a little relieved?" Zoe asked.

"Of course I'm not relieved!" Holly cried. "But I'd be lying if I said I wasn't dreading having to explain to his face why I abandoned him for the entirety of the drive here." She looked around nervously. Across the lot, a trucker stared at the girls from the front window of his cab. "Let's just get back in the car."

"Maybe the person working in the mini-mart saw him. I'm sure there aren't many six-foot-tall people in hot-pink wigs and bedazzled nightgowns passing through . . ." Zoe glanced at a sign in the distance. "Bear Creek Village Rest and Refreshments."

"If they did, that was this afternoon. Whoever was working clocked out hours ago. Now they're home. Nice and cozy in their bed . . ." Holly trailed off wistfully, her head drooping just slightly on her neck.

"Holly, no!" Zoe snapped. "We have to power through. For Genesis. We need to keep looking."

"Where else are we supposed to look? We can't check every inch of Idaho for Dustin! Face it, if we don't find him, someone else will. His picture is plastered all over the news. He has no cell phone, no resources—he's going to have to take that wig off eventually."

Zoe knew she was right, but she couldn't face the sheer obviousness of it all. Of course Dustin wouldn't still be here. Did they expect to find him peacefully relaxing by the Icee machine? He was a boy on the run.

"Just humor me," she said. "Let's take the next exit and drive around. Maybe he left here on foot. If we don't find him after another half hour, we turn around and go home."

Holly yawned. "Both options are equally unappealing."

. . .

The closest town to the rest stop looked a lot like Violet before the Reapses got their hands on it. Abandoned storefronts and a dilapidated old church. Not a soul in sight.

"I can't do this anymore," Holly said.

Zoe rubbed her eyes. "Fine," she relented a little too easily. "Let's go home."

"No, I mean, I can't drive anymore. I'm exhausted. I think I need to pull over and sleep for a couple of hours before we get back on the road."

"Okay. Maybe we should turn back to the rest stop and take a nap there. This place feels a little too murdery."

"I don't think I can make it." Holly yawned a rolling, uncontrollable yawn. "Oh God, it's really hitting me."

"Fine. Pull into that church parking lot."

Holly turned the car into the gravel drive in front. The building was tiny, more of a chapel than a full-size church, with a tall steeple and wooden siding with white paint peeling off the sides. At first, it was unclear if it was abandoned or just in serious disrepair, but then Zoe noticed it had one of those signs out front with interchangeable letters, in pristine condition.

HONK IF YOU LOVE JESUS,

TEXT WHILE DRIVING

IF YOU WANT TO MEET HIM

"Good night," Holly groaned, and shut off the ignition.

Zoe opened the passenger door.

"What are you doing?" Holly asked.

"Going inside." Zoe shrugged. "We're too exposed out here."

"You can't go inside!"

"It's not like I'm trespassing! This is a house of God, and *I* am his child. Plus, it's Saturday night—Sunday morning by now. If anyone catches us, we can just say we showed up early for the service."

Holly hesitated.

"C'mon! We can rest our weary heads on some pews. Nothing bad will happen," Zoe said.

"Why do I feel like I've heard that one before?" Holly mumbled, begrudgingly unlocking her door.

· · ·

The back entrance of the church gave in with a pitiful nudge of Zoe's shoulder.

"Does your phone still have any juice?" she asked Holly before fully opening the door. "Mine's dead."

Holly pulled hers out of her back pocket. "I'm at fifteen percent. Why?"

"Flashlight."

They huddled together arm in arm with the glow of Holly's phone leading the way. The church was fancier than its humble exterior suggested: plush red carpet covered the floors, and the dark wooden pews had thick cushions of velvet.

Holly flashed the phone to the windows, revealing ornate stained-glass depictions of the Gospel. "Whoa."

"See?" Zoe said. "This place is basically the Four Seasons."

While Holly continued to explore the walls with her phone, entranced by the details of the glass, Zoe felt compelled to sit down on the front pew and stare at the pulpit. Instinctively, she bowed her head.

"I know we're not exactly on speaking terms," she said quietly so Holly couldn't hear. "But I was just thinking—if you're as real as I once felt you were, then maybe you could just help me out here a little bit, okay? I know that's not how this works. I'm not supposed to make this conditional, like, 'Hey, God, if you give me this thing, then I'll totally believe in you!' I know that's manipulative. But also, you know my feelings about *you* dying for my sins. *That's* what's really manipulative in this scenario. But whatever. We were both at youth group that night when I got sent home for starting that argument. I won't get into that again. The thing is, Genesis really needs you right now. She's really all about you, and it would just *suck* if you ignored her! I think that'd really be the final straw for me. So many people are totally faking their faith; they abuse it for all the wrong reasons, but she's not. She's the real deal. You need to show up for her. So this is me asking for your forgiveness. And your guidance, I guess. To find Dustin and bring him home and settle this whole mess. His parents have really done a number on him. Maybe I took advantage of that, and I'm sorry. And maybe help me patch things up with Delia, if you have the time. I know a lot of people say that you think us being in love is a sin, but I know *you know* it's not. You know? Anyway, I'll wrap this up. Amen."

Behind her, Holly yelped, her phone slipping from her hands and falling onto the carpet with a thud.

Zoe jumped up and rushed over to her where she stood at the back of the sanctuary. "What's wrong?" she hissed.

Holly pointed down at the last pew, where Dustin Reaps was curled up into a ball, sleeping soundly and clutching the pink wig to his chest like a teddy bear.

40

HOLLY

"Dustin!" Zoe cried, shaking him by the shoulder. He jolted awake and squinted at the light coming from Holly's phone, his shoulders tense, then frantically put the wig on his head sideways.

"Holly?" he asked, his shoulders relaxing upon realizing it wasn't a stranger. He pulled the wig back off. "You came back for me?"

"Well, I—"

"*We* came back for you," Zoe said. "C'mon. Get up."

"Zoe? What are you—No. I can't. How did you even figure out where I was?"

"Funny story: turns out divine intervention is real. Very cool, huh? Now let's go. It's time to go home, mister."

Dustin sat up in the pew. "Why? So you can just use me to get the reward money?"

"*Use you?* We made a deal, Dustin, and you didn't hold up your end of it."

"I did some thinking, and I decided no amount of money is worth returning to my old life."

"Oh, please," Zoe scoffed.

"They arrested Genesis!" Holly interjected.

Dustin's eyes widened. "What?"

"We don't know all the details, but it seems like they want to pin this thing on the Astralians, and . . . I guess she was an easy target. I don't know."

"Shit," Dustin mumbled.

"You have to go back and show that you're alive and well. Explain that it was all a misunderstanding," Zoe said.

"Look, I'm sorry, but I can't show my face there again. I can't go back just to have to say goodbye to them all over."

"Oh, get over yourself, Dustin!" Zoe snapped. "Do you even have a plan for what you're going to do if you don't turn back?"

"I'll get a job," he said. "Find a cheap apartment. Start over. I turn eighteen soon anyway. My parents won't be legally responsible for me anymore."

"Have you ever held a job in your life, Dustin?"

"No, but what does it matter? I'll become a dishwasher or something. Who cares?"

"Do you know how little you'll make as a dishwasher? You'll barely be able to survive. Do you even have ID or your own bank account?"

"Well, unlike you, money isn't everything to me," he mumbled.

"You think that's what this is? That I just *like* money?" Zoe yelled. "Do you know why I even got into this whole mess? My mom spent the modest amount of money my father set aside for me before he died on your mom's freaking meal-kit scam. And look, I know that's her problem. That's not personally your fault that my mom's terrible with money and emotionally vulnerable to con artists. But remember how you told me you're not like everyone else at church, but your parents never listen to you, so you just never speak up? Well, they'll listen now. The whole town will listen. You have the power! Besides, if there's anyone else in this world who knows that exact feeling of being completely stuck and doomed to a life inside a family who doesn't understand them, it's Genesis. You don't have to go back for me. But maybe you could be *cool* for once in your life and do this for her."

Dustin sat up in the pew and gave Zoe and Holly a long sideways glance, then finally slipped the wig back on.

. . .

Back on the road, Zoe passed out almost immediately in the passenger seat, leaving Holly and Dustin to endure the most awkward of silences. She turned the radio on low volume in hope of easing the tension.

"I kept playing it over and over in my head," he said after about forty-five minutes, staring out the back-seat window at the rising sun. "It was the cigarettes, wasn't it? That's why you left."

"Not the cigarettes, exactly. Though smoking *is* really bad for you." She glanced in the rearview mirror. "I think it just kind of . . . sobered me up. Made me realize that we weren't doing what *I* really wanted. It was what you wanted, and I went along because I don't know what I want. I still don't. I just try to impress people instead of thinking about what I actually want. But from now on, I'm going to figure it out. I have time. That's the thing, we all have *time*. We don't need to have it all figured out."

Dustin rested his head against the back seat. "I still wish I hadn't ruined things with you before we even had a chance."

"Yeah, well," Holly sighed, suppressing a smile. "You can always blame it on Orlando."

"God," Dustin groaned, putting his head in his hands.

"How did you even think of that name?"

"One of my sisters was watching *Pirates of the Caribbean: The Curse of the Black Pearl* earlier that day when I first met you . . ."

"So it *was* inspired by Orlando Bloom?" Maybe it was the delirium from lack of sleep, but Holly started to crack up. Dustin threw his head back and joined her.

"What's going on?" Zoe sat up and looked around, her eyes settling on the radio. "Oh, wait, Dustin! This is your song!"

He froze mid-laugh. "What?"

"Yeah, last night this lady on the radio dedicated it to you." Zoe turned up the volume and "Every Rose Has Its Thorn" started blasting from the old speakers. "Oh, oh, here's the good part . . . *every rose has its thorn . . . just like . . .* I don't know the words. C'mon, guys!" She waved her hands like a conductor.

"Zoe. How do you expect me to know the words if you don—" Dustin mumbled, then proceeded to belt out the entire next verse of the song.

Reluctantly, Holly joined in, and there they were, gliding down the mostly empty highway, belting out a ballad that was a hit long before any of them were born, and for a fleeting moment, they felt like a regular group of kids who were just coming home from a wild Saturday night.

41

ZOE

After a brief pit stop at McDonald's to ensure Dustin didn't pass out from starvation upon return and Holly had enough coffee in her body to not steer them off the side of the highway, followed by another brief pit stop in which Zoe desperately peed off the side of the highway, the trio arrived at the outskirts of Violet around nine.

"What day is it?" Dustin asked. "I lost track."

"Sunday," Holly answered.

"Oh nooo!" he groaned. "My parents are at church."

Zoe craned her neck around the headrest and stared at him. "Yeah. Where else would they be?"

"No, I mean . . . I was thinking you guys would just drop me off at home, but they're not going to be there. I'm going to have a make an entrance in front of the whole congregation. Now this is going to be a whole thing."

"Honey, if you thought this *wasn't* going to be a whole thing, well, you've got a big storm coming for you," Zoe said.

They passed the NOW ENTERING VIOLET sign, which had now been dwarfed by an even bigger temporary sign that said:

FIND OUR BOY
#PRAYERSFORDUSTIN
1-888-DUSTIN
$100,000 FOR INFORMATION
LEADING TO HIS RECOVERY

"Is it too late for us to turn around a second time?" he asked, putting his head in his hands.

"Yes!" Holly and Zoe said in unison.

"Don't forget," Zoe added, "you're doing this for Genesis."

Holly turned the Buick down Main Street; it was quiet from everyone being inside Hope Harvest. "So what do you think? We drop you out front?"

Dustin shook his head. "No. You guys have to come in with me."

"Oh, uhh . . ."

"I'm not really dressed for that . . ." Zoe demurred.

Dustin leaned into the front of the car between them, his eyes terrified. "Please."

. . .

"Excuse me, miss! Miss, you can't go in there." One of the ushers had spotted Zoe, no doubt recognizing her from her attack on Pastor Reaps, and blocked her from entering the sanctuary.

"She's with me," Dustin said.

The usher eyed his pink hair and gave him a quizzical look. "And?"

Dustin pulled off his sunglasses and wig then threw them to the floor. The man gasped. It was truly incredible how effective that stupid disguise had been.

The usher pulled a walkie-talkie from his belt. "The young eagle has landed. I repeat: the young eagle has landed."

Dustin ignored him and pushed through the sanctuary doors, Holly and Zoe following behind.

The lights were dim and the music slow; congregants had their hands raised to the ceiling for the praise portion of the service. Some had their eyes closed in devotion, but the ones who didn't quickly noticed Dustin Reaps bolting down the center aisle. They tapped on one another's shoulders, murmurs spreading, until finally he jumped onto the stage and asked for a microphone from one of the Praisemakers, who was so stunned by him in the flesh that she nearly passed out and fell backward.

"Um. Hi," Dustin said into the microphone, feedback echoing. "I just wanted to let everyone know I'm okay." For a moment, the audience was stunned to silence, but then they erupted into applause and cheers.

"Thank you for all of your kind thoughts and prayers," Dustin continued, and the applause intensified. "But . . . I did not want them."

The congregation went silent like a scratched record.

"See, no one did this to me. No one hurt me. Um, I chose to leave. I was feeling quite alone in this world, to be honest with . . . all thousand or so of you. Ugh. Oh man." He raised a hand over his eyes to block out the stage lights, looked at the audience, and cringed. "Anyway, I think what I realized is that sometimes when we feel alone, it's exactly that—a feeling. But it's not a fact. I know you guys are probably expecting the next thing for me to say is that

I realized I wasn't alone because I had God, but that's not what happened. I realized that sometimes when we feel alone, we're not really alone, it's just that we haven't taken the time to get to know our neighbors. Um, this week I got to know some people I never really thought about before but who've always been there." He squinted into the audience and looked at Zoe where she stood in the back. "And they made me realize that I'm not alone. That sometimes just talking to each other about what makes us feel so alone actually brings us together. And that I actually have a lot to be thankful for. Sorry, I don't have a more eloquent speech prepared, but . . . I just ask that if I can be a lesson to anyone after this whole mess, it's just—don't judge your neighbor before you get to know them. It's a lot harder to make friends than it is to make enemies, but we should try. I'm sure there's a good Bible verse about that, but I'm honestly too tired to remember it right now. Okay. Thank you."

He gently placed the microphone on the stage floor and walked away. Everyone in the congregation gawked, aside from Zoe, who was smiling from ear to ear.

. . .

"So. What now?" Zoe asked Holly.

They were standing down the block from the church where all the members huddled around, gossiping in circles about what they had just witnessed. Moments after Dustin's speech, the police descended onto the stage, and the rest of the service was promptly canceled.

"Should we go to the station and wait for Genesis?" Holly asked.

"Yeah. That sounds about—"

"You!" a woman's voice behind her yelled. Zoe turned. Faith Johnson was pointing her finger at her as she stomped over in a pair of wedge sandals. "You had something to do with this, didn't you, you little troublemaker!"

Heads from all over the crowd stared at them. "I don't know what you're talking about," Zoe said quietly.

"The ushers told me they saw you burst through the church doors with Dustin. I knew you were a bad influence. First on my little Delia, then Dustin. You're just as bad as those devil worshippers over at the ranch."

"So maybe I am." Zoe shrugged.

"You might have gotten away with something this time, but I don't want to see you over at our house or in that sanctuary ever again."

"You're such a hypocrite, Mom!" another voice called out. Zoe glanced at the circle of people increasing around their confrontation. Delia emerged and stood next to her.

"All of you are," she continued, looking around at the crowd. "Zoe has never done anything to harm anyone. She's just asked questions. Questions that scare you because they make you think outside of your little bubble for even just a second, so you treat her like she's some kind of freak. Are you all forgetting that Jesus treated outcasts like family? Not that I think Zoe is an outcast. Because she's cool. Cooler than any of you. And smart. And special." Delia grabbed Zoe by the hand. "So if you want to forbid her from church or our house, then you're just going to have to forbid me too, Mom."

Faith stared at Zoe's and Delia's hands intertwined for a long moment, then turned away in a huff.

"Um, so I'll go pull the car around," Holly said, throwing a pointed glance at Zoe, and left.

"I put two and two together," Delia said. "Why you've been acting strange . . . I don't know how or . . . why, exactly . . . but, unfortunately my mom is right. You had something to do with all of this."

"And why would you think that?"

"Well, for one thing, I've definitely seen your mom in that gorgeous nightgown Dustin was wearing . . ."

"Oh jeez." Zoe cringed into her hands.

"And, of course, everything he was saying up there just screamed 'Zoe's impact.'" She peered into Zoe's eyes. "*Why?*" she begged.

"My mom spent all the money my dad had left for me," Zoe admitted. "Our 'get out' money. I really didn't want to tell you before I figured out a way to earn it back. Conveniently, Dustin was interested in defrauding his parents just as much as I was, but as you can see, that didn't really go as planned. I'm sorry. I was hoping you'd never have to know."

"So let me get this straight," Delia said, raising an eyebrow. "You put aside your flagrant hatred of Dustin Reaps for the greater good of committing a crime to get money so that you and I can one day live somewhat happily ever after?"

"Well, I mean, when you put it that way . . . Are you mad at me?"

"No," Delia said, a smile spreading across her face. "That's the most romantic thing I've ever heard."

42

GENESIS

"Genesis Astralia," an officer called into the cell like it was a formal announcement, even though Genesis was clearly the only person detained there. "You're free to go."

She sat up from the concrete bed, moving aside the shabby woolen blanket. "What's going on?"

"Dustin Reaps came home. Cleared your name. Lucky girl," the woman sighed. "Your family is waiting for you outside."

As Genesis emerged from the police station, she felt like a little bird released from its cage. The sun beat down on her face, so it took her a few seconds to register that the group of people standing outside weren't just a random collection of strangers; they were there for her.

Zoe, Holly, Grace, Ocean, and Sage were calling her name and cheering. She looked at this strange assortment of people and realized, fondly, that they *were* her family.

"I'm sorry," she said to Zoe and Holly. "I messed up the whole plan, didn't I?"

They shook their heads. "No, Dustin did," Holly said. "And I helped him."

"The plan was screwed long before you even got involved," Zoe added.

"I didn't say a word about either of you."

"Of course you didn't! I know you're not a snitch. Hey, remember that thing we talked about a while ago?" Zoe said, whispering in her ear.

"What thing?" Genesis asked.

Zoe pointedly looked at Sage where he stood a few feet away from them in the police station parking lot. "There's no better time to express how you feel about someone than when you're coming down from the high of being released from jail for a crime you didn't commit."

"How would you know?" Genesis begged.

"Just trust me on this one," Zoe said, flipping Genesis around by her shoulders, then moving her forward to face him.

He smiled at her. "I was so worried about you, Beginning."

"There's something I have to tell you," she said.

"Sure. What is it?"

Genesis reached up for his shoulders and leaned in to kiss him. She waited for the sparks to fly, but instead she felt like . . . well, she felt like she was kissing her brother.

She pulled back and stared at him. "That was . . ."

"Weird," he said quietly.

"Yeah, right?"

"I mean, no offense, Gen, it's just—"

"I think some things are probably better left to my dreams."

EPILOGUE

ONE MONTH LATER

"My course catalog has arrived!" Genesis exclaimed, bursting through the diner doors. She sat down in a booth across from Holly and slammed a manila envelope on the table. "I need your help picking my classes."

"Now, Genesis, this is very, very exciting for you, and I don't want to rain on your parade or anything," Zoe said, walking around from behind the counter. "But be forewarned, the offerings at Violet Senior High School are extremely limited. Like, last year when I suggested they start a women's history class, I was politely told that that was what home economics was for."

"Well, I don't know that much about economics. Or homes, honestly. So, sounds good enough to me."

Genesis had made an agreement with Grace: she wouldn't pull any kind of stunts again if she was allowed to start attending public school in the fall and wearing colors besides purple. She would be allowed to visit the library to use the computer as much as she needed, and for her safety and convenience, she was allowed to have the most basic of cell phones. It wasn't how Genesis wanted to live forever, but it was a start.

"Biology could be good," Holly suggested. "You already know so much about how plants and animals work. This could help you understand it on a deeper level!"

As Holly and Genesis continued to pore over the brochure, Zoe noticed a figure pacing back and forth and talking to themselves in the parking lot as if they were rehearsing lines for a play. Upon further inspection, she realized it was Dustin Reaps. At first she hadn't recognized him without his signature hair; it had all been buzzed off.

None of them had heard from Dustin since he returned home. Zoe assumed he was grounded for life or that his parents had sent him off to some kind of disciplinary camp for "troubled teens."

After a few more minutes of pacing, he walked inside.

"Zoe." He nodded politely.

She raised an eyebrow. "They cut all your hair off at Boys' Wilderness Mountain?"

He brushed the back of his smooth head with his palm. "Nah. I haven't been. I did this myself. I heard somewhere that when you're starting a new chapter in your life, it's a good idea to get a fresh look to go with it."

Zoe stared at his face, trying to put a finger on something different about him besides his hair. "Well, you look . . . nice, Dustin," she admitted.

"I quit smoking too. I have you to thank for that. Going cold turkey worked."

Before Zoe could ask him anything else, he walked over to the booth where Genesis and Holly were sitting.

"Ladies," he said. "Hello."

They looked up at him, stunned.

"Hi, Dustin," Genesis said. "How are you?"

"Good, good. It's great to see you, Gen. You look well. Um, do you mind if I talk alone with Holly for a second? If that's okay with her, of course."

Genesis looked to Holly. "Suuure." Holly shrugged. Genesis got up and joined Zoe at the counter, and Dustin took her place in the booth.

Holly took a sip of her Coke and gulped hard.

"How've you been?" he asked her.

"Good. Just spending a lot of time with my dad to make up for my absence during the first half of the summer. We tried getting into hiking, but that didn't really work out. Now we mostly just watch *Diners, Drive-Ins and Dives* reruns together. My dad had never seen it before, but it's really inspiring him to be a better diner owner. He keeps talking about how he wants to invent his own version of 'donkey sauce.' I'm kind of worried for him, honestly. Next thing I know, he'll have bleached-blond highlights."

Dustin smiled, then looked down at the brochures on the table. "School enrollment? Are you moving here for good?"

"No," Holly said, a note of sadness in her voice surprising herself. "These are Genesis's. I go back to LA next week. Public school. A whole new start."

"Exciting." He placed his palms on the table and stared down at his hands. "So I came here because I was thinking, before you go home, we should go on that normal date." Dustin peered up at her through his long eyelashes.

Holly's face was unreadable. "Really?"

"I know we got off to a rough start. Twice. But maybe third time's a charm. Or it doesn't have to be. It can just be a date."

"What about your parents?" she asked. "They wouldn't like that."

"Yeah, well, my parents are just happy I'm alive. Plus, I'm a grown-up now."

"And Heather?"

"Heather broke up with me. Over text. She's convinced I've been possessed by a demon." Dustin grinned wickedly.

"Hmm," Holly said, turning to look out the window. "She might be onto something."

Silence hung in the air. "I'm sorry," Dustin said, sliding out of the booth. "I should have realized you would never—"

"Pick me up at seven," she said, then grinned back at him just as wickedly as he had a moment before.

Dustin blinked and sat back in his seat. "Oh. Great. I mean, amazing! Um, where do you live?"

Behind him, he heard someone cackling, and turned.

"You were going to run away with her and start a new life and you don't even know where she lives!" Zoe exclaimed. "Lord, grant me his audacity."

. . .

When Zoe got home from work, she parked her bike against the fence and stared fondly at the blue glow of the TV coming out the front window.

After hitting rock bottom, Marla had finally cut back her spending, gotten a job at Hope Harvest Market, and managed to sell some of the junk languishing in the basement on Facebook Marketplace. She didn't realize how much stuff she really had down there until she returned home to find it all neatly organized; Zoe just pretended *she* was the one who sorted out the essential oils by vibe.

Tom was also doing surprisingly well for himself. After discovering Zoe has torn into his case of Four Loko, he was devastated, but then quickly realized that selling individual cans à la carte on eBay was actually much more profitable than selling an entire case. Turns out people didn't want to be responsible for *that* much of a bad thing.

So as Zoe walked up to the front door, she was concerned to see a package sitting there. She started to internally prepare a monologue for her family, that online shopping was a slippery slope, that next thing they knew they couldn't pay the water bill again, but then she realized the package wasn't addressed to Marla or Tom; it was addressed to her, in neatly drawn handwritten letters.

She tore the tape off the box and looked inside to see about thirty one-inch stacks of one-dollar bills. On top of them all was a single folded piece of paper. She pulled it out and sat down on her front step to read what it said.

Dear Zoe,

I'm sorry our first money-making venture didn't go exactly as planned. That was my fault. However, I wanted to let you know I've discovered a new business idea. See, for the last month I've been secretly selling designer shoes and clothing on eBay that my mom has purchased for me over the years. She has yet to notice. So far, I've made a total of $3,047, which you will find in this box. I got it all in ones because I know you're a waitress and this way if the IRS or anyone asks, you can just pretend it's all from tips. Also, sorry for giving it to you in this sketchy way, but I didn't know how you'd react, and I thought it'd be best to keep it discreet. I know it's probably nowhere close to your entire college fund, but it's a start. Consider this a payment for the oh-so-generous hospitality you showed me earlier this summer, or maybe it's just my dues for all the times I was an asshole. All I ask in return is that when you leave this place, you remember me fondly from time to time, not just when you're imagining running me over with your bike.

Your friend,

Dustin

AKNOWLEDGMENTS

I somehow wrote most of this book during the darkest days of 2020, and it would not have been possible without the support of many incredible people.

Thank you to my wonderful agent, Dana Murphy. I think lots of other agents would have rightfully looked at me sideways when I first described my idea for this book, but she completely understood my vision and encouraged me to pursue it when it was just a humble mustard seed in my brain.

I had the privilege of working with not just one but two amazing editors, Alex Sanchez and Ruta Rimas, who pushed me in new and challenging directions that made this book so much better than I could have imagined.

Thank you to the rest of the team at Razorbill and Penguin who worked so hard to make this book happen without a hitch in such a chaotic time, including Casey McIntyre, Gretchen Durning, Jayne Ziemba, Marinda Valenti, Ariela Rudy Zaltzman, Krista Ahlberg, Maddy Newquist, Sola Akinlana, Delia Davis, Kelley Brady, and Vanessa DeJesús.

Thank you to Louise Zergaeng Pomeroy for bringing the characters to life through your beautiful illustrations.

Thank you to Mike McGrath, Sarah Schechter, Greg Berlanti, and the team at Berlanti Schechter Productions.

Thank you to Mary Pender, Katrina Escudero, Olivia Fanaro, and Orly Greenberg at UTA.

Haley Mlotek, my sophisticated confidant and beta reader. Estelle Tang and Emma Straub, for supporting the launch of my first book and also being beautiful geniuses.

My Portions Family of Allegra Millrod, Joey Vincennie, and Rika Mady.

Lastly, Brendan O'Hare, there is no one else I would rather be trapped inside with for months on end while on deadline. Thank you for the endless encouragement, thoughtful feedback, court jester antics, and warm cookies.